David Alvarez
Chicago, XII 98

A STATE OF FEAR

Menán du Plessis was born in Cape Town in 1952
and went to school and the university there. She
was co-founder and later national chairperson of
National Youth Action, an organization which
sought to fight racial discrimination in education.
Her poetry and criticism have appeared in various
small magazines, and she is contributor to
*Sometimes When It Rains: Stories by South
African Women* (edited by Ann Oosthuizen,
Pandora Press 1987). Menán du Plessis is at work
on her second novel.

A STATE OF FEAR

Menán du Plessis

London

First published in Great Britain in 1987 by Pandora Press
(Routledge & Kegan Paul Ltd)
11 New Fetter Lane, London EC4P 4EE

Originally published by David Philip,
Publisher (Pty) Ltd, Claremont, South Africa

Printed in Great Britain
by The Guernsey Press Co Ltd
Guernsey, Channel Islands

British Library Cataloguing in Publication Data

Du Plessis, Menán
A state of fear.
I. Title
823[F]   PR9369.3.D8/

ISBN 0-86358-167-6
ISBN 0-86358-168-4 Pbk

This is a work of fiction and any resemblance to persons living or dead
is fortuitous

CHAPTER 1

i

It's raining over the city, raining down steadily over all of us who live in the mountain's rain-shadow. Raining over the Cape flatlands, over the dense growth of acacia in the sand dunes; over the factories and houses and shanties and office blocks; over all the million of us who live here. The sky must capitulate easily to those vast surges of icy air in the upper atmosphere: to come tumbling so weakly afterwards, helpless against gravity, melting down uselessly in straight pencilled strokes of cold air and glinting light. Raining down over the two wintry seas with their separate islands and bays and harbours.

Up in the mountain the granite faces must be glistening now behind the dense mist; there will be ephemeral waterfalls, hundreds of tons of water crashing down each second over the boulders and rock faces; and those quartz pebbles smoothed to opacity in ancient streams will be stirring in the beds of the steep ravines. Ja. It's against these rainy, graphite-smudged skies that the colours of protea and aloes achieve their full power of sustained incandescence.

It's hard to believe that in a few months' time the earth will be restless with dust and wind, rather than rain; that instead of mistiness there will be a richness of scents in the air – the faintly foetid, lemony scents of the fynbos. And beyond any doubt, instead of water racing downward there will be gigantic flames that sear upward into the rocky kloofs within seconds, let loose by carelessness and the summer's gale-force winds – and fuelled by the fragrant resins in the cracking trunks of the pine trees.

Ja, hard to believe. When right now the gutters in the street outside are thick with the streaming water. And tomorrow morning if there is any light at all it will be scattered across the plains and over the low hills of the Tygerberg, where the rain-wet roofs and panes

1

of glass become a strange litter of pure light in the blazing forms of rectangles.

But this is not the true state of affairs after all. 'It's been a fairly quiet week-end. Just the usual unrest, you know.' That was how a policeman summarized things in this evening's newspaper.

Violence seems so easy to tabulate: over the period from Friday evening till midnight on Sunday we had nine deaths – three of them in road accidents; two cases of rape; and two hundred and fourteen assaults. Figures like that always seem so exact, and yet I wonder what they really mean. How do you define an assault. A person's face is slashed, or a watch is torn from someone's wrist. People brawl in those clubs in the sleazier streets of the city, near the docks. Doesn't the Sunday duty-reporter simply sit disconsolately at a desk phoning the mortuary, the police, the ambulance station, the fire chief, the metropolitan emergency squad, the mountain rescue team, the sea rescue institute. . . . While a cigarette in an ash-tray slowly changes to a column of brittle ash, and the milky coffee in a polystyrene cup draws a dead film over itself. They call some of those incidents criminal, others the signs of civil discontent; but the boundaries sometimes become confused. In cases of minor arson, for example. It seems that fires break out frequently these days in school strongrooms or the school clerk's office. People seem almost grateful when they can trace these things to an electrical fault, or a still-smouldering butt-end that must have been tossed aside by some exhausted, alcohol-blinded tramp who'd broken in for a night's shelter. At other times, though, a wary, grim-faced principal will explain about two kids who'd failed an exam and were harbouring a grudge . . . that sort of thing. Suppose in the end, however these episodes are explained away, they're simply flickering reflections of our permanently violent state.

Maybe even that stoning was merely an image: something coming back at me out of glass panes with a silvery darkness behind them. It happened out at Philippi, along that neglected, pitted stretch of road. Someone drove out that way last week – alone, in a bakkie. The bleak light from the mercury gas lamps lit him up every ten metres or so, under the flickering shadows of the bluegums: giving away the pallor of his skin. Seems there was a road-block, a make-shift barrier of old tyres and oil drums that some teenagers had set up; and then a dozen kids were hurling stones, half-bricks, gravel-packed tins at the windows of the car. He was stunned almost immediately by one of the bricks and veered to a skidding halt; as the windscreen sent a fan-shaped scree of broken glass out across the tar.

There was a photograph in the newspaper. How, do you think? I want to understand how anyone . . . how they could have stepped back impassively to focus and steady the camera. There's an invisible dead space in the foreground of the picture, and people seem to cram their own emotions into it – maybe to compensate for the fact that the subject is a dying man whose personal feelings are already mysteries. That man sitting in the road, slumped forward in a sick daze: you sense that the world around him is slowly dying down, while the crickets must seem to him to be stirring and singing restlessly, endlessly.

Apparently the kids went berserk with rage, once his car had come to a stop: closing in on their victim, to hurl their most painful frustrations at him in the solid forms of stones. Another dispassionate bystander related afterwards how he'd seen one of the youngest of the group begin to tremble all over, once it was finished – even though his face still glinted with the passion of triumph. He was beginning to retch, and had to be helped urgently away by a friend as they clambered across a deep ditch and then disappeared into the uncertain shadows of the eucalyptus trees and acacias.

The revolution here always looks, on the surface of it, so hideously like a racist conflict. Even though most of us know that these incidents are only the most extreme and most superficial manifestations of the class struggle. And yet, while I know that, I still battle sometimes in the long hours of the night, sleepless and anxious for lack of a dream that will encompass both the heroic war for a national identity – that unification begun by Shaka – and the endless war between the workers and their clear-eyed oppressors.

I don't know. The comments in the liberal Press were so predictable. About the legitimacy of people's grievances and the depth of their everyday suffering; and about the tragic folly of resorting to violence. You can imagine the other phrases. Acts of senseless violence only detrimental to a decent cause. That sort of thing.

Wonder how you define sensible violence.

Suppose you could make some diagram of force vectors, calculate the mass of a baton; the biochemistry of energy surging through a policeman's arm as he lifts his weapon. Why don't they call police-men soldiers. Soldiers when the war is in another country? Namibia, Zimbabwe, Angola, Moçambique. And they use guns. But there's a picture in the paper of a police reservist outside Mowbray station, hugging a sub-machine gun to himself; obscurely grinning. It's a trick of the photographer's maybe, or something in the developing process that makes his face seem louring and heavy. The police are protecting the bus company. That's what it's about. Because of the boycott over the new fares. The police are intimidating the people from the townships who run combi-bus taxis, demanding to see their licences – when everyone knows that 'legal' status costs a fortune.

I don't go out much these days; except to buy bread and milk, and newspapers.

Sit at my typewriter in the evenings, staring at the sheet of paper I've rolled into place: wondering what elaborate fictions could ever repair its blankness.

Maybe Memmi was right. When he said that those among the colonisers who dissent will inevitably find themselves in one of history's curious impasses. Surely not? I find it almost impossible to accept that.

The neighbours have their television turned up loudly: seems to be a Western on tonight – I can hear the music, some grandiose sweeping of melody on the strings with an edge of brass to sharpen it; and the occasional crack and whinge of a bullet. It would be easy to despise these people with their laughter that seems grotesque to my ears. Easy to loathe them for the thick-voiced obscenities that form their conversation. Self-righteously, abusively racist they are too, although that's hardly surprising – the relative whiteness of their skins being all that sustains them. But then: they're also working-class – artisans mostly, or railway employees – and it'd bother me, you see, to have only a selective respect for labourers. In any case, they're neighbourly. The father brought me an alyssum plant from his garden, once, with the dry earth still drifting away from its fine roots as he held it out. And their little boy sometimes lets his tennis ball bounce strategically over the wall so that he can come knocking, breathless, and be allowed the adventure of wandering through the house and out into the backyard.

School starts again in a fortnight's time. In principle, anyway. I'm

4

not sure that I can go back.

Two days before term ended we had a visit from some people on a tour of inspection. Mr Bezuidenhout escorted them along the verandas and then into the middle of the courtyard's tarmac: where they stood chatting, with their hands in their pockets. Mr Bezuidenhout with his hands clasped in front of him, and smiling. One of them made notes in a wirebound book, while Mr Bezuidenhout pointed up at the windows of the second storey, where whole rows of the smooth, light-reflecting surfaces were interrupted by jagged edges of darkness. Marianne and Nicholas and I went to watch from the foyer. Nothing else to do. I don't know where the kids came from, how they heard about it: the end of term usually fizzles out in mass absenteeism anyway and this year, of course, with the boycott – almost all of the students had already abandoned school about a week before. But within minutes they'd managed to gather about two hundred people, and hurriedly lettered posters were being raised on all sides of the quadrangle. DON'T FIX WINDOWS, FIX THE SYSTEM and YOU CAN'T PATCH UP A STINKING INSTITUTION. Things like that. Some of the kids started up a chant – we couldn't hear the words – but it was ragged and uncertain, until someone broke into that British song about the 'Brick in the Wall', and then the voices became aggressively coherent. The stooges from the department stood their ground for about five minutes, pretending to ignore the protest, but in the end Mr Bezuidenhout led them away slowly to the school parking-lot and their cars, so that they could abscond with their dignity saved. It was just as well, because the kids had got hold of a loudhailer by then and one of the seniors was beginning a speech.

That girl from Zimbabwe who teaches history turned to Nicholas and said peevishly, 'Well, I just don't know what they want: first they say they want the broken windows fixed – now they want to have a riot just because they're getting what they asked for.' Marianne and I looked at each other. Felt incensed – I might even have said something rude – but Marianne was struggling, I could see, to stop herself from roaring with laughter. She hates Sally, energetically, because she speaks about 'Rhodesia' still – blithely, almost, yet with a shade of hurt and incredulity to her voice. When we were still teaching regularly she'd have a showdown with her class at least once a fortnight. She'd come into the staffroom still sobbing to catch back the breath that had caught itself shallow and quick in her chest; with her fine floss of hair sticking damply to her flushed cheeks. Perhaps it's callous, but few of us manage to feel any sympathy for her; except a few of the men who like to mutter supportively about Mr Naidoo having no real strength, and about children who really 'need' caning.

As for that remark of hers. Seems ludicrous that a history teacher should have no conception of struggle as a dialectical process.

And the police have already shot children dead in the streets: they fire at the children here in cold blood, children whose hands are empty, whose faces are aglow.

I'm not certain that I can go back now. Don't see how I can ask the kids to open the same old books and expect them to carry on from where we left off – as though nothing had happened; as though all their earliest impressions and beliefs hadn't been shattered into tiny splinters and painfully stuck back together into this new, stiff, almost adult consciousness.

I've spent the past week trying to evade the problem. Suppose housework is capable of infinite extension although it's real enough too. I've washed and ironed all my clothes; rescued a few hems that were beginning to unfold; sewn back dangling buttons. Scrubbed the bathroom floor a few times. The rain leaves a small tide of earth and dust and shrivelled earthworms – everything flowing in under the door. It's cold now too – I keep wondering whether there hasn't been snow up-country. Whenever I stand still for a moment I'm reminded of my own bones, and everything in me seems to shrink further inward. Keep bumping into things, clumsy with the cold; and the bruises show up yellow on my arms and shins.

Anton sent me a few postcards last week, to wish me happy birthday: bright prints of old-fashioned modernist art. I suppose because he has some inkling of remembrance that I used to delight in European culture – a decade ago, when I was in my teens. Funny, rambling, serialized sort of poem he scrawled on the backs of the cards. And he sent me a book as well: French translation of *Glas het g'n Kristalstruktuur*, printed on thick, creamy paper, with a glossy white cover.

The cards were ruined a bit by the rain – lying at the bottom of the letterbox, along with a tabloid advertisement sheet for a hire-purchase furniture shop.

What else. Constance is away, taking her annual leave. The university is also on holiday now, so there's not that much work for the secretaries. She's gone off to visit Gran in Natal - although I think the train journey itself is part of the holiday for her. Once she confessed to me how she enjoys the feeling of being in transit and unknown: liberates her to study other people, listening to their intimate secrets.

Sometimes I wonder whether Mom isn't becoming eccentric. She doesn't care about other people's opinions, of course; but it's disquieting to see the way she holds on to her solitude so proudly now that it's become a freakish travesty of individualism. That rich, coarse shock of hair is almost entirely grey now, and part white: she never goes to a hairdresser - trims it herself from time to time, snipping away with a pair of nail scissors. Even her vehement frankness scares me a little. Lately her anger has been directed mostly at the government's corruption - this Information scandal. Last time I visited her she was being abusive about 'the bloody Afrikaners': 'Thirteen million rand - of tax-payers' money, mind you, *my* money. My God, they think they can just do what they damn well like. . . .'

It's difficult to understand her attitude to Gran. She must be fond of her, I suppose, and yet when she talks about her sometimes her voice is dry with irritation. It exasperates her, she says, that Gran is letting herself drift into a perpetually querulous elderliness. Gran's rather a small-built woman, thin-shouldered - and most of her joints have been transformed now into cartilaginous knots of quietly raging pain. Mom seems to resent that for some reason. She herself is a tall, strong-boned woman. Once - bitterly - she said that people will seldom allow her to be weak in spirit: incongruous with her physical stature, they must imagine. I have a suspicion that Mom may be suffering from rheumatism herself, but won't tell anyone.

Gran gets up at five in the morning, apparently, to begin her ineffectual pottering around the cottage. Listens to every news bulletin she can, grumbling about the loss of her old valve radio that used to pick up the broadcasts from the BBC and Radio Moscow. She was a member of the Party in the old days: a fervent believer, before Stalin. She must have been idealistic. And yet I wonder how hopeful people could have been even then. Gran would have been a tiny kid when the First World War broke out; and then there was

7

the second war, just when Constance would have been verging on adolescence.

And when Granpa finally came home from the war he was sick with some invisible mental wound. I can see why Gran wanted Constance to take that typing course after she left school – so that she would have a proper skill and be independent. Maybe Mom felt humiliated, though, that Gran had such low aspirations for her. Still, in those days women could only really be nurses, teachers . . . and typists. Although Gran herself was a journalist, so there must have been some alternatives. And now in any case Gran trails through her house in old slippers and a threadbare, wrap-around dressing-gown, while the radio hisses away because she can never get the needle dead on the right waveband. The trivia of officially sanctioned news and advertisements splinters through the house all day; loudly, cheerfully mouthed by the announcers.

At least there's a garden at Gran's place. One of the things Constance looks forward to each year, I think: putting right as much of that neglected smallholding as she can. Almost snickering, she's told me how Gran sometimes tracks across the dewed, grey grass with the ends of her pyjama legs tucked into wellington boots – to 'prune' the decrepit roses. Mom still misses the garden we used to have; won't have anything to do with indoor plants, though. Once I offered to buy her a few pot-plants – begonias, perhaps, or cyclamen, in those knotted string hangers – but she turned them down aggressively: 'Oh God no, Anna, thanks. I can't stand women who keep cats and pot-plants. Amount of attention they give these things, when basically as far as I can see they're too damned frigid to give anything to real people. Er, thanks for the offer, though.' And she paused before the final firm expostulation: 'I don't really count that as gardening, you know: fussing away with special fertilizers, that sort of thing.'

I know that I ought to be kinder about Constance than I am. After all, she must have made endless sacrifices for my sake – when I was still a minutely boned, milky infant in towelling and flannel. There must have been times when she didn't want to leave the sleepy warmth of her bed at two in the morning – just to let me clutch her swollen nipples to my angry, small mouth.

Trying to think of Constance in the late months of her pregnancy, suffering through the dusty, drawn-out heat of March – time when

8

the arid warmth of the berg wind withers the flowers, and the sick and elderly grow thinner. Constance: blundering her way heavily through the still, stifling rooms of the house, or listlessly sewing at the small flannel vests. She was in her early twenties then. Younger than I am now.

That agony too, at the end of it all – for forty-eight hours, poor Constance racked by the tearing spasms, and I refusing to be born. Not yet an 'I', I suppose: a nascent awareness in danger of losing – and so already having lost – the inchoate, lightless, insensible state of nothingness. In the end perhaps I lost hope, or fainted: when I was finally born my entire forehead was purple-black and yellow with bruises – must have been battering myself half to death – against my own fright; against Constance's aching body. I feel guilty about that.

What else. What else to tell you.

Seem to have put so much energy this last term into devising lessons that were never even tried out. Marianne gave up long ago: she simply shuts out the other teachers in the staffroom, folding her long, thin arms into a barricade across her chest and, frowning, struggles myopically to concentrate on Zola. When I talk to her at tea-time she begins to smile and eventually dismisses my projects with laughter rich in derision, 'Anna, man, why can't you rather save your efficiency for something real?'

One of our setworks is *Julius Caesar*: and I really had thought that I could help the kids towards engaging ideas. Naive of me, perhaps. One thing I wanted was to read them some passages from *Arrow of God* and then ask them what they felt Achebe might have been saying about classicism and primitivism. Thinking of that race that Antony runs, and the ritual cleansing race that Ezeulu performs.

It was hopeless from the beginning, though. There weren't enough copies of the text to go round, so that very few of the kids could read the play on their own at home. Although perhaps that wasn't a bad thing: many of them battle with the unfamiliar vocabulary, and having to turn to the notes all the time just spoils the drama for them. Thought it would make the play come alive if we read it aloud in class, without dwelling pedantically on difficult words. And I suppose that I was relying on Felicia to help me – the child who played Juliet last year in the school production. When I

9

asked her whether she'd like to read Antony she shook her head, though, and sat staring, scowling almost, straight down at her desk. I felt thrown; but perhaps I wasn't totally surprised. Some of the other children eventually volunteered – the poor dutiful ones who inevitably act as monitors, cleaning the blackboard for me or helping to hand out papers. It was miserable, though. None of them could read fluently, let alone put the curving sound and rhythm into the verse. And throughout the whole abysmal lesson I was conscious of Felicia's stolid withdrawal. A few of the others picked up her attitude, even if they didn't perhaps know its basis, and perhaps they sensed the same heavy well of boredom at the heart of the lesson. But there was nothing I could do about it. They at least attacked it by murmuring incessantly; banging down their desk lids; unwrapping sandwiches, more or less candidly.

Had a comprehension exercise already roneoed off for the next day: thinking I could leave the problem aside for the time being. But the kids themselves took up the issue.

Secretly I was impressed. They'd drawn up a petition saying they felt Shakespeare was irrelevant to their own lives, their current concerns, and that they would absent themselves from any future classes on the play. Oddly, Felicia stayed right on the periphery. It was Debbie Johnson who handed me the document and then, thrilled by the situation and the approval of her classmates, launched into a brief speech. Explaining firmly, with her young face lit up, that she wasn't interested in the old, dead classics; that she wasn't going to struggle with an outdated kind of English, just to read a play that was only important in some other country, centuries ago. I could sense that the kids were eager to surge up on the same wave of emotion – there was a splintering clamour as people began banging on desks and stamping. Someone in the front row began aggressively humming that Bob Marley song, 'You gotta fight for your rights'. And when one child smartly folded his comprehension paper into a paper dart, he inspired the entire class, and for a few minutes the room was filled with flying paper jets, crumpled balls of paper, insistent stamping, catcalls and laughter of that odd, whinnying kind that insinuates a jeer. I waited until I could get a word in, and told them, 'Okay, well let's talk about alternatives then, shall we.'

It was another five minutes before I could say anything else, and it took Debbie's leaping up on to her desk to bring down the uproar

10

finally.

I like that kid. She brings a guitar to school sometimes and sits on top of her desk at lunchtime, strumming and singing to the other kids. I have a mean suspicion that she's not very good, but her friends enjoy the concerts at any rate. She often has one of those facile love stories under her desk lid and I imagine that she spends her afternoons at home lying dreamily on her bed, lazily pressing down chord stop configurations on to the half-tuned strings of her guitar; perhaps nibbling biscuits; fantasizing adolescent miracles of true love.

I noticed as things were quietening down that some of the children looked disturbed. Cynthia had left her desk and gone to sit with her cousin at his desk against the wall; and my trio of quiet, almost overly-demure girls were sitting together, with their faces very still – obviously troubled by the disorder. Those three are always immaculately neat: they wear their hair hidden under those long, pure white scarves; shoes polished; slim-fitting, home-tailored blazers; and their handwriting still the perfectly rounded script they were taught in junior school. When I could speak again I made an effort to keep my voice calm, so that the quieter kids would sense a restoration of control and order. It sounds calculated: but you have to help children when they're afraid. You can't just abandon them, leave them to feel that no one knows how to cope? Don't you have to make them feel that someone cares enough to take the responsibility. I know it's playing a role, deliberately being the teacher. Maybe that's inauthentic. But you can't just abandon kids?

I asked them whether they'd be interested in reading some African novels. A few of the kids were roused by the idea, but none of them had any idea how much African literature there is, so I ended up having to feed in suggestions and do most of the planning myself – which I'd have preferred to avoid. We took a vote and there was general agreement that we'd collect as many copies as we could of *Things Fall Apart*. Even my three timid kids raised their hands in discreet assent, after the two shyer ones had glanced first at Rachieda for their lead. I left the classroom with a blazing of happiness in my lungs; and that afternoon I went through to Rondebosch after school and bought two copies of the book to put along with my own in the school library.

I didn't imagine that everyone would have found a copy by the next day, so I went on planning lessons as usual in the evenings, keeping the emphasis on language and comprehension. Maybe neurotic this – always needing to have a small, mental map of a lesson clearly plotted in my thoughts before I feel confident about going into class.

For the next few days I kept coming ready to teach, but everything would slowly disintegrate into protracted, rather pointless harangues about the absurdity of studying Shakespeare. When I tried to find out how many people had begun reading the Achebe, the only response was bleak evasion: the kids staring sullenly at their desk. Willie Peters came up to me after one class. I think his habitual response to everything around him is bewilderment, but he hides this demeaning truth from himself by sulking and turning a belligerence on his teachers. He looked directly up into my face, avoiding my eyes though, and asked me aggrievedly to repeat the author's name for him. I'd written all the information on the blackboard, but perhaps he'd taken it down on some scrap that got lost. I wrote it out for him on a slip of paper, and he went away. Looking mollified.

The next day there was a formal notice on my desk from the class to announce their unanimous feeling that as 'the whites' got their textbooks free, they didn't see why they should have to pay for any setworks out of their own pockets. So the Achebe project was dropped. Perhaps it was the letdown that made me pusillanimous: I couldn't help a fleeting, uncharitable suspicion that the kids' apparently political decision was based fundamentally on apathy. At least I had the grace not to accuse them outright, and I'm ashamed now I ever thought it: even if the kids are lethargic sometimes – that's not an explanation of anything, is it. Need to know why.

I spoke to Marianne about it, but she was feeling disillusioned herself just then – so she interpreted the episode as cynically as I had: 'You know, sometimes I think these children are never going to change . . . inwardly.' In that husky accent of hers that always half lisps, half rolls when it has to glide around the ar sound.

Nicholas was listening in to the conversation. While I was filling in the background he kept saying, 'Hey that's tremendous.' When it came to the bathetic climax though, he put on a grave expression and tried to say something serious: 'Jaaa, but maybe you know you can't expect the kids to manage everything . . . like all at once.' He

12

was shocked, I think, by Marianne's brutal pessimism and tried to counter it with a formal analysis: 'You've got to remember they're in a tough situation, hey, I mean in the class structure – like their parents man, just the ultimate petty bourgeoisie, they're starting to get in there along with whitey.' Marianne was sitting with her arms tightly crossed, but when Nicholas came out with that she relaxed and breathed in more deeply. Grinning at him, hugely, 'Man, you and your long words always.'

Privately Marianne's assured me that Nicholas is yet another arrogant fool: her words gurgling helplessly somewhere near the roof and towards the back of her mouth. I don't think he really is though. Maybe she thinks he's vain because he's got that rich sandy-red hair on him and that confusedly curling beard. But it isn't his fault. He's a bit like a kid himself really; why I get on with him, I think. He came and spoke to me about the incident again, later. Beginning, 'Heeeey, Anna!' Ready to reason with me, affably. 'You've got to realize that maybe some things are more important for the kids *at the moment*. Like they've got priorities, okay. So, all right, you teach English, so you think they should be involved with it too. Well, how do you think I feel, hey? Because, let's face it, the kids are going to call a full-scale boycott soon. For sure. And I'm not going to get to teach science for months now: and okay, maybe they learn something from literature, what you want to teach them, but really, like – science education is what really frees people.' Stammering ardently. 'Anyhow, the thing is that they still want to sort out – key things, for themselves, okay? So maybe we're just going to have to accept that Achebe's not so important for them *now*; or science. Maybe later . . . ja, maybe later we can come back to these things. D'you get what I'm saying?'

I suppose I did get it. He's right, isn't he? Disconcerting thing about Nicholas. He lives in a commune where most of the other people are still students: so he's always in touch with the current leftist line. Leaves me feeling disadvantaged; out in the cold. I'd like to follow whatever that line is myself. Just sometimes. . . .

Last year he took his standard nines to the building-site of the power plant at Koeberg. I remember how excited he was, priming his kids beforehand with questions to raise about political implications, the problem of disposing nuclear waste, safety measures, damage to the environment. Apparently the guide parried most of

13

the questions deftly, suavely – statistics and latest scientific reports stacked neatly behind his white teeth – until one of the girls stumped him finally with an innocent question about the effects on marine life if the coolant is pumped out into the ocean. He managed to temporize, still glib and assertive, but the kids weren't satisfied and after that they probed him sharply, even coming out with fairly blatant political attack. Nicholas says he got a cool, rather tense glance from the guide as they were filing out of the building.

But this year. . . . The subject came up a while ago, and Nicholas just shook his head: 'Naa, I was all into that last year, but like I don't really think it's so relevant now. Politically man, these no-nukes people are naive . . . you've got to face up to the reality. For one thing, hey, a power plant isn't dangerous er . . . kind of auto-nomously: it all depends on who *owns* it, okay. So once Koeberg gets to be owned by the workers themselves, then the threat aspect just doesn't exist any more. And that's another thing, see – a place like that creates jobs, and you know we need that here in the Cape. People need *work*, hey, it's basic.'

Feeling bewildered, I offered Nicholas half of my sandwich: and left him enthusing over the lentil sprouts and marmite while I tried to unravel my own perplexity. Managed to work out eventually that his argument was phrased in a language that seemed perfectly co-herent, sufficient in itself, yet had no compulsory, irreducible term for the preservation of the sources of things. Life, culture, work, progress – all of those need a fairly elemental substrate: or at any rate an undestroyed environment. I asked him unhappily about that. He passed me a cup of bitter tea from his thermos, and I sipped it slowly as he explained that a lot of the outcry against nuclear power is emotional over-reaction.

'Look, we have to be realistic, Anna. Once this country gets free, we're going to need massive projects for development. So we're go-ing to need more and more sources of energy, okay? And nuclear power, if you like it or not, just happens to be one of the most ef-ficient sources we've got. There's far *less* pollution from a nuclear power plant than from coal-burning, hey.'

He must have seen my bleak, unconvinced expression.

'Sure, look, the waste disposal is still a big problem: but they're working on that all the time. And they're working on better safety precautions all the time as well. Heeeey, it's far more likely we'd

14

get hit by a tidal wave than Koeberg's going to blow up! You can't get hung up on these wild ideas about disaster and all that.'

Think I glanced across miserably at Marianne; but she was peering determinedly into the pages of *Germinal*. Convinced, I suppose, that I was a fool for wasting my time talking to an 'arrogant scientist'. Nicholas didn't seem arrogant even then. Just excitable; with his blonde hair sticking out over his collar and that spurious tie he wears half throttling him. Keen-eyed with conviction; and a few grains of wholewheat still clinging to his reddish beard.

I suppose it's true: that you daren't let your personal moods dictate your political standpoint? Maybe it *is* just a kind of mass, millenarian hysteria, this agitated envisioning of nuclear disaster. I don't know. Isn't it also a real possibility? Maybe the smooth disavowals are the myths. Feel so precariously adrift in this sea of facts and feelings. Afraid to be an utter fool and allow myself to be swept along with the unthinking, populist drift; and also much more simply afraid: afraid in the absolute.

I seem to have been writing for ages. The neighbours' television was switched off ages ago: there's only the sound of their chained Alsatian barking now at the wind, or the darkness perhaps.

ii

Had a bath half an hour ago – feeling warm and more relaxed. And now there's a whole evening ahead, that I feel compelled as always to fill up with letters. I wonder why. Why we're driven to speak all the time, to ask questions in stammers. Why we can't just say a thing for all time, once, then be finished. Silent.

Maybe that's why I like writing to you. Because it's speaking, I mean, without sound. You. You are not Papa, are you. I thought at first you might be, but then I began to doubt that. Briefly I thought also that you might be Marianne Hofmeyr. But I love Marianne – why should I write to her? No. In reality, I suppose, you must be a stranger to me. You who alter this fragmented print into a flowing pattern of remembered meaning within your own mind. I feel almost afraid of you, but I sense that there is something luckily keeping us apart: some glassy, impenetrable barrier that holds

15

me safely back from the reckless world where I imagine you are capable of flexing real fingers – to turn a page, or to stroke the spine of a novel.

But it seems real enough to me – this world that I inhabit. It's even beginning to break apart in places: there are holes gnawed in the skirting boards, and some of the window panes have cracks in them. The bathroom door is beginning to look rickety, I noticed. There are gaps between the planks, and that extra panel I nailed over the bottom part last year has come half away again. A few weeks ago there was a stormy night, with the rain lashing down in heavy swathes of metal-cold water, and the wind at gale force: I heard a kind of soughing from the roof, and then there was a colossal clattering din and splintering suddenly. Leapt up, racing to see – and the door into the yard was hanging listlessly, half stoved in by a giant sheet of iron from the roof. It must have been loosened by the buffeting, then lifted away from its rusted bolts to come slithering down, maybe ricocheting back from the alley wall.

Afterwards I couldn't get back to sleep, somehow: remembering the split-second feeling of utter terror, of violation. That razor-edged metal might have crashed right through a window. . . . Although it wasn't even that, really: more some obscure sense that glass or wood or even flesh were not nearly as fragile as the web of one's thinking, as the world one dreams about.

Feeling cold again. But at least it's stopped raining.

Thinking about Marianne's disillusionment again. It was only a temporary mood; and yet her kids quite often leave her desolately angry. Maybe her class is a special case, though: it's the lowest ranked stream of the standard nines – the kids Afrikaans-speaking, and taking practical subjects for Matric. Woodwork, needlework, typing. Seems they're looked down on by the English-speaking kids, as well as by the other standard nines from the upper streams. Marianne told me once, depressed, that her kids almost seem to believe in their own inferiority. They keep to themselves – a belligerent, morosely inward group: defying anyone to think that they care a damn, and loathing any teacher who singles one of them out with humiliatingly difficult questions. I'm supposed to have them for English lessons. Well, there were only a few weeks of real teaching this year: but I left their classroom despondent each time.

16

Maybe it's something wrong with the syllabus. Not the kids, I mean. Irrational to teach English and Afrikaans separately to kids who're bilingual, and switching all the time. Because there's a difference, supposed to be, between societal bilingualism and the cultivated bilingualism of an individual.

There are two girls in that class who always sit together, often in the same desk, at the back of the room. They have a way of wordlessly looking you up and down, obviously making a detailed, contemptuous inventory of your clothing. Marianne says that she's often nearly thrown the blackboard duster at them: 'Anna, they are so unliberated. . . .' Her eyes glittering painfully. 'They think you just nowhere unless you wear high-heels and, and stupid fashions.' She really believes her feminist preachings have made some impression on the three boys in the class at least. Because they come into the staffroom at lunch-time and fawn around her, enticing her so softly, so considerately, to let them use her car.

And Nicholas. Once we were both waiting at the bus-stop after school. The road running past the school is too narrow, really, for the traffic it carries regularly: buses, heavy trucks, light panel vans, as well as all the ordinary traffic, and bicycles and horse-carts. There was one of those vegetable-laden carts creaking and jingling past us, the old, blinkered horse plodding stolidly across the uneven tar; and a bakkie came up, far too fast, and hooting continuously. Of course there's no centre line painted in the road either. When the horse cart didn't pull over, the driver of the bakkie leaned out of his window to shriek abuse at its owner, then stepped on his accelerator and overtook him on the left, going up on to the verge and hurtling past, half skidding on the loose sand and slippery grass before he hit the tar again to continue, still speeding, and still blaring on his hooter. You should have seen Nick . . . he'd stepped right out into the road; had his arm raised, fist clenched. Don't think he was even aware of it. Indignantly glaring after the bakkie. He turned to me swiftly, his face all solemn with outrage: 'Shit, hey, I bet you don't get drivers like that in *England*.' With a proud, furious stress on the last word.

Of course I started to giggle then; and Nicholas was still so worked up that he couldn't see why – baffled, and quite angry with me for a minute. In the end though he saw it as funny too and began to laugh, perhaps a bit sheepishly.

17

Maybe that naive utopian enthusiasm is almost an instinct, the
_laborate outward manifestation of something graven into the
psyche.

Doesn't everyone dream about a mythical country. Once when
the kids wrote me an essay on *A Journey*, Willie Peters handed in
his usual twenty lines, with the words written out laboriously huge,
about a train ride to England. Not sure he knows that England is
an island, or that there's a sea between this continent and Europe.
Mostly the concessions to any actual geography were minimal: a
few lines extended with references to 'many pretty flowers along
the way' and 'many interesting animals'. Why not, in any case. How
do you persuade whole ranges of mountains, colossally folded and
broken layers of the earth's crust – to take on a papery existence.
Nature isn't tractable in that way.

And maybe the real journey Willie wrote about was taking place
in his mind, in some region of meaning where there wasn't the need
for seriality or the careful specificity of realism. Think his imaginary
experiences in England were probably the fanciful fulfilment of
his own dreams. I wouldn't call them idle, though. They were
focused on some central, ultimately invisible spot that had to do
with the absence of a colour bar. In England he was recognized as
a brilliant soccer player and paid vast amounts of money for con-
senting to play in a top team. Went wherever he liked, bought
anything he wanted, visited a dozen cinemas in less than a week.
The return journey wasn't even spuriously graced with more pretty
flowers: instead he crowned it triumphantly with a radiant satisfac-
tion, symbolized for him as a silver trophy.

The self; one's own sated sense of being: I suppose that's the real
prize.

When Willie handed in that essay he made a special point of
waiting behind the others so that he could give it to me personally.
There was a look in his eyes that I've rarely seen there – pride, I
think; but it amounted to a deep, almost luminous happiness.

I wonder why Willie's story seemed facile. I don't mean to sound
disparaging: I really would like to know. Maybe it's because his
questing wasn't complicated by any of the elemental struggles with
some oppressive monster; lacked the multiple, ambiguous relations
with doppelgängers. And it seems that there was no need for him
to overcome obstacles – merely entering the charmed country was

18

enough to ensure the romantic resolution. Maybe they're essentially similar: Nicholas's England where everyone is a courteous driver; Willie's England where he's welcomed as a hero. Maybe also that unreal domain you find in comedy? The Forest of Arden, where man and beast fuse briefly and bizarre inversion and licentiousness can occur with impunity. Because of bewitchment, the changeability of moonlight, the rite of theatre.

Once I was caught up also in a tumultously disintegrating dream of romance, a dream that swept us off the rain-wet steps of the cathedral in the city – and backward, till we were staggering under the blows of those men, falling back, aghast, into the sudden void of silence, of stained bright, glass-coloured air. I was too young then – eight years ago – far too young to understand that I'd been hoping for something fierily transcendent: nothing that could possibly have come to such an ending on the stone steps of a church, amidst tear-gas, before the bland faces of the crowd that watched us being kicked and beaten. Something was ripped apart that day, in a true enough sparagmos. Except that it wasn't human flesh, but a dream of the world, or words maybe: some language in which it was still possible to speak about heroes, redemptions, radical transformations. . . .

One of the things I've been doing is clearing out the old papers from my desk drawers. Found receipts going back five years; scraps of paper with cryptic Dewey numbers scribbled on them; bundles of old letters, pages and pages of them – that I never even posted. Phantom correspondence that I used to keep, although a few of my letters were even tentatively addressed to actual people. Wonder why I never sent them. Some sort of deception, I suspect. Pretend that you're handing over something of your real self, but then withhold it after all: maybe just a feint. That reminds me of Papa's poem, 'Die afstand'. It's about – well, it's impossible to paraphrase, but I suppose it's about the paradox of love poetry. The form that belies its own content. The writer of that poem grows steadily more and more conscious of his own action: the fact of the pen in his hand and the small, cryptic marks of his own writing seem merely to estrange him from the person he is addressing – and by the end of the poem from his own meaning, as well as from love.

I found adolescent poems too: those childish, unhappy rhapsodies of my teens, all of them written - though he never knew it - for Papa. I think I might have gone on writing that embarrassing nonsense even at university, if its real meaning hadn't been pointed out to me. A clever honours student who stank of cigarette smoke and who spoke with a dizzying rapidity while the coffee in his cup went cold: explaining to me that by imitating Anton, while I might want to please him, I was only entering into a kind of rivalry with him - winning his animosity rather than his affection.

Got up to draw the study curtains, and accidentally touched the glass with my finger-tips; suddenly realizing again how cold it is. There's a draught gusting right through the house: must be coming in from under the kitchen door. Or maybe it's the kitchen window. The top frame won't close completely, and the darkness seems to get stuck there sometimes and lie low in a long, thin rectangle along the wood.

The neighbours are watching television again tonight, so perhaps I won't have to be flinching under the pointedly loud curses I sometimes get for this constant firing of cold metal letters at paper.

François has been on my mind a lot, recently. It's six months now that he's been gone from the city. I keep wondering whether he's managed to find his way into Botswana, or whether he's still simply walking aimlessly somewhere in the veld. We had long conversations during the few weeks he stayed here. I pressing Constance's idea, that he might enjoy working as a nature conservation officer.

François had his thin, troubled answers, though. 'Jeez, Anna, *you* telling me that. . . . You really think I want to patrol some game reserve, and when the cabinet ministers come up for some shooting, I'm just going to head off in the opposite direction - see nothing, say nothing.' His words falling away in a jumble of impassioned incoherence. After a long silence he raised his head and looked at me quizzically. 'I don't get you, you know. *That's* establishment, hey - game parks and all that, mainly for the benefit of the rich. What does a worker in Guguletu give a stuff for kudu and elephant, hundreds of miles away.' François has always been sceptical about my political convictions - he was only saying that to win me over, I think.

I should've known that he'd resist - absolutist that he is. Unwil-

20

ling to work within a particular society, because he thinks of human beings as creatures who are part of a single, global ecology.

'Anna, listen, I just don't think that conservation's about setting up little separate enclaves for a few animals, hey. It's got to be re-educating people, till . . . till they see that the environment is all around them, always.' There was a glistening film beginning to form itself on his upper lip. Frans looked at me swiftly; scared, I think, that I wasn't following.

'It's already too late for these people here: that's why I'm heading for the Okavango, Anna.' His voice lost its urgency, becoming wistful instead. 'Hey? Like the people there already understand: they don't need to formulate. . . . How to make use of the natural resources around them, without just fucking them in till there's nothing left. Hey Anna? You don't have to fence off the swamps and call them protected. People still live there: only they know how to do it.'

It's difficult to understand François. He certainly wasn't naive: he didn't like the glamorous, middle-class conservation movement, and he had little time for unrealistic sentiment either. Told me once, frustrated after reading an article about some virtually extinct species: 'Ja, you know, it isn't natural objects you want to preserve, but natural systems. Sure it's sad when a species goes extinct, but that isn't the real issue.'

And I think he also sensed that his desire to go and live in a tiny village amongst strangers might be a selfishly tactless thing. He used to think aloud about the implications. 'Of course, I wouldn't want to impose myself: like I don't really think I'm some big deal from civilization who's going to show the locals how.' Later he'd add: 'And I won't be a drain on the local economy. I'm pretty strong, I can work. If people really wanted, I could help out, because I do have a skill, you see – knowing about insect pests.'

Isn't it another story about paradise. About relic societies 'somewhere else', where people still live in an innocent harmony with nature.

Think it must be horrible to live in a society where the common beliefs sustain your own personal myths. Like being insane. Except that you wouldn't know, would you. There were things that François believed in quite literally – about the original of all human questings: that primal, unimaginably courageous journey towards

21

the unknown of the outer world, through the dark, rigid, near-impasse of bone. I think he also believed in the utmost necessity of the hope held out by the foetus in the last moments of its drifting, watery life before it is choked fatally and drowned in a cataclysmic searing of light and the brittle, hurting air. I suppose that beliefs like those might have made Frans technically insane: because myths have no intelligible meaning unless they're collectively held – like language. And in any case, isn't it one of those aetiological fallacies? When people try to reconstruct something essentially pre-verbal or pre-rational – using words, and reason. Trying to find the beginnings of myth in some actual past, they end up only with other myths. Suppose you have to try and move away from those things, even if once they had a certain truth: because that truth is nothing now but an obsolete, burned-in circuitry capable of generating endless patterns for idle dreams and myths, romance, mysticism. . . . Didn't someone say that the earliest people may have been the prisoners of words at times, convinced of their substantiality, so that an utterance or a name might sometimes assume the deadly, terrifying beauty of godliness. Then there would have been some sunlit, leafy-coloured abyss of nothingness between words and objects, and nothing to interpose, except perhaps a burned, bleeding gift.

We're also trapped though, aren't we? By certain visions that we simply take for the mundane truth of our existence. I think so. In a state like ours the people in power are so terribly afraid that they are driven to acts of murder and torture: and our minds have been so poisoned that it's difficult to know whether those thick-set, uniformed men rise up out of a real world or out of thallium-induced psychosis. It's an unspeakable deadlock, that nothing can end except nothingness itself. If there were a space, I mean, between my body and the other person's thick-knuckled, blue-veined fist; or if there were some words with more dignity than mere screams; or if there were even someone else – a third person: then I think it might be possible to start discovering where fear ends and the real world begins.

After Papa left us, there was no longer a third person for Frans, I imagine. I still think that the only way to make much sense of his breakdown would be to look into his childhood. To try and find out how his own earliest experiences were given more and more elaborate symbolic expression by events in the world around him.

Because it doesn't help much to look at isolated moments. If you take Frans's last day at the museum, there doesn't seem to be anything significant about it at all. He was sitting at his desk as usual, sketching. I imagine he'd have had his technical drawing pens neatly ranked at the edge of his blotter. And there would have been a small, creamish larva in the watchglass under his microscope. Suzanne says he seemed to be quite happy, perhaps just a little thoughtful that morning. She was drifting around the department, flicking naphthalene back to the sides of the drawers. Way it sublimates, then recrystallizes under the glass lids in those fine, ghostly fronds. She must have been humming to herself – habit of hers; stopping every now and then to meditate on the shape of a fingernail. François teased her, apparently, about her crimson nails. Daily ritual of theirs: he'd always find something – the height of her heels, or the dipping of her neckline. She did notice, though, that he was mumbling something to himself: the same phrases over and over. Some problem he was having to determine the right level, I think; the significant division. Which may have been why he kept saying, 'There must be some other time for them, it doesn't exist for them in the same units. But how to watch more slowly. Time of a different duration; then what time is there?'

I wonder sometimes whether it wasn't a reference to his ants: I know that he spent hours watching their rambling, haphazard work activities.

Mid-way through the morning he stood up and began to tidy his desk. Scrupulously, Suzanne says. All his drawing sheets into manilla folders; a pencilled label slipped into the vial along with the specimen in alcohol. He switched off his miscrocope, covering it with its plastic dust hood; folded his white coat over the back of a chair: and wandered out of the building. Suzanne wasn't disturbed – thought he might have been going downtown, or maybe to the library; maybe even just off for a quick wee. He didn't leave any message where he could be found, which was unusual – but then he was clearly in an abstracted mood.

It doesn't explain anything, does it – that scene. I've been thinking almost obsessively about François for months now: and no matter how many other tiny episodes I come up with, it still doesn't make much sense to me. I want to know why, not how;

why that happened to him.

How *do* you? How do you add together discrete moments and then suddenly understand them as a single flow, all interrelated and meaningful. How do you get to those moments. Selecting facts. You can only pick them out if you already have some theoretical principle that decides what is critical. Isn't it all self-referential? A relevant fact is anything that controverts or proves a particular hypothesis. Objectivity of science. The Press too. Newspaper stories: always about the unique, the spectacular, the momentous. Supposed to be a realistic account of daily event. What makes people see some events, not others? The kids at school might like to talk about that some time. Debate we could have: whether a scrapbook of newspaper clippings would constitute a genuinely historical account of a period. Maybe even get them interested enough to think about reportage, and realism in the novel.

Maybe it's only while you're actually at the heart of the moment, living out something, that your actions have a fixed quality; the immediate meaning of them bound to place and instant. It's only afterwards, when you stop to think about it, that meaning frees itself and becomes a symbol, a story. You get people who imagine it is false, somehow, to recount the action. But there would be no human language if we couldn't re-create things. If we never stood still and tried to make out the sense of the wind, the warmish rippling through the light hairs on your fore-arm – then we'd be like tiny flies? Dipping and hovering always, just swaying in the air at the whim of the breeze.

There's a curious, brief poem of Papa's: about those number squares that you sometimes find in lucky packets. Do you know them? A kind of puzzle: a cheap plastic thing, usually, with moveable ill-fitting little squares set into it. Numbered, but out of sequence; and the trick is to shuffle them back into order. The point for Papa is that the whole manoeuvre is only possible because of the existence of one empty space in the frame. That's one of the constant ideas in the *Sprakeloos* collection: that it's the breathless, wordless pause before an utterance that makes most spoken meanings possible. And it is also stammering inarticulacy that may precipitate new languages – and with them, new worlds. The children at school know this. They never speak of themselves as 'coloured', but as the disenfranchised. Just a game with words? Not really, I

24

think. Isn't it a way of recreating one's vision of reality. It'd be rash to imagine that those particular words lack substance: they're as heavily real as the weight of a father's hand on his daughter's neck – while he touches those hollows of flesh and bone near her throat; or as real as the pent-up force that's contained in the rigid rubber baton of a crouched policeman.

If I tried saying that sort of thing to Marianne now. . . . I know just how she'd sit there with her shoulders hunched up, aloof, and her collar-bones standing out. And finally saying, 'But that is so theoretical. . . . How can a ordinary person understand it. It's arrogant, arrogant, Anna.' She believes that committed literature ought to be about the misery of life in a re-settlement camp or a squatter's shanty. Looks at me bleakly when I try to suggest that realist novels only help to preserve the status quo. 'But I don't know what you mean,' she'll cry indignantly. 'Now you sounding like Chrisjan. He and his friends are always talking about, about Barthes, how wonderful this man is. But now I want to know what is it about?' And when I try to suggest also that there can hardly be out and out racists still left, or that mildly liberal conversions are useless now, in any case – she looks at me with a scathing grin, and then shakes her head slowly, unhappily. 'Anna, I don't know. Maybe you haven't been in the country. My parents now – they literally believe that the black people are just not human.' Fretting, she'll stammer slightly. 'My mother goes on and on about the concentration camps in the Boer War, still to this day she won't speak to an "Ingelsman". You know that? But if you tell her about the Eastern Cape, the camps there, with kids dying, fifty thousand a year, and the women too depressed and hungry to move from in front of their shacks. . . .' Tears often surprise her when she talks about things like this. All she can do then is fumble for her glasses, or pretend to be setting the thermos upright in her basket. 'Ag nee. I think if you can just get people to *see* that suffering.'

I wonder what Marianne really thinks of Papa's poetry. Suspect it might make her impatient because it's never overtly political; often not even set distinctly in this country. And too private? Thinking of *Liefdesverse*, and *Glas*. When I was at university I used to get stupidly enraged sometimes – sick with doubt about Papa's political standpoint. Writing his opposition sentiments on the ballot ticket only, with an X – like a poor illiterate.

25

He'd already left the department of Afrikaans and Nederlands by then, and few people ever connected me with him even. Well – Rossouw's a common name. Once, I remember, an older student picked it up when she heard my surname. She inclined her head shrewdly for a few seconds, squinting at me; and then said, 'You related to Anton Rossouw?' Funny, I felt embarrassed, almost. Not certain whether to admit it or not. Disowning Papa?

I still feel confused about parts of his work. And that's mixed up with a bitterness I used to feel about his abandoning our country, with its particular historical struggle. Now though. . . . I suppose the life he's chosen really is the most authentic he can lead. He must love Karen, I'm sure: I've always known – it's hardly unobvious – that she is the woman in *Liefdesverse*. And it feels odd to read the fragments of erotica in that collection. One's own father delighting so feelingly in the dark, tangled mass of a stranger's hair. Well. And as for his living in France now – he could have chosen almost any country, couldn't he. Perhaps the soft rain of the Paris winter, and the pigeons, remind him of Cape Town.

Suppose it's inevitable that a certain nostalgia creeps into his work every now and then. Wistfulness of the exiled. I know Nicholas would probably whinny with laughter at the idea of any deep attachment to a landscape. It might be another of the things he'd call a myth. . . . 'Hey I can't get that, you know. Like a city's a city. Living in London's going to be just the same as Cape Town – huh? Maybe no sea, okay. And sure – the mountain. But there's no . . . er *mystique* about the place, you know.'

But couldn't it be like those feeling-experiences that are inchoate forever, because they imprint themselves long before you have any language to protect yourself. The first bush-scents, and the cold, streaking rain; the wet earth and the termite alates grounded after their feeble flight, helplessly crawling in circles.

Suppose for Papa his first landscapes will always be the Transvaal veld – the hard, dry earth there, and hardly any real mountains; in some parts still the tall, slender, razor-edged grasses. Winter for him a dry, bitterly cold season, rather than these cold, grey-black rains of the Cape. Now, I wonder. What is his winter now. It's inconceivable to me: winter in France, in Paris. Perhaps also a thin, trickling, endless rain: chimneys and rooftops darkened to the colours of slate, of water, of doves.

26

I've never been able to let Papa go. I remember how I used to pore over his poetry when I was a teenager. He'd only published *Sprakeloos* and *Die Stedelike Kuns van Landskapskildery* by then.

I never spoke to Papa about his work. I wonder why. Maybe because we grew up with such a stern respect for Papa's working times, Papa's need for silence, Papa's inviolable privacy when he was locked in his study; and perhaps those observances extended themselves to his poetry for me.

I don't even know whether François used to read him. Odd, never asking that. But there were such distances between us as children. Think he did try reading some of Eugene Marais's poetry. Of course, because *The Soul of the White Ant* and *My Friends the Baboons* were his two favourite books, next to *African Insect Life*. I remember how tattered his copies were of all three till he mended them finally, painstakingly restoring the torn pages with fine tissue paper overlays and tipping in the ones that were coming away. He covered them with plastic wrappers and after that no one was allowed to open them without his permission.

Ja, François. . . . Way he used to storm at his friends if they knocked things over in his room. I liked going in there. To look at the caterpillars in those empty shoeboxes he kept along one side; bringing him arum lily leaves to feed them, that time he was entranced with hawkmoths. Once he explained to me about the scales on the wings, handing me a dried specimen he'd mounted and the little metal-cased loupe that Constance had given him for a birthday. I couldn't really see properly through that lens though, clutching the moth by the tip of the pin; moving it nearer and further. And suddenly felt nervous. If I dropped the moth, maybe crushed a wing with my clumsy fingers? Even my breathing – maybe dusting away all the tiny scales: would François shout at me? I handed it all back to him, sick deep down inside myself, and crept away to my own room, to find a book. Feeling flushed; ashamed, somehow.

Things became better as we grew older. Maybe we just got accustomed to the constant, almost inaudible murmuring of petty squabbling that we used to express our kinship.

And then when he was working at the museum, after he'd left university. I loved to visit him there, in my holidays. Nobody would frown at you, thin-faced, for disrupting the schedule of the working day; and if François was busy with something he couldn't leave im-

27

mediately I'd walk up and down, pulling out drawers from the cabinets to gaze, half covetous, at the metallic colours of the beetles' elytra. Staring at the cryptic shadowings of beige and grey and cream on the wings of moths. I always stopped for a moment in front of the glass nest where François kept his ants; to watch the workers out on the foraging tray. And Suzanne would glance up from the insect she was busy trying to re-pin. Flicking her dark hair from her eyes to give me that quick, radiant smile of hers. Funny thing – she almost always chose English when she spoke to me, though I know that she and François used Afrikaans.

I felt at home there, feeling that there was no one I had to placate with my usual strained, complaisant smily or sticky, stringy bits of compulsory conversation. Always trying to hold everything together. What? The whole world, maybe. With my dry, uncertain search for words. But at the museum there was a kind of peace. Suzanne would continue with her work, chipping in if she wanted to: but mostly oblivious of us, lost in thoughts about the coming summer, I suppose. Or wondering about the chemical nature of that coppery-green, crystalline thread that was snarled around the corroded pin she held.

Sometimes François would push back his chair to go and speak to Dr De Wet. He'd stand there almost languidly – the height of him in the doorway that separated their working areas. I'd sit quietly in the background, listening to them. François liked him, I think. Could tell from the way he'd stoop forward slightly, with a solemn attentiveness in his eyes as he listened. Or maybe that was just his habitual manner: because of being tall? Perhaps he'd picked it up from Papa. There was something in his voice, though, as well. The way he used to try and draw Dr De Wet out always, unconsciously encouraging him with little nods and humming sounds. I know Dr De Wet used to pretend amiably to grumble away at everything – the weather, his work, inflation; but really he was dedicated to his projects. Think François was always trying to learn more from him, because he's one of the world authorities on the hymenoptera of southern Africa. He spent about six years in the field collecting specimens and information for his monograph on ants of the western Cape. Frans was assisting him with his huge programme to describe the larval stages of all the local weevil species. A necessary task, Dr De Wet thought: even though it meant abandoning his beloved work on solitary bees. I remember: his commonest plaints were about frivolous research. When he needed to rest his eyes for a few minutes he'd stop peering down his microscope and swivel round in his chair: mumbling aloud, as if purely by chance, and to no one in particular, 'Mos 'n klomp bôls. . . .' But knowing that François would always be there within earshot, willing to come over and listen. He worked in the Transvaal for a long time, almost fifteen years – in one of the government departments. Pest control, I suppose. Maybe crop spraying. So maybe his aggressiveness was partly from a loyalty to the people that hand out the funds. I don't know. Perhaps it was partisan-allegiance to the state. But the way it worked out it was also a real concern for the welfare of the country. Maybe? Believing it important to tackle things that are directly urgent. Like that project on the weevils. If a whole granary gets infested the price of bread can go up, or of mealie-meal. Then people go hungry; maybe even starve.

François said he was almost always the first person to arrive at their department in the mornings, and sometimes only packed away his miscroscope at six in the evening. Ja. I remember now why I thought Frans admired him. He used to take Dr De Wet small presents often, of bees and sometimes ants that he'd found in the veld. Suzanne says that Frans could get into an astonishing rage if Dr De Wet didn't seem to him to appreciate the gifts enough. Grow murderously taciturn, and treat everyone around him with exaggerated respect. 'Ja,' she murmured, lowering her eyelashes reflectively, 'ja, dit was so effens . . . snaaks, eintlik.' Then dazzling me again with her dark-lustred eyes: 'No, but really, that was just a few times. It was just – his way, you know.'

I suppose it must be quite late. It's hushed outside, with just the rain still always streaming – innocently. Even if it's falling in such constantly drifting patterns of straightened light. There's the sound of the darkness too. But then they say that's something in your own ears. Molecules of air.

iii

Spent this morning sitting at the kitchen table, tilting the salt cellar

29

to and fro in my hands; trying to persuade myself that staring at the drizzle against a cracked window pane is thinking. What would I do if a storm blew that window in. But I can't even panic. It would be easy to find a glazier, or I could measure the frame and buy new glass myself. Ask the man in the hardware shop how to mix putty. Or do you need a helper to do these things? It's hard to believe in catastrophes as long as you sense you still have reserves of self-sufficiency.

Find myself tidying books into neatly squared piles, or petulantly tugging at the hem of a curtain till it hangs plumb straight. For a fleeting moment even seriously considered sleeping on top of the blankets, underneath a sleeping-bag – just to avoid rumpling the bedclothes. Stopped myself though; can still keep myself from entering these maze-like geometries of insanely patterned behaviour.

It must be about half past five: It'll be falling into evening quite soon. I've been going around the house, ritually drawing curtains across the face of the night and the shining window panes. At least the garden will be thriving on all this rain. Suppose it's settling into twilight now, glistening with spider webs and the shaken rain in its leaves.

I've been thinking again about François. About the time he took me on that camping trip to Clanwilliam – organized, I half remember, by people at the museum. Looking back I can see that Frans was withdrawn, perhaps a bit eccentric even then; and that would have been about two years ago. No: it was summer – two and a half years ago.

Yet he didn't seem unhappy – his movements were unhurried, with a certain serenity to them. Made me think of Papa, that peacefulness. I remember how on that camp Frans would wander off in the evenings to puff away at his pipe, crouched down on his heels at the edge of the ridge. The second night we were there I saw one of the children set out along the track after him, trying to imitate his leisurely, long-legged stride. And a little while later there was a second, miniature version of François squatting next to him in the twilight. It was quite a distance away, with the light mostly gone into shadows and settling dust by then; but I could make out the little kid as he secretly broke off a twig from a bush. Experimental puffing movements. They seemed oblivious to everything around them; even to each other. Lost, with the scents of the bush around

30

them, and rising woodsmoke, and the hush of the dying light. When they came back to the campfire it was separately still, and the small boy went without a word to find a low rock within a few feet of his father.

So many single parents on that camp, with their children.

And that little boy. There was an incident that just stuck inside me, for weeks afterwards. After supper his father wanted to take him off and settle him into his sleeping-bag for the night. I was sitting nearby, and the little kid suddenly scrambled up on to the rock and held out his arms to me, asking very softly to be picked up. It seemed strange, because the rock was only a few inches high, and he couldn't really have needed help. But I lifted him anyway – such a thin, long-limbed child – and I felt his hands come round my neck, fluttering there timidly as if he were afraid to clasp me properly. I understood only as I was setting him down that he'd been whispering 'Good night' into my ear, over and over: and then I guessed, already too late, that he'd simply wanted someone to hug him.

Maybe it was because we'd had an exhausting day: walking along the foot of the ravine, having to duck under branches, getting scratched, with the sun concentrating its heat stubbornly on the napes of our necks. Could have been the firelight too. Flickering up vividly, without really illuminating anything: you feel a constant darkness behind the eyes, watching flames. And the smoke swirling up on the breeze, veering into your eyes. Smarting. After the child had gone to bed, though, I found myself left almost hollow, as though there were some void inside me, that nonetheless burned and burned.

I remember that morning, the way the sun's rays came piercing down on to us, acutely angled. It was really the second sunrise for us lying on that ledge, facing the west, and sheltered by the steep rocky overhang from the dawn rise. I had my bare shoulder stuck out of the sleeping-bag – could feel it beginning to tingle, and I turned over drowsily to lie there and sunbathe. One of the things I liked about that camp – the way no one thought it necessary to rouse us all instantly and begin delegating energetic tasks. Of course, the children were up early: I heard a kid shout out occasionally, triumphant – who must have been finding tiddlers in the stream. Self-sufficient mostly, they'd pull on bathing costumes and tee-shirts before wandering away to amble dreamily over the smooth rock of the ancient river-bed: breaking off branches and peeling them for something to prod at stones with, or for scribbling signs in the dust.

The expanse of rock all around us was pitted with wide basins and funnels that must have been scoured out perhaps a million years ago by small, grinding pebbles and the constant flow of the river. Now they formed isolated pools of warm, still water where the children liked to splash and wade.

I inched myself closer to the cool face of the overhang, and stared up at the shadowed colours of the stone. That was where I found a small fly clinging intently to the rock. It had the look of a creature just emerged from its chrysalis; wings still drying, hardening. It was about as big as a mosquito: but then I saw it had two pairs of wings. Not a fly. François's rucksack was lying within my reach, his collecting kit sticking out from the outer pocket. I took it out, stealthily, with one hand, and found a glass bottle. Stirred back towards my ledge and softly fitted the open mouth of the vial over the insect.

François seemed to have gone off into the bush – his sleeping place was already tidied – so I couldn't ask him what it was. I lay quietly, looking at the strange fly. A few minutes later it had managed to duplicate itself, and I was amazed; not quite certain whether mature insects ever cast their skins.

Lazily I dressed myself then: beginning to feel uncomfortable and sticky. Sponge bag over my arm, I found the little trowel leaning against its rock, next to the roll of paper, and set off, picking my way down into the ravine, through the bush. Already the day was singing, with the light melting on the stones. I walked on, brushing through a waist-high scrub that was sometimes irritably thorny, but sometimes velvety, or powdery, or scented with wax. A lizard occasionally slipped away discreetly from the crest of his rock.

François was crouching next to the gas burner when I came back, brewing coffee in the stained, blackened billy-can that had belonged to Papa when he was a boy. I showed him the insect then, but it was silly – as I put the vial into his hand I began to realize – thinking it, stammering the word 'ephemeral'. Frans, who was watching me, grinned and was about to tease: but we said at the same moment – 'It's a mayfly.' Ephemeridae: of course. Probably the September Brown, Frans said.

Was it only spring then? Seemed so hot at the time. Françoi
didn't want it, so I let the living creature fly away; keeping the
translucent, skeletal replica. Tried to interest the small boy in it
later, but he seemed reluctant to reach out and actually take the
vial to himself – held back, and wouldn't talk properly. Pretending
to be more a baby than he was, I think. Fretfully mussing at his
pale hair with a slender, fine-boned little hand. I felt convinced that
he'd have liked to have it – saw his face flickering uncertainly
between eagerness and timidity – so I left it on his sleeping-bag,
next to his folded pyjamas. Where he could find it in his own time.

That offering – I suppose it was meant to be conciliatory. Isn't
that what people do? You volunteer some fragment of yourself or
any kind of substitute: in recompense. The way a lizard will shed
its tail when it's caught beneath the vivid, racing shadow of a plun-
ging kestrel.

In extremity I suppose one might offer up anything, or anyone.
Anything to spare yourself from the vision, let's say, of a man's
torso rising above you, muscular with fury, while his right arm is
drawn back and flexing with the power about to seethe into his
knuckles.

I even think I'd offer up words: throw some flimsily clouded
trace of screams into that deadly space between us.

I found it hard to keep up any vital interest in the paintings we
saw that day. Secret confession. Even though we'd slept where the
San themselves must have slept on their rustling mattresses of sweetreed with their frieze of painted elephants and warriors on the
stones at our backs. Suppose that art is most meaningful when you
don't even regard it as something special. Isn't living art inseparable
from the dynamic of the society that produces it? Maybe. . . . But
we were struggling to revere those rock paintings as Art. Capital
letter A. As though it were the same as that kind of modern art
that serves no cultural purpose except to add a chic kind of lustre
to the lives of a few wealthy people. We were even driven to use the
idiom of the bourgeois critics: people feeling obliged to speak
about the delicate artistry of line, or about the illusions of contour
and depth created by such subtle blending of ochre into chalk into
ash. The 'beauty' of rock art. Constantly we resorted to that word.
Proof, I suppose, that the paintings had lost all significance. And
yet we had no other way of understanding. Not being San.

Who were we. Our straggling band of old-fashioned, off-beat sightseers. Pricking our way through the arid scrub – constantly casting nervous glances at each other's trouserlegs for signs of ticks; irritable from the sunlight that was wrinkling our faces, making the backs of our necks feel sore and stiff. I remember someone wearing a pair of binoculars around his neck – a nature lover. Every now and then he'd stop still and raise them authoritatively to the sky, to track some speck that must have been sailing slowly just above the stony outcrops on top of the ridge.

François detached himself from the main group early on, to go stalking across more sparsely covered terrain – on some independent quest.

We ought to have taken a water-bottle, of course. Some families stayed behind at one of the swimming-holes. Better really. The guides giving a shout every fifteen minutes or so, and we scrabbling up some bushy, prickly incline to join them at the overhang of rock. You had to crouch down near them then, or lean up against a boulder while someone pointed out the way the white pigment had disappeared from an eland's neck. I tried to prattle about the binding agent that might have been used, but it's difficult to keep on enthusing when your lips are beginning to crack and all that you can smell or taste or feel is dust, stone, the dry flowers of the grasses, and wild herbs.

How do the farmers in the district make a living, I wonder. Not to know such an elementary thing. They could farm sheep in that dry country. And people breed horses, I think. But cattle? You need a lush pasturage for dairy farming, don't you. We saw a few herds, even so. And there were those goats nibbling at the bushes alongside the dust-track when we drove up to the camp: how they withdrew to berate us, reproachful from a thicket of acacia. Remembering now – someone in the group pausing to show us a buchu bush. Suppose they package bush teas then. And there's citrus farming, of course: we saw acres and acres of dark, glossy orchards. Maybe people grow vegetables too, and fruit. Vine things – spanspeks and watermelons. And the dam is big enough to take speedboats, for waterskiers: suppose there's a hotel trade in the summertime, and in the spring too – when people drive north from Cape Town to see the wild daisies opening across the veld.

Suppose there must have been a smaller village on the outskirts of the town – there always is, in the country. To house that whole other class of people who find their bread and alcohol by tackling the dirty manual work at the base of all the town's enterprise. Or else there must have been clusters of white-washed, single-roomed cottages on the farms; inconspicuous next to a dried sloot, in amongst stands of bluegums.

I feel ignorant, not knowing enough about these basic things.

Not knowing the names of birds either, or even of the animals we saw. There was that tiny buck that came skipping, almost flew across our track and sheered into the bushes, with hardly a crackle of the twigs under his hooves. So quick that only a few of us glimpsed him. One over-tired kid insisted tearfully that he'd nearly seen him, and was ready almost to bring out his fists when an older child teased him, echoing the words in mockery. What would it have been? Such a small buck: a klipspringer, or a rietbok? What is a steenbokkie. A duiker isn't that small, is he.

But then: maybe it's not so important to pin down any creature to specific level. More interesting to understand what general features make something a bokkie, than which particular clusters make an animal a steenbok, rather than a rietbok. Suppose you'd even find features in any single animal that make him separate in turn. But those are not significant, usually, are they. Except for farmers, maybe. Critical level does vary, doesn't it, even within a single society: if you think of zoologists, hunters, farmers – and children in a city. I suppose there must be some people who are content to define creatures as human or animal, with some of the animals wild, rather than domestic. Maybe it all depends on the form of your everyday exchanges with nature.

There was plenty of time for reflection on that walk. Something else I've never forgotten. There was one mother with a look of perpetual anxiety in her eyes – one of the single parents. She had three small children that she kept shooing ahead of her, desperately harrassed; not realizing perhaps how much of an edge had crept into her voice. I was walking behind them, and heard. The two older children were long-legged and managed to keep up: pacifying their mother. But unconsciously they'd picked up a nagging sharpness from her and kept glancing back officiously to urge on their small sister: 'Emma, Emma, come on.' And from the mother, bitterly, 'Oh, hurry up, Emma, we're going to be left behind because of

35

you.' I began to feel myself smothered in shame for the child's sake. At one part of the track there was a slight scramble up over a wind-eroded, keen-edged rock. As the little kid was struggling to fling herself up on to it somehow, a bit of thornbush brushed across the back of her knees. Unable to help herself, she gave out a poorly stifled wail, and was instantly panic-stricken, knowing there'd be another exasperated shout from her family. There was too. Because the mother herself was lost: I think she sensed that there never could be any catching up again. Only scurrying along, too afraid ever to rest; and being scratched by dry twigs that leave a slow, searing welt across the skin.

I saw Emma glance rapidly behind her before trying again: her eyes wide, as though she were afraid she might begin to cry. She was about four, four and a half. Rather pale under her freckles; had her hair in two scraggly-ended, shining plaits tied with cotton ribbons. I knew she was trying to pull her small self together, bracing herself for another rush at that rock; and I hurried up, trying to pretend that I'd just happened casually along. Swung her up over the rock on to the upper path, as if I weren't really even thinking about it. I'd have liked to walk with her the rest of the way, keeping my pace slow and even – let her know that there were grown-ups who could dawdle peacefully along at the rear. But I'm too clumsy to manoeuvre these things. Always moving too quickly myself, in any case. And she couldn't concentrate on anything beyond the fierce necessity of keeping up with her brothers.

Stopped being so conscious of my own thirst after that. But then it was a different ache that stuck in my throat, dry and floury. Like the feeling of futile anger; or the knowledge that there is nothing to be done about the dryness of the mesem scrub and the ashy dirtiness of the hot sand. Perhaps I am sentimental. I know that for weeks after that camp it really wasn't the paintings I remembered. Closing my eyes at night, the feeling of bush would come back briefly: memories of a broken keurboom that trailed its dusty flowers in the sketchily shaded water of the river; finches darting away to leave their woven, straw-coloured nests quivering where they hung in the tall reeds. But mostly it would be memories of the children. And then a familiar burning, just before sleep: the way your eyes feel when the wind shifts

36

suddenly at twilight and the smoke veils your face, stinging and darkened with the tiny smuts of the lifting ash.

iv

'Well, what have the future generations done for me?' That's a witty one-liner quoted in this morning's newspaper. Some visiting American was speaking to a group of businessmen, and they asked him for his views on conservation.

I wish I never had to go outside again. Ever. I went up to the main road to buy the paper this morning, and some apples, lettuce, milk. It's strange, but there seems to be so much noise outside – I can't even locate it strictly; perhaps its nothing, or only the cold air rushing through the folds of your own clothes, or the leakage of muzak and hiss from people's radios as you pass their doorways. But the traffic is real enough, along the main road: buses, mostly travelling empty, boycotted; and heavy trucks, delivery vans. And the number of people – it must have been tea-break at one of the small factories: clusters of people, some of them swathed in plastic overalls, buying milkshakes and samoosas at the café. Waiting in the background, I felt my head begin to swim. Maybe from the cold; or because of the noisy giggling and calling. Saw childish fingerprints smeared across the glass panes that front the counter. Brittle, brightly-coloured sweets in the drawers. Apples gone over-ripe, beginning to yellow where they were nested in the window; and the pungent smell of bruised guavas. You hear snatches of talk – emphatic, supportive: 'Maar 'n supervisor kan nie so nie. . . .' And when your tongue moves in your mouth, silently rehearsing the purchase, the roughness of your palate is a dry reminder, I suppose, of certain things about human beings and sociability.

Cottages are being refurbished everywhere in this suburb: the builders snatch every hour they can, in between the rain showers. Laying bricks, hastily plastering. I saw one semi-detached place having a new roof put on: people hauling down the old sheets of corrugated iron – that will go to make shanties for other people, somewhere in the dunes. Thought the builders were taking a risk in this weather: it's one of those sullen, dark days, coldly hugged to itself.

37

Almost every road has a house in it with the Sold notice stuck across its gate: seem to be quite a few young, newly-rich couples buying up the houses. Because of the petrol price going up, maybe – much closer to the city from here. It's almost as though the city is spiralling around on itself, re-locating its centre. I wonder who still lives out in the 'countryside' – Constantia, Bishopscourt, Tokai. I've never really been into those suburbs; can only guess at things like silver cutlery, fine porcelain dinnerware, servants, mirrored bathrooms, stables, guestflats, swimming pools. And sometimes at a petrol garage you see a sleek, softly gleaming car pulled up, with one of the occupants maybe carelessly resting a hand on the rolled down window pane. See a tiny wristwatch: looks like light dripping from it, and the slender strap not silver – more subtle, probably platinum.

There was a family about three houses down from here. . . . I always thought the husband was a fitter and turner, some kind of mechanic. With a shrill-voiced little kid, who used to ride up and down the pavement on her bicycle. They moved away to Parow North a couple of months ago. Mrs Conradie told me.

And the house on the corner: with a garden even smaller than mine – just a rank, weed-thick area about three yards square; the veranda boarded up with a lattice-work of weathered planks, and old Nespray tins with succulent plants growing in them balanced on top of its ledge. I could hear their television blaring when I passed their front door in the evenings: used to glimpse someone, an indistinct, hulking shadow directly in front of the set. While the children played on the doorstep, virtually on the pavement, wearing worn, greyed vests and little else. They've also moved now. Suppose to Vasco or Parow, or beyond Milnerton, maybe. The renovators have put a high wall around the house – makes it more private; with a brass-coloured carriage lamp set into the plaster. Don't know whether some people have bought it. You get speculators buying, you see. There's a thin tree sticking up over the wall of the place – looks as though it could be a poplar. But it's been muffled in a complicated, vast hood of hessian, to keep the leaves from falling, maybe. Seems a bit futile: part of the twine has come unravelled at the seams, and the Observatory winds are whipping straight through the contraption of sacking – you can't help seeing that the few wiry branches are already stripped and rattling against each other.

I'm thinking about the newspaper again. Tempted to say that there's nothing new in it at all, but I know that that would be reactionary. Better to believe in a steady escalation of the struggle. Imminence of change. Better to remember the strikes and the boycotts, to remember the latest ANC victory: ja, I'm certain the resistance must be growing daily.

And yet. There's an advertising supplement in full colour: model girls with dark, shimmering hair, and narrowed eyes made to look glittery round the rims with kohl and mascara. The way advertisements encroach on everything. The news stories themselves report that there have been incidents of arson in several parts of the country. Mostly minor - school store-rooms, or principals' offices. And some directed at the buses here in Cape Town, although usually the attacks against the tramways come as stonings. Half-bricks hurled through the windows. There's a picture of a bus with its front windscreen smashed out, some of the jagged pieces still in place, but whitened. Shatter-proof glass it must be. I remember when we were kids, picking up hundreds of those tiny cubes from the roadside sometimes: diamonds, we called them. But even on that page of the newspaper - elegant sketches of winter coats billowed airily from the margins. 'Hurry hurry hurry limited number in stock.'

For the middle classes, and the aspirant middle classes, this is their secular dream of reality, perhaps? The fiction they read most avidly each day, to find their own history given an impress of veracity by paper, print, colour photographs, advertisements. Maybe why those people subscribe. If the newspapers weren't tossed daily down on to their doormats they'd slowly waste away, as surely as if the farmers in the country had given up their struggle with drought and the drifted topsoil - and stopped sending Cape Town its wheat and mealies and milk, cheese, sunflower seeds, dried peaches and meat in those rickety trucks that travel steadily through the long nights, inching their way up over mountain passes along with the sunrise, to reach the city's markets by four in the morning.

Sometimes wish I could still indulge in wild premonitions. You know: visions of catastrophe just around the corner. I remember four years ago, when Soweto rose up. The excitement so many of us on campus felt, filled with a tense, ardent hope. I was struggling

39

then with my conscience in any case: whether to go on with the teaching diploma course. University had begun to seem amazingly irrelevant, and especially then - when the schoolkids had been pushed to the very brink, were almost desperate with frustration and anger: while we were studiously preparing papers on Piaget, or practising our script on the chalkboard. I was living in a commune then, in Mowbray. Used to be unable to get up in the mornings - my skull just felt impossibly heavy. Instead I'd lie there on my mattress, listlessly aware that the day outside was steadily swelling; hearing people outside in the street. Secretly I was hoping, praying for deliverance. The fierce thought each morning, 'Will this be the day at last?' Lying there under the sheet, inert; dull-limbed. Trying to hush your own breathing, quieten your heart-beat, so that you can listen for the sounds. Of what, I wonder now. Gunfire? Explosions? A prolonged, rumbling drone of aircraft in the skies? Machines; gods too, maybe.

Revolution in the air? It seems to have been in the air of this country forever. Immanent rebellion. And there *is* always struggle, isn't there? Why you have oppression. As well as history.

By the time I was born this current revolution must have been burning for decades already. When I was five, I remember, there were roadblocks along the old road to the airport. Constance was driving to fetch Papa. Where, I wonder. Where had he been to. Giving lectures somewhere, maybe; perhaps at a convention, or reading his poetry. Mommy was driving to fetch him, with Frans and me sitting in the back of the small Morris, each on our 'own' side of the carseat. It was late for us to be awake still, and we were already bathed and dressed in our kitten-printed, flannel pyjamas.

There were dark wattles in the night outside the car's windows; a cool, damp smell of sand; perhaps night fires; a smell of paraffin. What was the hissing sound, and the acrid stench of hot, perished rubber as we slowed down, the car jerking us forward. There was a fierce white light in the window, a man holding a torch there that blinded us, close up to our faces; and a deep voice growling that was asking questions. What did Mommy say. I don't remember. How did we get to Papa. . . . I wonder, did he pick us each up, Frans and me in turn. That bleak, echoing arrivals hall. Papa's briefcase in the crook of his arm, bumping against us as we were crushed against his chest. There would have been a tiny present for each of us - a soft

40

toy, a tin motor car. Hugging Papa was always strange for me, a confused, struggling problem of angularities and my face burning unhappily: keeping my small elbows locked together, stiff to interpose themselves between his body and mine. And Papa protesting, joking, trying to win me back with his strong arms gripping me around my pelvis, or between my nervous, quivering shoulder blades.

We didn't know then, Frans and I, about the Sharpeville shooting, about terrified white men who had closed off the city with cordons and roadblocks to keep in the prowling menace of their own anxiety.

We must have driven back home, of course. Smell again of eucalyptus from the trees lining the worn, bumpy road. Window always open just a crack; Mommy insisting, for fresh air. Almost hypnotic though, the steady streaming of the white centre-line dashes melting towards us in the car's headlights. Think Frans and I must have fallen asleep; our cheeks against the clammy vinyl of the back seat.

Twenty years ago.

Twenty years. To think that the Afrikaners had come to power just a little more than a decade before that. We've lived under Afrikaner Nationalism all our lives, Frans and I. Growing up with a sense that the leaders of the state were contemptible, while the true heroes that one learnt about slowly over the years were dead, or in prison, or in exile, or banned. And yet if you think how recent that rise of the Afrikaners was. Papa's own language has only been officially acknowledged for about sixty years now. Important part of the struggle that must have been – winning that recognition, and establishing cultural academies. What is that word. Hegemonization?

I feel afraid to think too much about Papa's place in that establishment.

Don't even know enough about Afrikaner culture. Ought to. Early poetry, I know, a kind of volksdigting, with sentimental, rural themes: not individuated much – common vocabulary, turn of phrase, theme. Then, there was a group called the Dertigers? Poetry becoming private. And with the growth of the cities, with industrial progress, with wealth being stored up, maybe that was the new cultural ideal. Is Papa's poetry bourgeois? I just don't know. Maybe. I'm sure that Marianne thinks so. That turning to the avantgarde movements in Europe; and his emphasis on personal experience; his concern with form.

41

But it could also have been revolutionary. I'm sure that's the way he and his contemporaries saw it. Because they were attacking complacent middle-class values, rejecting the stifling cosiness of the family, looking for some natural, unrepressed humanity of spirit. He and his friends often seemed embarrassingly like middle-aged hippies – because their quests coincided with the dreams of the flower children, I suppose. Free love; mind-expanding drugs. Well, perhaps not quite. But it was almost like that.

Romantic idealism always makes me feel a quiet, murmuring kind of fear: it's glamorous and alluring, but so dangerous. . . .

It's true that Papa's poetry incensed people – particularly the *Liefdesverse*, because they were most obviously immoral. Stories we heard about women's circles burning copies of his books. But then why has he been so ardently admired in other circles – the upper middle-class Afrikaner élite? All those prizes he's received. What is the role of Kultuur in our society. Big letter K.

Marianne's told me about that set of people – who reject her, she claims. 'Ja,' she drawls wryly. 'I haven't got the sophistication. You know? Die aksent moet hoogs modieus wees. And you supposed to wear these beautiful imported peasant clothes and look unusual. Preferably–' she gurgles, 'preferably you must have a nervous breakdown every other year, because you know, you suffer so much, being an intellectual.' And underneath her ridicule, I know she is silently growling at me: 'It's the people in Langa and Ndabeni, man, and Bonteheuwel and Manenberg and Silvertown and . . . and . . . they're the ones who suffering right now, Anna. People like Beverley–' A surge of anger to hide her own wordless despair from herself, 'Her father beating her up when she was a little girl. The women are the only slaves they got . . . those men. And alcoholic, alco, alcoholisme is such a problem. Those are the people who are struggling, Anna man; they just so poor, so poor.'

I know that Marianne is right – that it's difficult to be entranced by the febrile, decadent brilliance of an élite when the near-starving, uneducated masses live in the same city. Rather than in some obscure Third World country on the vaguely remembered map of another continent.

And yet Anton isn't blind to all that. Perhaps he feels that it's honest only to speak to your own class. You get people who'd say dogmatically that it's not enough. But Papa's language would create

42

problems, for one thing, if he wanted to identify with the working classes. Also, I know that he left partly because the rising Black Consciousness movement disturbed him. I think he was afraid that the struggle was being reduced to some trivial polarity. Stasis, it'd mean. And no more contact for him with his black intellectual friends. Maybe he couldn't accept that it was a necessary phase. Of course now, with the strike action, the emphasis seems to be getting back to class struggle. But Anton didn't wait to see that happen.

Even as early as *Stedelike Kuns* there's a strong sense of foreboding in his work. There are allusions to a description he'd read once; of an aerial view into the eye of a tornado at sea. It *wasn't* totally still: there were craggy, storm-black mounds of water hurtling and crashing near the vortex of the thing; while the general area of the trapped, splintering sea was surrounded by a circular wall of towering, impenetrable cloud. Well, of course, it's one of the ironies running through that whole collection that it's not so much about nature as about the city-dweller's false enthusiasms for it. Partly I think Anton was commenting on something that was a recurrent theme in the work of his contemporaries: sceptical, you see, of an irrational fusion between inner and outer realities; sceptical that a turbulent landscape could contain the same energy as human history. And yet: given that, I'm uncertain why Papa didn't admit the value of estrangement, of that very falseness. Doesn't the science of biology arise from an inharmonious relationship with nature. I suspect there must be so much about my father that I'm still far from understanding.

I want to know, to understand. Maybe it's naive. To believe that if you pursue 'truth' for long enough and determinedly enough it'll break out all around you one day, blazing, painfully brilliant as the glare of wet potassium. Probably it's just something I learned as a kid.

I remember I began reading the newspapers when I was about thirteen, terribly earnest about it: because our history teacher had remarked, faintly chiding, that we were 'old enough by now'. I remember stealing away the creased news section once Papa'd finished with it. Used to spread the pages out across the carpet and kneel over them, solemnly poring over every last item.

That was when I discovered the word Apartheid. Strange that you can know something for so long without knowing that you know it. Of course, I'd always understood that there were children called 'coloured' who lived with their mothers (at least the ones we knew) in backrooms in the yards of other people's houses. The room would have a tiny ventilation grate instead of a window, maybe some exposed piping along the wall: always musky somehow, with the half-light and the smell of paraffin. I have a memory of a Dolly Varden, crimped out in a mass of nylon frilling, with a row of china shepherdesses arranged on the top, next to a painted tin canister that reeked mercilessly of violet-scented talcum powder.

That was years ago, when we were still living in our house in Claremont. I couldn't have been more than ten: because when we moved to Rondebosch, when Papa became a senior lecturer, Frans and I were still in primary school. It never occurred to me then that Jo-Anne couldn't go to the same school as us. Suppose because there were several other children in the neighbourhood gang who didn't go to the same school either. Or maybe I did know? Forget-fulness is perhaps a mimicry of innocence. I wonder now if she went to school at all. But she must have: I can see her still in a navy-blue gymslip too short for her, and with the bodice straining across her chest. She was skinny, I remember. The boldest at tok-tokkie, because she knew she could always outrun anyone. And when the season's game was rope skipping, she was the only one who could run in without tripping. The gang found out one spring that you can walk on top of a really old, tough myrtle hedge if you're sure-footed and light enough; and not prone to hay-fever – the tiny-leaved, greyish twigs sent out dust-storms if you did stumble and slip down into the mass of prickly spikes: so Jo-Anne was usually the volunteer sent up to test Mrs Cartwright's hedge.

I really believed I was the first person ever to recognize the in-iquity of this apartheid and went around for months with a con-stant simmering of indignation inside me, trying to pummel Papa and Mom into argument. Papa was patient: let me carry on, listen-ing with a silent restraint that allowed me to feel he was absorbed in my revelations. Now I can see that he simply understood my need to cry out. Trouble is I suppose that I really wanted answers, even attack: not his kind, wordless assent. Or is that true? Mom found it hard to be as tolerant. Eventually she spoke out in self-defence, rather sharply, 'Anna, perhaps it hasn't occurred to you, but we've felt all of these things ourselves you know, for a little while longer than you've been alive.'

I learnt from the newspapers that there was a tiny opposition party, and I came to think that Helen Suzman was one of the most admirable people in the world. I was so intense then – thirteen and newly wakened: if there was a picture of her in the paper I'd stare at it for so long that all the words in my mouth simply dried away, turned into darkness. Remember finally asking Constance, warily, expecting more rebuke. Wanted to know what she thought of the Progressives. She explained matter-of-factly that there wasn't a candidate in our constituency. The stiff apprehension in me seeped away to a subliminal, grey aching of unhappiness. 'But what happens then?' She explained that she and Papa didn't vote.

When I was in standard nine some kids started the Youth Action movement. Not sure exactly how it began; except that a girl at our school wrote a letter to the paper, about some kids getting free schoolbooks while others from poorer homes, still had to buy their own. A group of people from various schools rallied and started to organize a huge project in response. There were notices chalked up in all our classrooms, I remember, announcing that there was going to be a public protest meeting. Recruits were wanted to help paint and put up the posters. Most of the people in my class felt obscurely embarrassed, though – wouldn't even discuss it. If you tried to talk they'd look away. 'I don't think it's our business,' was the usual demurral. I tried enlisting François's interest, but the kids at his school seemed to be just as distrustful, self-righteous even: 'Politics isn't for schoolchildren to get involved with.'

Strange about François: believing that politics didn't remotely concern him. When I was a kid – fifteen, sixteen – that attitude used to incense me. I was intolerant, perhaps. Never understood either how he could accept military service. Of course, it was much easier for me to be a pacifist than for him: I wasn't confronted by any actual choice. Even so. To fight for the white government?

He was very changed after his two years in the army – almost taciturn for a long time afterwards. Maybe there were things that took a while to forget. What do soldiers do. Military exercises, I suppose. Run ten miles every morning – weighed down in full battledress, heavy pack on your back, the rifle cradled in your arms, bayonet fixed: don't dare break your pace, but keep on steadily running, ignore the blaze in your chest, running towards some un-

45

real hillside. Slope of hardened yellow sand scattered with prickly succulent and a slithering scree of disintegrating stones, perhaps dusty crystals of quartz, stinging your palms as you come down. A weathering pegmatite there at the surface, maybe. Eyes burning, you stare briefly at the mineral forms; maybe just beginning to recognize the beetle that's scurrying into the sand next to your grimy, scratched fingers. Then back again on the run, heading for the next koppie. When you fling yourself to the ground, how do you? Men's bodies are so vulnerable. You must take your full weight on the forearms, on one side of the pelvis? But the jarring, as you land on hard, stony ground.

Soldiers: they have to run with some imaginary purpose always in mind. A picture of the enemy that's been tattooed across their thoughts, so that it stands midway between their vision and the real world. Residual retinal image.

These last few years I never raised politics with Frans. Better not to argue. It isn't an easy thing to reject your own brother even if he does give unthinking assent to oppression. If we bickered and squabbled as tiny kids, and if we were hostile to each other's opinions as teenagers – well.

And at the time of the Youth Action movement our family was rapidly breaking apart: Papa had gone to live in the bachelor flat; while Mom and Frans and I were moving to the flat in Rondebosch. There was the smell of new paint in our rooms still; and so much silence full of meanings that I couldn't detect. Used to imagine, morbidly, that there was something appallingly sad hiding in the shadows of the tall, nameless shrubbery that crowded in the grounds of the block. Maybe François was really as frightened as I was. Maybe why he didn't want to be involved in anything impersonal. He seemed to transform his panic into something constructive, though. Why I imagined, jealous, that he must be secure. I remember the way he spent several weekends diligently installing burglar bars across the windows. For Mom's protection, he told me gravely. The care he took over every detail: filing down edges where the metal was rough, and afterwards retouching the damaged paintwork on the walls.

Perhaps the upheaval was also partly why I couldn't make my own decisions: wanting to go and help with the posters; but uncertain. I went to Papa for advice in the end. It was about March –

with the February heat still settling, like dust, in the suburbs. Dryness in the nostrils and throat; people at school coming down with flu. The sun's rays were at a lower angle by then, streaking out a weak, etiolated light: yet they still blazed painfully at the back of your neck. Walking home from school, one shoulder drooping with the burden of the leather briefcase. And that day I hadn't slept properly the night before. I was insomniac often at that time. I'd be all right in the mornings, intoxicated almost, with the world around me miraculously bright. Staring almost dizzy with excitement at the traceries of light in the oak leaves at school. But I'd begin to flag at about lunch time, and the last two periods of the day always dragged themselves out intolerably. I'd find myself beginning to lose consciousness, and then have to flinch awake and try to find ways of fastening my mind on a miscellany of trivial detail about the nineteenth-century migrations of the semi-nomadic, pastoral whites in southern Africa.

Usually I had a poem to take Papa. That day I had nothing.

There was a bed of geraniums growing on top of the low brick wall around his block of flats. I remember: the light was gathering there into a still pool, and the petals were lit up – rather pale ones, almost white. Glistening very faintly: you don't expect that, somehow. Thought of picking one to take to Papa; but a geranium flower isn't a real present.

Papa didn't have much to say. He offered me tea, and I was on the verge of saying yes when I guessed, my courage sagging, that I was supposed to feel a surge of filial pleasure at the thought of going into the little kitchen and making the tea for both of us. Felt too tired to do anything right then. Sitting there hunch-shouldered in one of his armchairs; my hands clasped stiffly between my knees. Silently I was storming at him. . . . 'But I don't want to, Papa, don't want to make tea for you.' I suppose it was a trial for him: he might have been tired too. Frans and I were supposed to feel we could go to him whenever we wanted, but it must have been a strain on Papa. After all, he'd have wanted to be decently discreet about his private life. We weren't supposed to know about things like mistresses.

When I began to talk about the protest meeting he listened quietly, lifting an eyebrow very slightly – his way of suggesting a courteous interest, I think. But he wouldn't give me any firm guide. A brief smile that disrupted the silence of his features – and then he rugged slightly, as if he were really at a loss. . . . 'Well Anna, I l that it's up to you . . . you must decide for yourself what you want.'

There was a dangerous, terrifying moment when there was nothing between us at all; nothing to cover up the singing, black space of our strangeness to each other. I should have had a poem, a piece of paper, anything to ward him off with, to deflect his attention from the uncertain wavering of feeling across my face.

Maybe he realised I was over-tired: he went off hurriedly to put the kettle on, and I heard him rummaging in the kitchen cupboards.

While he was out of the room I glanced at his desk. The chair was turned outward – he'd obviously been working when I knocked. I saw the pile of essays he was busy marking. So I was intruding.

I leapt up and went into the bathroom. And stood there staring at the light green tiling over the bath tub and the daft fluffy mat around the pedestal of the lavatory. There was a vase filled with sweetpeas on the window ledge. Slender, transparent column of glass with the flowers crammed into it so that the heads were all tumbled together. You know the little keel they have, and those wings in pastels of pink and mauve and blue and white; thin, groping tendrils springing out from the crowded leaves and petals. And that scent of theirs: almost naive in its sweetness. A kind of darkness in the glass, hard to locate . . . behind the vivid green stems? Except that they were silvered with tiny bubbles that clung to them. Blew my nose with some toilet paper eventually, and ran some cold water into the basin to wash my face. In the bathroom mirror, before I could escape my own glance, I saw. Who does she think? Anton Rossouw's stiff-faced, awkward daughter. Constance should have done something with me. What. I saw the pallor; the straight, listless hair. What?

When I went back into the sitting-room Papa had made us each a cup of tea and was proudly bringing in an arrangement of biscuits on a saucer. He'd even mixed some orange juice. Perhaps you'd prefer this. More refreshing, eh? It was fragrant and sweet, I remember. You taste the sunlight in the rind, the pith, the translucent segments: isn't that what the advertisements say. I prattled about my schoolwork while Papa listened with a grave interest.

As I was leaving I gave him the closing formula that he expected: 'François's fine and so's Mom. They send their love.'

48

CHAPTER 2

i

It's been two days now. Two days, or is it nights, they've been here. When the knocking came, I thought calmly, At last; as though I'd been expecting it.

But as I got up to answer the persistent tapping I felt the strength seep away till there was nothing left inside me, under the skin: except some internal honeycombing of dried bone and tissue. I wanted to call out, No. No, let me stay as I am. There was no choice, though. The typewriter keys had been falling back stiff under my fingertips for more than an hour in any case – clammy as an iron grate in the morning.

I unlatched the door. Stared at them for a second only: they seemed numb with exhaustion, hardly able to speak coherently. I saw how the streetlight was casting a dull, pewtery gleam across the boy's cheekbones.

Once I'd let them in, once I'd shown them to my room – I didn't know what else was expected of me. They were speechless, wanting only a place to sleep. Foolishly I toyed with the blankets, trying to cover their stiff limbs: but they were heavy almost immediately with sleep; the girl's knee jutting defiantly out from under the rug.

I went and made two cups of cocoa – the proper way, warming the milk till the bubbles were just rising at the rim of the saucepan. Carrying the cups slowly along the dark passage, I spilt some: the tremors in my hands magnified by the china and the liquid. The kids were too far plummeted into sleep though. I could only gaze at them; after putting down the chinking cups. And then I began to see that they weren't properly resting, despite the low, steady hush of their breathing. I think it was that that left me more helpless than anything. I could see a sporadic jerking of Felicia's shoulder: fitful. And I heard the boy half cry out once. It wasn't words, but muffled, smothered chunks of pure sound that might have been trying to tear themselves a way out from nightmare.

I came back here into the study, although I'd lost all my heart for letters. I just wanted to lie down on the spare divan.

When once we could lie on our bellies in the warm, sweet grass, discovering the microfauna – ants, beetles, leaf-hoppers, millipedes.

I don't know how long they're going to be here: it's been two days already, and they've given me no indication. They're not very talkative – with me, I mean. I find myself lapsing into brooding, irrational doubt; wondering whether children ever simply go away again, once they've come to you stricken with tiredness in the small hours.

They slept until noon yesterday. Yesterday? Yes. I wasn't sure whether to wake them: spent the morning tip-toeing up and down the passage, peering in at them uncertainly. All I could discover was a whitish flickering of nervousness in my own wrists and ankles, and the burning ache in my chest; while the children remained an enigma. Even waking, they keep to themselves – they spent the whole of the afternoon yesterday reading in the sitting-room. I think now that they were resting themselves, consciously working for a calmness of mind. Because they were going out again: Felicia came to the study door to tell me, politely, that they'd want a light meal at eight. The boy doesn't speak to me at all.

It's no good is it, succumbing to emotion. I keep explaining that to myself, trying to wrench the words around to make them face me. We're going to be all right, after all. I spent that night on the divan worrying minutely over a domestic inventory, with an insistent belief in my mind that each new detail, each careful specification would restore a sense of realness to my thin blankets and the darkened study. There was powdered milk, sugar, half a loaf of bread that I could think of; and a sack of onions in the vegetable rack, mouldering slightly, with bright shoots beginning to stick out through the plastic mesh. I had the calm detachedness of that person in the corner of one's skull, the one who witnesses dreams. The jars were well stocked with lentils, split peas, soya beans, brown rice. 'Realism, this is realism,' I tried at one point to whisper: but the words were small and hard as seeds. 'Rice'. I remember how the word lodged itself under my tongue, against the ridge of my teeth. In the museum there is that ancient pottery – earth-coloured, but incised with patterns and fire-smudged: made by the early nomads here; then smashed by a child perhaps, or some animal, or simply time; and reconstructed by modern scientists. The form is there still – perfect really: except that the meaning of that earthenware, its wholeness, its use remains in those shards that were littered in the dust, underneath the crystalline leaves of mesembryanthemums. And I continued with my small catalogue: there were raisins left, and a packet of masala. Tomato paste somewhere, there had to be.

Perhaps it's all a fiction. I feel tempted to believe that none of this is real, that the outside world, our invisible Revolution, the children – that none of these exist at all, but rise up out of my own sleeplessness, blazing chaotically at night behind my own burning eyelids: nothing more than fantasies of light pressing against my own retinas. If that were true though, then it might be correct to speak about despair. If there were no one else, then where would I be?

They came in at four again this morning: and it was uncannily similar to the scene before. The way the children huddled in the doorway, as if embarrassed by the spill of light from the streetlamp. But this time I was perfectly calm, knowing what to do. To grow accustomed so swiftly? I have an uneasy feeling that it's almost immoral: yet it's a flair I've always had. An ability to change in an instant, in response to someone else's whim or some new situation. Slip into the next gossamer costume, quick: before they notice the naked flesh of the actress. How else should I try to be. Natural? Just myself? When you need to be knotted in, I think, bound up into some social existence before you can forget the absence of your own being. . . .

I don't know what it is they're involved in and I daren't ask them anything – sensing that I have no right. Or maybe I'm unwilling to take a snub. Wilson has such a frozen, bitter-faced method of ignoring me. It's easy to speculate; appallingly easy to conjecture some shadowy, glamorous venture. People keeping on the run all night, hunched low but moving rapidly from street to street to street. Easy to imagine kids taking the terse words of a code from someone who waits for them in the backroom of a shanty, where the iron walls gleam in the darkness – hinting at illuminations of

51

old mattress springs and empty bottles on a dirt floor. Easy to guess at kids being picked up and taken out by car, hidden under earth-stained hessian sacks: perhaps to those long, inconspicuous buildings low in the dunes near the coast. Munitions factories, aren't they. I can almost see a supple, slight figure being hoisted up towards the tiny squares in a window frame. Both of the children wear dark clothing – indigo denim, black jersies. Perhaps it is fighters' clothing? But no. No. Because you can paint almost anything if you allow yourself. And I don't want to give in to a deluded, wistful, tremulous, rushing kind of imaginary anarchy.

Whatever it is, this mission of theirs, it seems unlikely that it should have anything to do with my own sickly presentiments of disaster. These children are bright, unsentimental; they know what they're doing. 'Children'. Ought I to say something else then? Soldiers, perhaps. Feel certain they're working to some thought-out, highly organized major plan. I must be only a small part of their scheme: irrelevant even, only the actualized version of some cypher for the person who would come up with shelter and food. And that's all right. I think I can be that for the time being – this alpha or delta.

They're sleeping now – not going out tonight. It's begun to drizzle again and there's a small, sharp hint of cold under all the wet, subtle as tungsten wire.

Supper was such a stupid affair of non-communication. Everything I murmured, trying to be sociable, was left unanswered – and ended up as an exposed banality. When Felicia offered, conventionally only, I thought, to help with the supper, I waved her away, smiling and flustered. But it was just a curry, there was really nothing for her to do. And I was afraid of the small-talk we'd have to make – both of us pretending a curiosity about the silvery-thin sheath between the onion layers, or admiring the deft edge to the steel blade of my kitchen knife. Then when we ate, neither of them would speak. I pressed things on them with a growing sense of anger; salt, chutney, more rice.

Felicia got to her feet at the end of the meal and said hurriedly, 'Thank you for the supper that was very nice.' Started to recover myself after that, wondering whether the original formula hadn't ended with the word 'Mommy'.

I remember Felicia in *Romeo and Juliet*. I'd seen the production in dress rehearsal and also disjointedly from the wings – helping backstage on the two previous nights. But watching it from the front on the final night, with the lights down in the hall . . . all my academic notions of the play seeped slowly away. Each time Felicia stepped out on to the proscenium and her eyes flickered shyly upward, there was a long shaft of amber light that brightened the darkness in them. You forgot about the latent imagery of the flower still budded, a sun not yet fully risen, the ascending flight of stairs still be scaled, a duke not sufficiently possessed of his own strength to govern. Of course, the lighting had a part in it. The two kids in charge were – well, gifted. Those effects they managed, deep umber shadows and muted light spilling over the cheap, dyed muslin of the costumes. And it wasn't only the designing: those same boys did all the wiring. One of them has a dad who owns a small electrical supply company, I think. They must have organized the PA system for the music as well. But Felicia. The way she could carve out a perfect stillness at the heart of the audience, leaving a deep, echoing hollow that she could whisper into, and still be heard at the back of the hall. How do actors do that. Something in their tone, or is it in their faces, or their posture. She didn't overplay either. In that tiny pause before she swallowed the sleeping draught there was desolate fear in her face – behind its pinched, blank mask all the imaginings that billow up gigantically in the mind of a child.

It hurt her badly, I think, that her father never saw the play. He's skipper of a fishing trawler and often has to spend days, even weeks at sea. It must be one of those factory ships. Wonder what kind of fishing it is, though. Pelagic? Do they go after pilchards and anchovies from Hout Bay, I wonder. Maybe it's mid-sea trawling, for whitefish. Cape hake. And they still take tunny, don't they, and snoek, in the season. And haarders and kabeljou, John Dory, squid and maasbankers.

It must be hard for Mrs Moodie too. I've only met her once or twice, at PTA meetings. Hardly spoken to her, really; but I've liked her. One thing I remember, a facial trick: as she is speaking to you a slight frown sometimes starts to set in across her forehead, but almost immediately smoothes itself out again – as though a conscious self-correction has forgotten about itself and turned into a habit itself.

53

I remember something now. It was at the end of last year that I spoke to her. Her husband's name had finally come up on the waiting list for a house at Mitchell's Plain – but it was troubling them that Felicia would have to travel all the way to Athlone to get to school. Mitchell's Plain is right out at the coast, near Strandfontein, way on the other side of all those flattened dunes and the Port Jackson wattle. No proper public transport for the place yet. There are a few schools but I think they're still struggling to build up reputations for themselves; and parents don't want to take their kids out of the better-known schools, especially once they're half-way through already. Some children, I know, are boarded with relatives in Athlone.

The parents. At least they're supporting the kids this time. I remember those mordant satires in the popular poetry after 1976. About parents glassily watching their television screens – anything to avoid seeing what their children were fighting for; parents sick with fear, and warning their kids bitterly to get back to school and stop their trouble-making.

There was a story in last week's paper. Well, impressions collected from people in the street – asked how they felt about the students carrying on the boycott. One mother afraid that her kids will be sent back to Transkei unless they settle down next term; and another, obviously convinced of the political rightness of the movement, but nonetheless despondent that while it drags on and on her child is learning nothing, except new habits of crowding a pavement in a jostling group of friends, or sneaking into matinée shows at the cinema.

I can't help wondering whether there aren't two different schools' movements. It's treacherous to think that. But can it really be the same for our kids and their parents as it is for the people who live out at Crossroads and Philippi and Guguletu? I know it is a common struggle. I know, I know that. But when we object to a ludicrously conceived technical course, and the parents back up that protest – perhaps it's partly because these kids have the potential to enter the economy at some fairly rich nodes. Everything is supposed to be shooting and blooming. Well, you can see it in the advertisements for jobs. Secretarial, managerial posts with salaries starting at R 700 sometimes, for young people. I think that there are some people, maybe even some of the parents, who still suppose our kids would be content if they just had the same education that the white kids get. Separate but equal: the way apartheid was meant to work.

So many people still seem to think that the issue here is race – whether they're conservative or liberal, I mean. The same newspaper story quotes a teacher who is tiredly angry because some of her best students have dropped out of school and gone to work in a factory. The editor even takes that up – talks about 'tragedy'. 'Tragic' because those kids might have gone on to university, or even straight into commerce. Could have joined the establishment, and instead they've been reduced to a working-class life. Well, maybe there are some kids at our school who'd want to perpetuate the bourgeois life-style their parents have struggled to create for them.

But what about the kids who can't even hope to come near that. There are a few thousand who might matriculate and then go on to a teachers' training college, or bush university. But for most of them, even if they stay on till standard six, there's no future in anything except the lowest kinds of manual, semi-skilled work. For the kids from those single and two-roomed, low-roofed brick cottages that each hold several families. Hok in the backyard with perches and sack-draped nesting boxes for a half-dozen spattered, grimy chickens; strip of grey sand in the front, with cabbage plants, or a stand of virus-infected mealies, with yellowed, streaked leaves; and at the side of the house, diagonal, tense streaks of whipping light and wires, where the wind tugs at shirts and blouses and children's vests. Those areas that we learned about as children – seen remotely through car windows, and beyond tall fences that seemed eternally semi-plastered over by a decoupage of litter and newspaper scraps that the wind held adamantly up against the mesh.

I used to suppose that those kids must be moving towards change with a much more profoundly sustained anger than anything our kids could possibly feel. But now I understand how arrogant it was to think that. After all, the students at our school worked out for themselves that their cause was allied to the struggle of the meat workers who're on strike. Because we also have children from petty bourgeois backgrounds – kids who are thin and fiery with imagination. Who understand that the rites of oppression in this country call for a double-bladed axe – racism on one cutting edge, and capitalism on the other. Children who are young enough still to sneer

55

at comfort and material security; and old enough to be taut-faced already from the strain of responsibility.

It's still raining. I was looking at the night through the bathroom window: not a darkness really – more the shapes of rain and misty cloud; and there's glinting everywhere, coming off the guttering across the alleyway, from the telephone wires, from the snail tracks on the bricks outside.

That strike is still on – did I mention? Would like to support it, but then I never buy meat anyway. Wonder about people that have no consumer power – because they have no money. Plenty of people living mainly off bread, beans and samp, or mealiepap. Sometimes get a sheep's head, I suppose.

Ought to go to sleep. Perhaps just lie down on the divan for a while, listening to the water: still get some rest that way. But it's more than that. One has to dream. That's what they say? More important, perhaps, than a respite for the muscles. Perhaps it's the dreams my body wants to ward off: whatever they are – remembrance of meaning. Can't be a physical fear? Of losing one's hold; slipping back into a chasm of guilt.

No.

ii

Wilson has still not spoken to me. He brought a book with him into the kitchen and kept it open next to him on the table throughout the meal. Not really reading; but it made the silence easier to endure, for all of us. Beginning to wonder why they came here, if he trusts me so little. Perhaps it was Felicia's idea. She offered to wash the dishes afterwards. There were only a few plates; frying pan; saucepan: but I couldn't refuse her, remembering my stupid rejection of her last offer to help. I fussed in the background, making the tea. Coffee for Wilson. Even made some squares of cinnamon toast with the last of the stale loaf. He ate some of it too. Considerate, perhaps: but how could he know the extent of my dependence – that his refusal, even of a bit of sugared bread, would have left me feeling forlorn. And perhaps he simply has a liking for sweet things.

56

I've begun to place him: he's one of the matric students, an orator, I think.

I remember one occasion when I saw him in action. It was the day the students swept out of the grounds on that spontaneous protest march down towards Klipfontein Road. Just before the real momentum of it began I'd been called out into the foyer. Well, not called out, perhaps. I was sitting in the staffroom, trying feebly to read. Marianne was in a slumped, introverted mood, with a book on her lap. I happened to look up suddenly, sensing something – and saw that it was Cynthia, wistfully hovering at the staffroom door. The kids aren't supposed to come in, you see, and the shy ones never conceive of themselves as special cases. I could see even across the room that her face had taken on that dangerous, bleached look, and went out to her immediately, trying not to make my hurry seem too wild. I didn't want any of the gym teachers to get to her. They're the ones that cope with sprains and cut fingers; and they've decided that Cynthia's an irritating malingerer. ('That child gets on my nerves. It's just attention. You must leave her. She's just seeking attention.') It's true that she's annoyingly vague when she's in that condition – she'll stand in front of you helplessly, avoiding your gaze, with her fingers working at a pleat in her dress. All she can tell you usually is that she feels 'funny'. But I think she's grown used to being abused for her attacks: and now she puts half her thin, listless self into placating people who want to grab her roughly by the shoulders and bring her to her senses.

Apparently the students' meeting inside the hall had turned into a crashing, rowdy, dinning rebellion of excitement. A few hundred children from another school had swarmed in across our fields to join the assembly, and something was beginning to stir. People leaping up to speak, shouting at each other, and the whole hall stiflingly packed with close on fifteen hundred kids, all on their feet, swaying and cheering. Some of the tougher boys were trying to clamber forward to speak, shoving through the crowd, without caring much where they put their feet or their elbows. I think Nicholas was inside there, somewhere, watching it all with Hennie.

Cynthia's own halting account was almost inaudible against the noise. I could see her on the verge of collapsing into a faint. Partly she may have wanted the fit, I suppose: at least it would release her from the intolerable demands of consciousness. Thank God she had

57

the presence of mind to get herself out of the hall. What if she'd fallen in there? She could have been horribly trampled by people in flight, in panic.

Got her to lie down on the bench in the foyer. Luckily I know where she keeps her tablets, top right-hand blazer pocket; and know how many to give when she's having an attack. The clamour inside the hall seemed to recede suddenly, but to replace it there was a more concentrated noise: one person speaking, insistently. The sound was badly distorted, so we could only hear hiss and bellowing, and that eerie, high-pitched electronic screaming. And then that got drowned out when the kids began pouring out of the hall. Cynthia went very quiet for a few minutes, but she didn't seem to be having a full-blown attack. All I could do was to hold her hand and try to shield her from the buffeting of the kids streaming out through the foyer. Didn't want to suffocate her with my own presence either. When she came round she was shivering badly. Her shoulders and upper chest began to jerk slightly, and then she was crying. Feebly pushing her hand through her hair; whimpering. The kids just kept coming, hundreds of them flying through those swing doors.

I began to feel shivery myself, sick with a double apprehension. What if Cynthia began to hyperventilate: I wouldn't know how to control it. And I was worried about the kids, so many of them, straining towards the foyer doors – plate glass, set into metal frames. You could feel the rough, shoving excitement. There was a welter of dark blue gaberdine. Striped ties were flung back over shoulders. People were trying to free themselves from the press by holding up their satchels and rucksacks over their heads. Underneath the pushing and shrill giggling, and the fragmentary protest chants – you sensed a sombre awareness that the whole experience was something alive, rich with significance. Finally some of the prefects must have managed to push open the side doors of the hall, because the flow suddenly lessened and we began to see the crowd moving past outside, as the kids came out in tributaries now, and smaller groups.

Nicholas came out of the hall with Hennie. He was grinning, burning almost with excitement. Made some waving, perhaps beckoning gesture in my direction, and then shouted something hoarsely, with the other hand cupped around his mouth. I couldn't make out what he was saying. Most of the staff were packed around the staffroom doorway – but not more than four or five people could really see anything, of course. Mr Naidoo was standing to one side of the main entrance, speaking to Rachied with an expression on his face of totally absorbed, intense concern. Rachied's head boy, and universally popular with the students. His face still has a kind of delicate, silvery gleam along the jawline, although he's begun a beard. And he has a hugely generous, crooked grin. I suppose that Debbie in my class is not the only child who's announced, ingenuously at large, that she thinks he's 'fantastic'. I doubt though that he's any sort of skilfully driving rhetorician on a platform.

The streaming of children through the foyer had ended by then: most of the kids were out in the grounds, or already beginning to rank up and march down the road. A boy came out into the foyer carrying a megaphone. I'm certain now that it was Wilson: that same thinness, slightly stooped, bony shoulders, the pallor of the face; the tense, unsmiling look about the eyes and mouth. He must have been the speaker just before the shouting in the hall changed into a more dynamic energy. He'd stopped trying to deliver his exhortations by then and looked emptied of all his strength. I saw him meet Rachied's glance, and they nodded curtly to one another, as though acknowledging some sort of failure.

Gavin suddenly appeared next to me, rather breathless. 'Miss, is Cynthie all right, Miss?' They're cousins, and I think he feels it his personal responsibility to look after her. A bit dazedly I promised him that Cynthia was fine. 'Did she take her tablets, Miss?' I reassured him again. He seemed to be at a loss. Noticed he was flushed in the face. He had his school rucksack with him, trailed over his shoulder by a single strap. 'What must I do, Miss?' he said eventually.

'It's okay, Gavin, there's no need to. . .' Then I began to wonder what he was really asking me. The schoolgrounds were steadily emptying. We could hear the chanting and singing of the kids out in the road, even though the vanguard must have been at least a kilometre away by then. Some of the staff had gone out to escort them, disturbed at the thought of real danger if the kids began moving out on to the busy highway at the top of the road.

Tentatively I said, 'If you want to go with your friends, I think Cynthie will be all right here with me. I'm going to ask Mr Abrahams if he'll drive her home just now.'

I could see the anxiety tightening the skin across his boyish cheeks. When Cynthia is sick he has to stay with her. I don't think it's purely his family's insistence either: it seems to be his own private rule. His small face seemed to turn coppery with unhappiness.

'But some of the other boys, Miss, they say we mustn't go, because it's irresponsible. That what they say, Miss: the action hasn't got a planned motivation.' And he looked at me, fixedly.

I made up a kind of solution for him then. Perhaps it was wrong: but I couldn't bear his tremulous uncertainty. 'Perhaps Gavin, if you don't mind . . . maybe you could stay here. I'd like to get some tea for Cynthie, and she might feel better if you stay here while I'm gone? Also, Gavin, I wonder if I could ask you to go home with Cynthie in the car: so she won't be alone at home, you see.' He put his rucksack down and settled himself next to his cousin, resting his hand instinctively on her shoulder. When I came back with a cup of tea for each of them, that dark, disquieted flush was still there on his face.

The wind outside is racketing. Such a dry sound. The neighbours' dog is upset; and that iron gate in the alleyway keeps fighting and listing against its own hinges. Wish it would rain again.

iii

Felicia came to ask me for a few more books. Caught a glimpse of myself drawn up into a thin earnestness as I was trying to decide. Wanted to give them something 'educative' I suppose. Embarrassed then: fumbled at the first things I could find. Had *The Social Contract* and *The Coloniser and the Colonised* on my desk anyway, so I held out those. I wished I'd had some Brecht for Felicia. Took down half a dozen books of protest poetry, and piled them in her arms.

There's a whispering feeling inside me that they're planning to go out again tonight. Wish I had some way of stopping them. I know, I know: I'm behaving like a fussing parent. And even if I dared speak to them, there's nothing I could sensibly point to. The sky is dark, but I don't think it will rain.

I saw Wilson reading in the sitting-room. Well, both of them:

60

they sprawl on the giant cushions, wedging the scatter pillows under their tummies or their elbows to make themselves more comfortable. I was standing in the kitchen, waiting for the kettle to boil – couldn't help glancing in their direction from time to time. Wilson seems to have a knack of centring all his concentration, without his body showing any angularities of tension. Think he was oblivious of me; all his energy had gone into holding the sense of the text in his mind. He shifted one arm lazily before turning the page. It's a calmness he has; as though his thoughts are greyish crystals he can turn over and over, peacefully, in the palm of his hand – like frankincense or myrrh.

And it suddenly seems a fatuous proposition that he should ever return to school. To be examined on the syllabus as it stands now?

I know that I'm not apart from it all. I'm beginning to understand what teaching English literature is about. Why the examination format makes it inevitable that I have to provide the kids with model character analyses. Why I have to teach them a sophisticated repertoire of eulogisms for the novels they study. It's really the form they're being asked to commend. The kind of society that gives rise to such a peculiarly intense, personal ownership of a cultural act. Almost a contradiction in terms. And there's an insidious side-effect. If the prescribed literature really has no living meaning for them and yet it's invested with so much apparent value – they begin to feel there's something lacking in themselves. Remember being discomforted myself, as a teenager. Why on earth they set us those dreary books. *Moonfleet*. *Mr Polly*. Used to feel a physical ache as I tried diligently to 'enjoy' them.

I wonder if it's different for Afrikaner kids. Afrikaans literature is genuinely their possession, and maybe reading it really does instantiate for them that notion of an 'eie kultuur'. There's a kind of beauty that you find in young, educated Afrikaners – something in their faces, their bearing. Assuredness, I suppose it is. Self-pride. Knowing that you belong to a community. Or rather, *not* knowing it: taking it for granted.

And I'm going to go back and teach. Am I? All this vacillating: surely it's false. I wonder what real alternatives I have. It makes me feel old-fashioned, almost prim to confess this, but teaching is my vocation. You long to teach, so you work at a school: where you end up not teaching at all, but preparing kids for examinations.

Where despite your best intentions you help to instil the values that will keep the ruling class in power.

Wonder about Marianne. What turbulences her teaching might set up. Because she's teaching Afrikaans literature to kids whose home language is Afrikaans, who're ostracized by the English-speaking students – and who probably detach themselves the more woodenly from that prose and poetry written by people like Anton Rossouw.

If I wrote to Papa, perhaps; asking for advice. He's always had that conscientious, gravely concerned side to him, as an educationist.

If it comes to that, why haven't I chosen him all along to act as my remote confessor. But this is almost the nub of things. There's a last, perhaps saving feeling that Papa is the one person I must never begin writing to. What I've wanted from him all my life is The Answer, I think. And I know, without really wanting to believe it, that writing out the endlessly insistent question on paper is one certain method of warding off response.

I've been directly to him a few times. Gauche with my abrupt demands that he never seems to have understood. Demands I've never understood myself.

The time I went to him about the protest meeting, and all he could tell me was that I should decide for myself what I wanted. When I was wanting him to tell me what my own desire was.

In the end I decided that I did want to go and help make posters. About fifty of us arrived that Saturday afternoon: meeting at a colossal, intimidating house in Kenilworth. (It must have been owned by some corporation: perhaps someone's dad was managing director of a big company.) The kids who were setting up the protest had arranged free cooldrinks for all of us, and there were cellophane packets of salty, papery chips being passed around. I remember the neatly stacked supplies of poster-size cardboard and different coloured koki chalks: you took your requisition and wandered off to find a working area. We all drifted across the pale, cropped grass of the lawns and let ourselves into the high-fenced tennis court. Because of the spacious surface, covered with smooth asphalt, the green kind. The other kids all seemed to know one another. They couldn't have been any older than I was – fifteen or sixteen – yet some of them had a kind of élan: something in the casual way they kicked off old, broken sandals and then strolled across the tennis court in their bare feet; or perhaps it had to do with their small, intense voices that sang and called and commanded incessantly. Still clutching my sheets of cardboard, I could feel the tendons in my upper arms beginning to stand out in an ugly rigidity. I was scared, suddenly, that I would be sick. Too young then to know that anxiety is always transient: a seizure that has to grapple for itself and struggle, until it slowly dies.

I began to have a glimmering of something about myself then, for the first time. I'd always been passionately excited about schoolwork - and I think I imagined that my classmates shared in precisely the same delight. The bliss that crowded my thoughts when we read Catullus. Listening to the small hops and chirrupings of Lesbia's sparrow. Or else the feverishness that would come during a lesson on electron orbitals. I mistook my own hectic state for communication: and it never occurred to me that I never confided in any special schoolfriend. Used to spend so much of my time reading in the afternoons and evenings that I fully believed I was talking endlessly - superbly gregarious in a void of silent pages.

Michael Bernstein saved me that afternoon. He came up with a box that held some small white cards, and squatted down next to me as I pretended to be gazing purposefully at the blank sheet on the tarmac. I was sitting cross-legged, but huddled, clasping my ankles. He introduced himself, and took my name and address to write down on one of his cards. When I told him which school I came from, he grinned and flopped down in front of me. 'Same as —,' he said. 'Are you in the same class? She's up at the house with Pete and Helen and the other guys. You know them? You know Dave? Mike Newman?' The panic was beginning to seep back into me and I almost cried out, trying to stop that cheerful streaming of assumption. Perhaps he noticed then that I was feeling out of place. He squinted at my poster, and I blushed for the few timid guidelines I'd dared to rule in pencil. I mumbled that I didn't know how to letter; and Michael responded with energetic kindness. 'Yeah, I'm not so fantastic. But look it doesn't have to be perfect.' He did have the knack, though. He took over the central parts of the posters, lettering the key words with dashing streaks of colour - and then passing them to me to fill in the less conspicuous details about the date and time of the meeting. Forget what it was we wrote. I suppose PROTEST MEETING, and FREE SCHOOL-BOOKS FOR SOME; perhaps UNEQUAL EDUCATION – that sort of thing.

He went off again later, to get names and addresses from the rest. Explaining that they wanted to draw up a mailing list – to keep in touch with everybody who was interested. About half an hour later he came back, though: with two bottles of coke and a packet of sharp, salty chips. 'Hey, Anna, break time.' He passed me one of the bottles and glanced at the dozen posters I'd managed to colour in – carefully imitating his first designs. 'Hey those are great,' he said. And I had a handful of chips to cope with suddenly as well. I asked him then about the other kids – that indefinable feeling of 'groupiness' that they had. I remember he began chuffing and giggling, and then the coke in his bottle started to fizz up and spill. 'Yeah you could call it that,' he agreed. He explained that most of them belonged to the Young Progressives: knew each other from working on election campaigns. 'Hey, wouldn't you like to see what we do sometime?'

I noticed that both of us had small flakes of broken potato crisps clinging to our jersies. Michael wore glasses – little round, gold rims, with astonishingly thick lenses. Yet his eyes shone so vividly. They were beautiful, I thought: a deep black-gold.

I helped him afterwards, once all the finished posters had been collected together. Most of the other kids had begun to gather their things, retrieving shoes and sweaters and jackets from the lawn, or the periphery of the tennis court. Felt slightly on edge, because the afternoon had grown late already, and the bus stop was at least twenty minutes' walk away. 'You going to the bus stop, Anna? Why don't you hang on just for ten minutes, then I'm going that way too.' He was busy punching holes into the posters. I took each one from him, and threaded lengths of coarse sisal string through them. So that they would be ready for tying up to the streetpoles. 'Lucky we managed to get the permit yesterday,' he said. My hands were beginning to feel stiff, reddened by the rough fibre: I couldn't make sense of what Michael was saying. 'Ja, permit. You've got to get a permit from the city council, you see, before you can put up posters.' We'd nearly finished our trussing of the posters by then. 'Anyway, now we can start to put them up. We're going out tomorrow night, cause Dave's got his dad's combi. Hey if you want to come and help you're welcome.'

It would be foolish to pretend that no one ever made overtures, that I wasn't urged, generously, to join in.

I was right about Wilson and Felicia. They didn't want to eat very much: Felicia came and warned me at about half past five. When I called them to the table, Wilson came in with the Memmi under his arm. Even Felicia seemed to be in a hushed, distant mood. Suddenly lost any appetite I'd had. Served up for them and simply excused myself.

They're still here. Probably go out at about nine or ten.

I wonder. My whole skull feels as though it's singing with noisy, scattered light. Perhaps it's only my own diseased imagination that makes me suppose this mission of theirs must be some violent activity. Perhaps they do nothing more than go out to meetings with other students? It'd make far more sense. Of course, yes.

Why on earth I allow myself obscure, foreboding fantasies, when I know that we're going to be all right.

We're going to be fine. Tomorrow I'm going up to the café for provisions: fresh wholewheat bread, eggs maybe; and a newspaper - so we can read the stories about the world.

That Youth Action protest meeting was about a fortnight after the poster-making day. There was a fair amount of publicity in the press, I remember; and then, unexpectedly, Constance began to talk about it. I hadn't thought of asking her, for some reason; but when she murmured, 'Oh, I'd like to come along, Anna, if you're going to that meeting' - something inside me flowered. Partly pleasure; but also, inexplicably, partly regret.

It must have been nearing autumn then: I remember that Mom wore her old, peacock-blue raincoat, with a scarf at her throat. We walked past the peach tree near the station, and I remember seeing that it was stripped of its springtime pallor and tawdriness: only thin, soughing, black sticks clapping together in the streetlight, and faintly damp. It felt strange to enter the main hall of the little civic centre: Mom and I were there twice a week always, but it would be the worn wooden stairs we took, up to the lending library. There must have been a few hundred people there already by the time we arrived: we could only find seats at the back. And more and

65

more people filed in after us. We could feel the press of people behind our trestle chairs. Small kids lifted up on to parents' shoulders; people craning their necks, trying to see what was happening on the platform. Constance and I didn't really talk much to each other: there was too much clamour around us. Scores of schoolkids in the audience of course – so there were people rushing up and down, giggling, catching at friends' elbows, parading, flirting. I saw Michael briefly: escorting a group of people: reporters, I think. They were trying to get themselves to the front of the hall; having to touch people's shoulders and then ease themselves through the narrow gaps in the crowd. We kept thinking the meeting was about to start, but it would turn out to be someone testing the microphones. And the hall went on filling up. Afterwards we heard people saying that the audience had spilled right out into the road. Maybe why there was so much noise all around us: dinning excitement, and chatter – and underneath it a curious solemnity.

I don't remember what the speakers said. It was impressive, of course. They must have spent a lot of their time researching: they gave us statistics; a breakdown of state expenditure on education. There were huge charts as well, to make the same points – stuck up on the walls. One of the speakers started out in English: he was polished (with vowels that were almost orotund, I thought in secret regret). Halfway through, though, he switched to Afrikaans, and you realized suddenly that this was his home language, perhaps because he became even more powerfully assured as he spoke it. The audience burst into applause almost unthinkingly at that point. And yet I wonder what it was about. I don't really imagine that many of the people there were Afrikaans-speaking themselves.

Mom was very still beside me. I stared at her once: and her face was lifted and half turned away from me. I'd never seen her looking that austere before. Occasionally her hand moved to her eyes. And afterwards, as we were leaving, I could tell that there was some kind of pride lurching inside her, but smothered down. The crowd wasn't really moving away: kids were shoving to the front to fill in membership cards; someone was hurriedly trying to organize a small table where people could sign a petition; and everybody wanted to hand over money. I saw a hastily emptied tickler box passed along over people's heads to the petition table. Coins streamed into it, an almost noiseless flood of the buttery silver discs, and plenty of

66

notes – sometimes a large fist ashamedly burying a couple of ten rand notes. And Constance scrambling at the watered-silk lining of her handbag to find some coins for me. I caught the fragrance of her perfume and lipstick. Crumpled tissues inside the handbag I saw too.

We walked home mostly in silence. A chilly, fine drizzle was beginning, and we stopped for a minute, so that Mom could take off her scarf and drape the pale, flimsy bit of chiffon over her hair. As we turned into the grounds of our block, I saw that ugly shrubbery: mostly in shadow, but lit up enough under a streetlamp to show me its shapeless, furred foliage, and the dead spires of its sharp, blue-black, sticky flowers. There was rain water dripping somewhere underneath it – a swift rippling of the light. I couldn't get to sleep that night: feverish despite the coldness of the air. There was the sound of trains shunting throughout the night: a long series of urgent clatterings, and then the deep, sustained whistling of steam. Shunting-yards? Ja, in certain recesses of the suburbs, alongside the railway stations. My straight, lifeless mass of hair burned on the pillow, burned against my neck. As always, I suppose I was fighting back that crazy, impossible ambition to go running out down the cold stairs into the night – to rush, striding along the pavements till I came to Papa's flat where I'd beat at the door, in my dreams, until he took me in.

It comforted me that Constance had come with me. I know that I felt much closer to her after that; wishing that I knew of some uncomplicated way to make my peace with her. Even so, the bitterly vicious tantrums of adolescence would still burst in my chest, and then, weeping, and with my throat aching, I'd scald poor Mom with my vindictive ragings and reproach.

And two years later, when I was at university, but childish and unsettled as ever – it was Papa again that I hankered for, incorrigibly wanting him to save me.

Thinking about the demonstration on the steps of the cathedral, that day the police stormed us.

It's odd that I remember the incident as something so nightmarish. The truth is that I was only on the very fringe of things: holding up my placard, ja . . . FREE EDUCATION FOR ALL . . . but teetering insecurely on the bottom-most of the cathedral's patient, stone steps. Conscious perhaps of someone else's poster obscuring my view; aware of our crowded bodies, fists and elbows in one's ribs, or the small of the back; bruised ankles and heels. Mostly it was the crowd opposite us that I saw: the gathering crowd of curious, lingering pedestrians. And our immense calico banner dipping and drooping just above my head. Police vans arriving: ja, I saw that. Saw the policemen swarm across the street on to the small traffic island opposite us. One man stooping forward slightly, urgently whispering the holding, alert commands to his pent-up Alsatian dog. They shouted something to us, and the man with the dog straightened up - shifted his feet slightly, till they were braced apart. That was when Dirk was suddenly speaking: he had a megaphone and he'd scrabbled up on to the granite base of a pillar. He clung there, one arm around the pillar, the other holding up the loudhailer; calmly but determinedly calling out again and again that the protest was peaceful. When they came for us. I didn't even know what was happening. Only that the world was lost then, shattered into some kind of roaring. Didn't hear individual screams, even: just a tremendous, dark roaring that seemed to keep on lifting all around us. Smoke, there was smoke at the end of the street, but also burning us. You felt a searing, a kind of singeing: and somewhere in the solid wave of black, pouring sound you heard a steady, weighty cracking. We were falling backwards - you couldn't help anything, the scratches and the jabs, the desperate, kicking pushes from behind. Someone got that side-door open, drew aside the iron bar that latched it: and we were staggering inside, into the church's immediate sanctuary of silence.

We were trapped in there for a couple of hours. Sitting on the floor of the transept, cross-legged; people huddling in small groups. One girl rocking a friend in her arms, I remember: not really sobbing, but staring blindly, and her face streaked and flushed with tears. It was wintry by then - there'd been rain that morning: and yet we were most of us white-faced, perspiring; sick with the heat that was stifling us. And then the quietness began to scare me. The faint smell of dust from the tapestried kneelers and the fine, crumbled pages of the hymn books. Saw a kind of lectern, ornately carved into a sinuously gleaming angel: brightness of the wood. Some high, persistent sound still tingled at the back of my skull; and as we waited, trusting in our eventual release, the light seemed slowly to die down all around us. All the lustre pieced into the

68

lancet windows came out blazing for a while, and then that also dimmed itself.

By the time they came to help us away my bare arms were painfully cold. Members of parliament came, I remember, and escorted us out through a side-door, down a narrow, rambling little path with a few embarrassed, rain-bedraggled phlox plants along it. The MPs didn't speak much: seemed almost stunned. There was still a burning, almost liquid feeling inside me – maybe only the memories of those colours there had been in the tall windows – but I was shivering when my turn came to leave, trembling so violently that my body began to ache.

Can't quite think how I ever got myself home that night. I must have gone with some other students – perhaps we hitched along De Waal Drive; or perhaps we walked down to the railway station. Strange thing though; can't remember actually speaking to anyone. There was a numbness inside my mouth: alongside the gums, and under the tongue – a chalkiness in my spittle. Think I went straight to bed: not to sleep, but to be warm, closely hidden under the blankets.

I stayed like that, sleepless, for the length of the night: with a patch of jewel-coloured light near my head, where the bedside lamp cast its steady glow on to the blankets; aware only of the rhythm given to my own consciousness by the pulsing of fear.

Hours later the warm colours disappeared, diffusing into the chilliness of morning. Mom and François were still asleep as I dressed, pulling on the jeans and tee-shirt of the day before. Let myself out of the flat.

In the stairwell there was that smell of cold concrete; and the pungency of the caretaker's old reed-broom, with bristles half damp still from swilled, pine-scented disinfectant. The first light had hardly begun to thaw from the surfaces of lamp poles and car doors outside in the street. I passed the peach tree near the station: saw the silver streaming light pencilled along the lines of its branches. It was too early for any shops to be open, so I kept on walking, wandering along side streets, along the canal of the Liesbeek; kept on walking until about seven, when I passed a café where a bundle of newspapers had just been dumped on to the pavement outside. Bought one, and a bottle of milk. Didn't want to look at the news until I was back home, but the whole of the front page was blackly

69

inked with unmistakeable headlines and photographs. I saw then. They called it a 'riot'.

I walked up to the campus later. Needing to be with everybody else, I suppose, and I had a vague idea that I might find Michael. When I got there the campus was already seething, and it turned out the SRC had called a mass meeting for lunch time.

I was waiting to cross University Avenue when the police vans arrived. How many were there, I wonder – ten, twelve? And half a dozen thick-chested men leapt down from each van while they were still travelling: beginning that advance towards the Jameson steps. They had dogs with them, wiry-hackled, half-starved. I heard the angry, sharp-edged barking, and I turned back: breaking into a run.

Maybe it was cowardly to flee like that. But there was a feeling – well, it's hard to define: in the midst of all the swarming crowd there was some sickly inertia, some frantic desire, almost, for martyrdom. Many of the people there hadn't been involved the day before; had only heard the appalling stories from those students who came back to campus from the city with their faces still blazing in the ghastly excitement of shock. And you see, as those hundreds of people on Jameson steps began uncertainly to back away, or else to linger in expectation, it seemed that a part of the frenzied, seductive shrieking was meant not to repel but to entice the predictable onslaught. I think that I wanted to escape that cloying falseness more than anything.

An extraordinary freedom it was: as I raced across the paving slabs I knew nothing more than the rushing grass with its patches of darker leaf – sorrel, clover, dandelion, oxalis. Hearing nothing of the screaming hysteria behind me, and feeling nothing, absolutely nothing beyond the curious lightness of my own body. Perhaps because there *was* nothing. I hadn't been hit; no one's fist had come near me. There were kids on campus who couldn't move their fingers for days afterwards – where the thick, rigid baton had smashed down on the back of a hand; and there were others with huge, crimson welts across their bodies, the skin broken by the impact of the weapon. It must have been weeks before the haemorrhages faded underneath that damaged skin, until the dead corpuscles left only the livid, bruised reminders. There were dog bites that afternoon as well, mostly at the backs of people's calves. It's a pain that sinks deep into you, apparently, and lingers there, throbbing for days, so that the leg feels stiff and inflamed. But nothing had actually happened to me.

Hardly slept that night either, though I was close to tears with sheer tiredness. A little sleep towards the dawn only. Sleep? The pain in my bones receding slightly; and wakefulness slipping away until I was conscious only of the morning light under my eyelids: crescents shaped from something insubstantial – clear, grey.

That morning I told Mom that I wanted to go to Papa. I could see the reluctance in her: her eyes taking on that golden cast they have when she's under strain. Papa was staying out at Hermanus then, which meant that I'd have to hitch a hundred and twenty kilometres to get to him. But I'd turned eighteen just that month; and Constance forced herself, unhappily, to say that I did not need her permission.

It's a bit after midnight. Still a few hours to go before the kids come home.

I hope the sound of my typewriter doesn't carry across the alleyway – might be keeping the neighbours awake. Why can't you get silent machines. Because the mechanism relies on a strong impact. And then? Energy, is it, dissipating itself . . . heat; shock through the air. And perhaps it doesn't bother them. It's only when you're lying awake: then you hear the heavy beating of rain dripping down from a corner of the guttering. Or that restless Alsatian prowling up and down the backyard, barking at the wind or the starlings in the fig tree. Reminds me of something. What. Is it some poem? Probably. So much of my world comes out of books. Although that rite of desecration on the cathedral steps broke apart most of the symbols I'd learnt up till then.

It was easy, finding Papa at that cottage near the sea. I left in the afternoon. Didn't take much with me: three rand that Constance gave me, and my old rucksack with a sweater and some underwear stuffed into it. Got a lift first with a salesman. His gaze shifting over me for a minute, and his voice trying out different registers: in the end he just shrugged, and switched on the car radio. He took me as far as the Strand. It's odd how intensely the memories impressed themselves on me over those few days: as though my mind were white-hot, molten into a state of radical, lit-up flux. Trivial details, mere contingencies seemed to sink straight through what-

71

ever mass it is of electrical fields, or tangible nerve-fibres even: and must have burned themselves directly into that region of mind where it's ordinarily only the constant things you hold on to – the general things, patterns, grammars, laws of the abiding world.

Had two or three other lifts before I found a driver who was going all the way through to Hermanus. Mostly the journeys dissolved into a warm, nodding half-sleep. I had a paper-cupful of coffee in one of the dorps: it burnt my mouth slightly, and the milk had wrinkled itself into a skin at the top – but the strong taste roused me. Felt wide awake again, light-headed with excitement as we came to the outskirts of Hermanus. Took me only about ten minutes of walking to locate the cottage: set apart from the main part of the village, with that massy bougainvillaea at the front. Wintriness of its coppery, shivering petals.

Papa must have been startled when he opened the door; but his face showed nothing at all. He drew me inside after an infinitesimal pause only; and then he was gently patting my upper arms and shoulderblades. Gestures that he thinks speak of fondness. Perhaps there was an awkwardness as we strolled towards the front room, both of us pretending to be happily at ease. As we were entering the room, Papa said hurriedly, 'You know Karen, don't you, Anna.' And I suddenly felt anguished – irritable, really. Of course I knew her. I'd met her at Papa's flat once. Also, irrationally, I was upset that he'd called me Anna instead of Antjie – the pet name he used to give me when he was in a warm-hearted mood. And so I stood there, tired again and rudely staring at Karen with my eyes rather wide, blinking; unable to speak.

A few minutes later, as I huddled on their lumpy, floral sofa, I realized that Papa had really been trying to inform me, warning and encouraging me with his tone, how I was to understand his relationship with Karen. Being deliberately 'adult' with me. Ja. The stern assurance that I was old enough to accept the fact of his living with her. When Frans and I had both accepted it for at least a year by then.

After a few minutes Karen excused herself quietly; so that I could have Papa to myself, I suppose.

We sat there in the front room; listening to the turning on of taps in the kitchen, and the clatter of china; listening to the old walnut-cased clock heave up enough wind for itself to begin chi-

72

ming. Think I asked Papa something about Paris – he was planning to leave soon, for France – and he began a kind of conversation, while I gazed at an enormous ceramic vase they had on the table. Branches of the bougainvillaea in it, listing and rich with the papery, translucent, burnt-orange leaves. It must have been one of Karen's pieces: simply shaped, with a creamy-white glaze that was crackled minutely all over.

One of the poems in *Liefdesverse* is about a woman working at a revolving wheel – her briefly lifted hands shining with the pale, slippery clay.

Karen came back carrying a heavy tray full of tea things – an old, cracked teapot; those tiny, silvery-yellow teaspoons with the figure of a saint for a handle; a plate of small, neat sandwiches and some round slices of cake. She turned to us after she'd put it all down, and then her face went suddenly taut, as she thought of something.

'My God. Anna? We heard about this riot in Cape Town. Were you in that? Some student demonstration, and the police – what they call it, a baton charge. . . .' She sat down, still looking at me. 'Were you hurt?' Saw Papa's elbow jerk slightly. He spoke more slowly than Karen. 'Antjie . . . *were* you involved?' And Karen said again, 'Did you get hurt, Anna?' I saw Papa glance swiftly at Karen. He had that drained, expressionless look he wears whenever any violent emotion is seething inside him. Unaware, perhaps, that the very stillness of his face is far from neutral.

I couldn't respond to their tense concern, though. Looking at the raised porcelain flowers on the teapot. Eventually I answered, since I had to, 'No, no it's all right. I didn't . . . nothing happened; I wasn't hurt.'

Karen got up to pour the tea. She was efficient, arranging cups and saucers, lifting that large, steaming pot; but you could tell from the set of her small shoulders that she was still trying, unconvinced, to work something out. She wore a long, slim robe – a kaftan, I suppose: bold blues and purples spread out across patches of waxy clearness. Her dark hair, drifting down her back, shone faintly in the light from the window. With my tea she gave me a plate laden with buttered bread and cake: but she seemed to forget her own cup, once she'd helped me and Papa – went and sat down again; chewing absently at a buttered disc of the Boston loaf. Finally she suggested, 'Anton . . . ek wonder miskien . . . net 'n idee:

73

hoekom vat julle dan nie die motor nie. Miskien sal Anna dit geniet as julle 'n entjie langs die see gaan stap?' Some momentary look, illegible to me, passed between her and Papa. Then she turned to me, trying to smile, 'Have you ever visited the old harbour here, Anna?'

When Papa and I went out it was already growing late. Karen's excuse - that she wanted to get supper started. We drove down to the harbour in the dented, puttering Volkswagen. I remember the feel of the air when we climbed out on that road above the inlet: a slight clamminess to it - perhaps there was a mist coming in off the sea; but it was scented also with the dampness that comes off stones and rocks high in the mountains. Could smell the fynbos too - senecio, felicia, kapokbos, erica, pelargonium. Papa and I picking our way down across the shingle and the wet sand; then ambling together along the old breakwater - part boulder, part massive concretion of bleached shells, pebbles, lime, grit, sand and smallish stones, with a couple of flaking, corroded iron rings set into the construction. Papa and I were both so gangling in our movements, each trying to imitate a natural, loping ease, and each conscious of the nearness of the other's stiff elbows. We stopped to stare down at the shallow slipway and the treacherous water that played at dashing and racing in the lee - an icy-looking, dull swirl of pale rack and coarse, stinging sand: strong, swift current there. I kept thinking about the few inches of chilly air and silence that lay between me and Papa. The sea had broken away part of the concrete block we stood on - you could see the collapse of it still, stones and crumbled cement scattered down near the foot of the wall.

Papa asked me, light-voiced, almost quizzical: 'Well Antjie, what brings you out here?' I was blinded for a minute, tasting salt. It had turned really cold: out towards the headland you could see the dense bank of mist coming in. I think I answered him in his own even tone, inventing something about a whim, wanting a break from university. There were other words that tried to shout out, frantically clamouring inside my head. Papa, Papa, I don't know how to hate you, I love you. But I couldn't speak them: I'm not certain that they even expressed anything like the truth.

There was a flickering across the sky - a white, dying recollection of the light; and then the dissolution of the twilight almost

74

immediately. The thick mist made the air seem dark, even stormy.

We hurried back to the car.

I slept that night: slept and slept, with my body buried heavily, almost earnestly in the soft, sagging mattress. Karen left me to rest, and it wasn't until well after lunch time that I began to make sense of the tall window opposite my bed, with the low riempie bench underneath it.

Later Papa came in and sat down on the bed next to me. 'Anna, Karen and I are a bit worried about you. Are you sure you're all right?' I stared up at him, still sleepy and with my hair blowsy over the pillows – sticky from the mist. 'Ag ja, Papa,' I whispered. 'It's nothing. It was just . . . the cathedral and all.' He looked at me, obviously bewildered; a little irritated. Carefully, formally, he said, 'Oh. But we understood that you'd not . . . that you weren't hurt in any way.'

Tiredness began to oppress me again. I couldn't begin to explain: not in any way that would satisfy Papa – clear, definite sentences with endings; elegant logical relations. Feeling sick again I tried to turn on to my side – but the sheets and blankets bound me too tightly, held down by the weight of Papa's body and his hand that rested uncertainly on my ribs. 'Papa, I couldn't sleep for two days,' I said, fretting. I felt hot; wanted him to go away. I tugged petulantly at the blankets.

Gentle again, he said, 'Oh. Well. In that case you'd better stay right where you are. You probably just need some rest.' I was silently incanting, 'Go away, please go away.' He sat there for a few minutes more, though. Without saying anything. At last he patted my shoulder, and got to his feet – releasing me.

I stayed there for another day or two. Papa was busy, editing that critical work on Afrikaans literature; writing some of the chapters for it. But there were books to read; I went for walks on my own; and they took me into the village to have tea before I left.

Papa insisted that I go home to Cape Town on one of those touring buses. And in the end I didn't really speak to him at all.

75

CHAPTER 3

i

It's become almost comfortable, having Felicia and Wilson here: we live indoors, sealed away from the rain and the funnelling wind, and there's no need for talk, as they read all day, and I type out my letters in the study. I plan the meals serenely, and when I come to prepare them find myself inexplicably hushed into an odd state of grace that allows my fingers not to fumble.

I know that it will have to end. Going to have to go out soon for bread and fresh lettuce. And the mundane truth is that we're not severed from the outside's realness. People still come knocking: beggars, but hawkers too. Fruit-sellers with basketfuls of leathery, reeking guavas. A tall, bony man who has a door-to-door trade in incense sticks and curry powder came round again a few days ago: this time offering some cheap calendars from Taiwan, with painted peacocks and apple blossom and humming birds on them. Occurs to me that the little boy next door will be getting bored one of these days, and then his toy soldier will be dropped into the weeds at the back and need rescuing. Still, if he did want to come trailing through the house – what harm would there be in it.

After all, I open the curtains during the day, and if it isn't raining too heavily, push up the sash windows to let in some light and clean air: otherwise the rooms fill up so quickly with a warm thickness of all the smells from dust, mouse-droppings and an ancient, dried memory of cat-spray from the skirting boards. Ja, it's quite ineffably ordinary.

This morning I ventured outside for a few minutes, to admire the pelargoniums and to see the black drop of water that slips, mercurial, at the centre of the nasturtium leaves. And there's nothing like apocalypse in the flimsy clouds; not even in the ugly temper of the wind that was tearing at the last few, weakened flowers on that

76

hibiscus. Someone across the street was using a vacuum cleaner, and behind its keening there was the noise of a radio serial - violin music, jingles, fake American voices.

I suppose it's really school that I don't want to go back to. To that staffroom. We've been trapped there for months now, stifled in trivia. So few proper classes for the kids that the day turns into a protracted, tedious free-period. You try to read, but no one believes you're concentrating and so you're interrupted incessantly for your admiration of the newly finished cardigan, or your corroborative opinion on the price of apples this year. Marianne is obstinate about her privacy and ignores people; but I've never had enough self-certainty to be frankly rude. Always have to yield my tense smile and the phrases people expect. Get a headache too, from the cigarette smoke.

Mr Naidoo spends almost the entire day in his office. Once I was asking the secretary for something and caught a glimpse of him through there: his long, handsome face faintly shadowed as he stared down at a pile of forms on his desk. He's in an awkward position - having to placate the sycophants from the administration, but also bound to keep the respect of his staff, some of whom aren't secretive about their support for the kids. Chris even had a charge laid against him. The police were here early last term: not doing anything; just aggressively present during a student meeting. The kids became restive, and a scuffling began at the back of the crowd after there had been some cat-calls and whistling. What the cops were after, maybe. One of the policemen found cause to begin smashing into the small of a child's back with his fists - Hennie told us this afterwards: and so Chris grappled with him. The charge was dropped later; inscrutably.

Mr Naidoo leaves the authoritarian announcements to Mr Bezuidenhout, who seems to take a gleeful pleasure in the business of switching on the intercom, even when we're mostly assembled in the next room.

Mr Naidoo. Sometimes he'll come into the staffroom, wearing a suffering, dull-hearted expression - to tell us about parents who've been telephoning him at home, at all hours, distraught that their children have dropped out of school. Once he told us, stunned himself, that a child had been unable to come to school because a group of gangsters had besieged him - waiting, armed with flick-knives and

77

sharpened kitchen knives, at the gate outside his parents' house. Another time the story was about a child in standard seven whose mother had drunk herself into a murderously violent state. The child escaped through a window and ran across to her cousin's house, where it took the aunt and some friends half an hour to quieten her screaming.

I can't find any adequate responses to such pitiful grotesqueries of 'event'. Mr Naidoo ends his narratives with a switch into suave, worldly-wise gruffness: 'Well it is tragic, but this is the way things happen nowadays.' Ja. And Marianne turns brittle with fury. Her face pinched with scepticism, she'll say, 'The hypocrite. He doesn't really care.' She hates Mr Naidoo, you see, for trying to smoothe his clichés over the unsalvable wound of a child's anguish. Can't bear his sad-voiced complacence about a child's discovery that terror is something thrilling, and even easy of access. Moved by her own extreme conviction she'll begin to blink and stammer; finally turning away, bereft of language.

Once, though, I was grateful for that placid reserve of Mr Naidoo's. It was during my first year at the school; when I was naive enough still to be astounded by a flare-up over religion. We were having a staff meeting, when Mr Korsten suddenly raised the question of Friday lunch break. I'd never realized that it was contentious; couldn't make sense of the strangled, vicious fury that seemed to lie behind his aggressive speech. Almost half of the school goes to Mosque then. Well, naturally. But it means that we come to a standstill between one o'clock and two every Friday, and because school closes half an hour later in any case, the afternoon is usually wasted completely. I hadn't taken much notice of Mr Korsten till then - he teaches woodwork, and junior accountancy, I think - but at that moment he seemed to create an almost palpable, hot surge of anger in the room. My gaze seemed to get stuck on him. Remember noticing how his face had gone a grim, suffused red. His words were spurting out of him like hot sparks of metal; and I noticed his forearms then for the first time too. Perhaps he was simply clenching his fists, but the gesture made his wrists look steely with crude power. Nobody else actually stood up to join Mr Korsten in that vehemence; but you could tell from the dispersed murmuring in the room that he had several supporters, with Mr Bezuidenhout among them.

78

Mr Naidoo didn't move, didn't raise his voice. Kept his face utterly impassive. He even let the other man interrupt him: and each time the sputtering, intrusive words petered out into the polite silence that was entertaining them, Mr Korsten lost face – without really knowing it. His objection was put aside, at any rate. Mr Naidoo controlled it all so calmly that you were left with the impression there had been a reasoned debate and resolution: in fact though, he'd left Mr Korsten to engage with himself, until his argument simply dissipated into indignity.

Marianne was next to me. She seemed to go terribly still; and afterwards she told me she'd thought she was going to faint. Mr Korsten had unleashed something horribly evil. I knew what she meant. I'd also felt physically afraid, close to nausea. She told me the story about Mr Korsten then. During the risings in 1976 some of the kids were caught up in a rampage of near hysteria and went rushing frantically down the stairs. I think there were police in the grounds: I'm not sure, but there was tear-gas around, everywhere, and someone had turned on a fire hose. Mr Korsten is supposed to have grabbed one boy who came flying past and punched him full in the chest, so that the upper part of his back went crashing against the brick wall.

There are several men at our school who believe that true authority can only manifest itself in brute force. After all, I suppose that is simply the tenor of the ruling ideology.

I miss Marianne. Who thinks that it is men who are to blame for most of our unhappiness – that it is purely through their arrogance that we're trapped in a city of violence.

She doesn't have a telephone either – can't afford one. The Department will only recognize her matric (something about her B.A. lacking one credit still), so they pay her about a hundred and eighty a month. Not sure how she manages, with those dogs of hers to feed, and a car to run. Living all the way out at Lotus River. Chrisjan helps her, of course, but Marianne won't take any rent from Beverley. It's really for Beverley and Chrisjan's sake that they live in that almost rural obscurity: people could make trouble if they wanted to. You'd think it would be peaceful at least – near the vlei, with all those birds breeding in the marshland there, in amongst the tall, clattering beds of dry reed. But it's a derelict place: an unused small-holding really, with the ruined wiring of old chicken-runs in the yard; perished tractor tyres lying scattered; unidentifiable, rusting knuckles of metal pipe. The roads in the area are untarred, so that when the wind blows there's a thin, irritating veil of grit and dust over everything, even in your hair and your eyes.

I think that Marianne dreams of writing a documentary-type novel about Beverley Samuels. She works at the school as a cleaner and tea-maker, in a role that with its implication of subordinateness seems to be destroying her from the inside. Cancer of the psyche. Always has bad headaches; and is often absent on a Monday morning – the worst day to have to face, I suppose. People are quick to dislike her for her weaknesses: Sally assessing it in a snipped little exclamation of distate, 'Beverley and her illnesses'. Well, Marianne offered her the spare room. Her husband lives there too, in principle: it seems he clings jealously to a debonair private life as well. Sometimes he'll come home swaggering drunk, take Beverley's savings from her and begin to beat her, forcing huge welts of sub-cutaneous bleeding all over her body with his fists and knees – bruises whose shadows I've often seen myself. Marianne has huge shouting quarrels with her over this, telling her she ought to divorce Benjamin. Beverley responds usually with a half-hearted show of resolve, and might even spit some raging words at Benjamin when she sees him again: but these things always dissolve into the more comfortable, warm tears of misery, and later she'll take him back. Marianne tells me this, trembling just perceptibly. Too tired for feeling, she'll stare at me and ask, 'Anna, Anna, why can't people just love each other?'

Maybe the trouble is that people persist in loving.

Beverley's father used to beat her up when she was a child. He'd do it righteously, convinced it was some solemn duty that came with paternity. But his daughter still worships him. Marianne says she goes to visit him once a fortnight, on a Sunday afternoon: looking pretty even, blushing, when she sets out. She makes him his tea, spooning in the right number of sugars; probably puts a batch of biscuits in the oven. Reminiscing with him; laughing, babbling away. How can you not love the idea of the father. Sometimes Beverley will admit, reluctantly, that her father is an ill man, or more simply, a bastard. For her, though, fatherliness is embodied in something self-admiring, maudlin, obscenely in love with its own crude strength, and she still adores that: even if it means that

80

her love is monstrously close to masochism. Some people would call it a form of slavery.

ii

I had a real conversation with the kids last night, for the first time. Well, it was mostly Wilson who spoke. He's an awkward child. How can I be so mean, though. It isn't his fault that his shoulders are narrow and meagrely fleshed out. Or that he's so pale, with freckles smudged over the planes of his face. There, you see: I'm freckled myself, though I hardly remember it ever. Seeing someone else's often brings the ludicrous thought, Do they feel the marks against their cheeks. When I think of my own at all it's when they've merged across the doubtful image of my face in a mirror. Tiny pebbles just below the surface of streaming, colourless water. You look into the distance of a mirror, always past the blemishes; or perhaps only cursorily in any case, at brush-strokes flicking through the strands of your hair.

Wilson is letting his hair grow out into an Afro. But it's the wrong colour. Find myself disproportionately moved by that mass of indifferent tawniness above his forehead. The way the general emblem of solidarity loses most of its force when it is adopted in some modified, more or less unique form by an individual. He still doesn't trust me altogether, I think. He's careful now to avoid the conventional 'Miss', but still uneasy about the 'Anna' I've asked them both to use: he addresses me rather stonily – without appellation.

At any rate he transformed some of his silent hostility into aggressive debate as we ate. At one point it was, 'You liberal whites make me sick.' Chewing steadily at his food. I'd made a lentil curry, tricked out quite proudly, I thought, with chutney, raisins, onions and brown rice. We had the light on in the kitchen, but the room seemed to sway heavily with shadows at times – less illuminated by the electric bulb than by the strange hostility of our arguments and the flickering of our forks in the grains of our food.

Felicia carried on eating quietly; but she was listening, I could see. Found myself staring at the light that gleams faintly on her temples and cheekbones. More than once during the evening I wished she'd say something to interrupt Wilson's burning speeches,

81

my burning words.

'Your bullshit about agrarian socialism,' he went on, 'that's just a pipe-dream. Suppose you've got some romantic idea about harmony with nature – all that. But you can't make history go backwards.' Like so many of us, he's an impassioned soliloquist. I began asking him something: 'Surely, Wilson, if Communism is working anywhere it's in China, . . .' But he completed my sentence for me: 'and in Africa. For sure. Suppose you going to talk to me about Tanzania now. But what you don't want to realize is, you have to look at the economic reality of the particular country. So for Azania? This is an industrial society, that's the reality. Okay, sure, there's the agricultural sector. But we talking about the future, okay, about growth, okay, about development – so we talking about the industrial development of this country.' It was impossible to break into his spectacularly swift rhetoric. 'We've *got* the raw materials in this country, right. So how long do you think we going to stay oppressed by the Western multi-nationals? When you going to wake up? We're fighting for development, for progress, okay.'

He pushed aside the remains of his food, leaving the plate bordered with a crescent of the translucent rice grains and the dark lentils. And I was thinking of François, who used to become angry sometimes too: similarly afire, except that he would stumble heavily over his own syllables. 'Listen Anna, I . . . I just don't give a stuff about politics the way you do. When they dump some drums of nuclear waste into the seas . . . hey, I just don't care who the country is, because they're fucking in the whole world, ja, the world I want to live in.' That was François's constant argument. 'Anna, it's a global thing: your economics, pseudo-Marxist, whatever they're supposed to be – you don't found them on the basic, fundamental, irreducible economics of the planet itself. So I'm not interested. Your concept of value – you just don't give a damn how much you take from the earth. The sea. The atmosphere. And that's primitive, Anna. Primitive. I tell you, the Bushmen are civilized now. They know how to leave aside – for tomorrow.' Almost always he'd end in incoherence, muttering apologetically, with his eyes gleaming a deep hazel-gold.

I couldn't think of any way to counter Wilson's oratory. Really, he must be quite exceptionally persuasive, speaking from a platform. And so much of what he says is hard to dispute. We sat drinking tea

82

after the meal: Wilson rather grudgingly, as though it irritated him to accept even my smallest offerings. He was in a mood to carry on talking though, even if he might have preferred a different audience.

The soothing, bitter drink swirled against my palate. I dared to press a point. 'All right,' I said. 'You want to assume that an urbanized, industrial society's going to be best for the future of this country. . . .' He was set to interrupt, but I felt suddenly vociferous, and over-rode him. 'Well, maybe *you* haven't realized that the last decade has changed people's attitudes towards industrialism pretty drastically. Or it ought to have. We've caught ourselves out thinking we were gods with limitless powers, when the truth is that we're only animals – pretty clever ones – but animals: and like all the other animals we're a part of the planet's gigantic, incredible network of living systems. . . .' I was beginning to get breathless. 'Ja . . . that, that's the network we've been so industriously clawing down all around ourselves; tearing it apart as though it were just something useless, disposable. When it was our sustenance.'

I wonder why we couldn't simply exchange our ideas peaceably? Why we couldn't reason quietly with each other? Know what François would say: 'Look, I'm sorry, Anna, but there're some ideas I can't afford to tolerate. What room for tolerance is going to be left when the earth is a stinking, radio-active desert?'

I was over-wrought, of course, speaking far too heatedly. The half-darkness in the room seemed to flicker, shift, sometimes blaze up around us, in random imitations of my own excitement. Wilson had set his mug down on the table, and was tapping at its rim with his fingers. But I still had things to say. Memories of François were overwhelming me just then, bright, trembling in the midst of that obscure shadowiness. Because I was saying the things he used to say. Or cry out, rather. When his private visions of a ruined, eternally darkened sky had tightened his features till his face was a miserable, glistening mask. But he was ill: depressed, suggestible. Watching him, listening, I used to warn myself against succumbing ever to the same failure of heart. Yet here I was, ranting at Wilson. These timeless, unchanging predictions of the imminent end. How do you tell what is most realistic? I pretended last night that I knew the answer – flightily, weakly rounding on Wilson: 'Do you know what is the real illusion? The real opium dream is thinking you can build yourself some towering, vertical highway to the future, all cables and steel and coal and oil, minerals, gold.... It's a fairy-tale castle; a ... a house of cards: all built on top of the dying earth.' My voice was beginning to choke up, but breathing in more deeply I added, 'Haven't you heard of finitude?'

I felt ashamed, a little. Why wouldn't I let him speak, for one thing. Perhaps I *am* the problem of my own personality. Too much storminess?

I stood up to refill the kettle; trying to think of a question I could ask Wilson in genuine perplexity, rather than rhetorically. He didn't need a cue, though, to resume his driving hisses: 'You know I can't stand this, the way you whites go on; it makes me sick. I suppose you've got some presumptuous little theory about misplaced aspirations? How everybody's just going to want a TV and a fridge and a stove and lounge suites and smart cars. . . .' His cheek was lean with contempt. A moment's pause, and then he sat forward in his chair – speaking slowly, emphatically: 'Maybe you don't understand that Azania's not going to need your bourgeois consumer trash. You know that? I'm not going to need a house full of possessions. Fuck that kind of decadence. I don't need it: just like I don't need the kind of education a white gets. Okay? Know what I want? I want education for freedom, not slavery: because I'm going to be living in a free society. Me . . . not my kids: me. My parents were waiting for Azania to come, and their parents sat waiting for Azania to come: and their parents before them. Well, I'm not going to have my kids waiting and waiting, and then turn around to me and say I was a sell-out.'

I began to feel dazed, listening to him. Kept reaching out for the tea-bags without knowing altogether what I was doing. His own anger or perhaps his eloquence had encouraged him to say more, I think, than he might have intended. Still sounding furious he interruped my activities: 'Haven't you got coffee? I can't take this tea all the time.' I blushed and fumbled even more clumsily with mugs and tea-spoons; trying to remember where I'd put the tin of instant.

He seemed to use my confusion as a convenient break while he recovered reserves of his own. Steady-voiced again, he went back to an earlier part of his speech: 'I suppose you've got some typical vision of people just going crazy after the revolution — looting the shops, just taking everything: stupid little crystal lampshades and

84

underwear and nylon bedspreads and curly, golden picture-frames. I suppose. Well, maybe they will. Drive you people into the sea as well. I don't actually care, you know, if they want to do that. But I'm telling you the real work begins with the reconstruction; and then nobody's got the time to go playing around in Mercedes Benz's.'

Neither of us spoke for a while after that. The wind was beginning to rise outside: I could hear the iron sheeting on the roof lift slightly from time to time, rattling at its own corroded bolts. Think I was regretting much of what I'd said. I've had so little practice at the living exchange of words.

Feeling remote from the children, I sat listening to the gusts of the dry storm. Beginning to worry again about the panes of glass in the splintered sash frames. I glanced at Felicia, who sat drinking her tea still, delicately silent. It is not Wilson's fault if his eyes shine hotly when he interrupts.

Interruption. Breaking in, yes. I also think it is everything – everything – that these children have called a halt to. Heard the rowdiness of a seagull veering past, stifled at the heart of a gusting wind. They come over from Woodstock beach, searching for shelter inland when the atmosphere turns stormy. What is it they sense? Turbulences in the air? Or electricity, scattering its dry, sporadic streamings over any gap that opens in the dark clouds: when the cumulus towers for thousands of metres you get a potential difference forming. It all begins to seem familiar, somehow. As though once before in my life there was some similar invasion: a similar collapsing inward of each vestigial image of the world. Someone surrendered then, I think: losing consciousness as they fell backward, staggering under the weight of an unthinkable blow. Someone near me.

My eyes had begun to ache: tried fixing my gaze on Wilson's hands. He moves them incessantly as he speaks. The bulb in the kitchen is really far too dim – only sets up shadows everywhere. When you're tired it's in the shadows that other images of darkness want to stir and grow. Dumbly I moved my gaze to Wilson's thin face. And suddenly I couldn't understand why we were antagonists. I am complicit, after all, in his actions. Even though I don't know what these two are doing, I support them in it. Blindly, but adamantly: I have always had a capacity for faith, I know.

85

Tiredly I offered him a last, rather empty question; meaning to put an end to this talk. For an instant we found ourselves entangled by accident in an odd kind of intimacy: both poised to break into speech; both with our mouths slightly parted. I felt a throbbing begin in my forehead, above my eyes. Doggedly I put my question - arranging my syntax, at any rate, to imitate enquiry. There was a stirring near me: Felicia, finally, was sitting forward. 'Yes,' she said, 'yes, of course: you *have* to have endless revolution. The world has got to keep on renewing itself, or else . . . or else it just freezes over. Can't you see.'

I was taken by surprise. Yet it was only as it should have been, I suppose: the sureness to her voice; the light come alive, almost golden in her eyes. I don't think she was tired at all. Wilson's face, I noticed, took on a certain opacity as she began to speak. 'Only revolution is life-giving,' she went on, now that she had begun. 'It's the only, it's the only true creativity. It's only eternal revolution that can liberate us spiritually - make our lives . . . works of art.' She seemed slightly feverish; stammering. Wilson kept his face averted; kept his eyelids lowered.

It seemed that there was nothing left for anyone to say. We wished each other goodnight eventually and the children wandered away in turn, subdued, to the bathroom and then to bed.

I stayed on in the kitchen, ill at ease - troubled by some point I was too tired to identify. Only the wind seemed to have an unrelenting energy. I could hear it still steadfastly tearing at the night's shining, flimsy fabric. Kept remembering Felicia's face. There are loose strands of her hair that stray across her cheekbones. And I was thinking, for no reason, of rain at night: the way the wind dies down when the rain comes.

What does Wilson want with Felicia's dreams of anarchy, with her erratically frenzied romanticism?

I keep trying to think back ten years, to the time I was Felicia's age. But then it was writing letters as well: to Michael Bernstein, whose lenses were so thick you saw the greenish colour of the glass in them. How we concluded - we were grandiose in our teens - we concluded that revolution was inescapable: the outcome of oppression itself. We could never escape that knowledge. It was our pacifism though, that anguished us. For a time we thought, but never happily, that an individual might choose a revolutionary mode:

but only after enduring the most extreme tortures of conscience first, as a kind of purgatory. Violent acts, but with a seared mind.

We were never tested, though.

And these kids. . . .

How can they cope? How can they possibly cope. When the world they're prodding at doesn't resist ever, but keeps on yielding to them. It must be like falling eternally through nightmare, with only an endless cold rushing of stars; the dark night wind; and nothingness. You need the counter somewhere; a checking. You need at least one brief moment, say, when your father will grip you in his arms and hold you to him with his lips in your hair and his fingers moving lightly, amazedly over your forehead, your cheekbones. Before surrendering you to yourself. Isn't it a dialectic? Of being; or love, perhaps. Yes: love — something cold, and so rough.

iii

It's cold again, but at least that wind has stopped its incessant rustling through my thoughts. It's been drizzling ever since we woke up this morning.

Feeling a bit calmer today. I was upset, distracted, the whole of yesterday - trying to write you a letter. Won't post it, though. Words kept uttering themselves that I hadn't meant at all. Partly fatigue, I'm sure. Had a strange sense the whole day that things around me were threatening to break up. Perhaps it was partly the wind as well: it was up yesterday, cold and forcefully persistent. Stormy too - a gale, probably: adding to the sounds I kept imagining, of wooden beams disintegrating or the crashing of glass in huge, jagged shards into the streets. At times I thought it was sheer form, symbol itself that was cracking apart along the black and silvery veins of internal flaws.

Now I think it was mostly irrational. There's a tranquillity about the quiet, steady dripping from the guttering outside. Perhaps it's absurd, perhaps it's even morally wrong to spend one's days braced in a rigid unhappiness against some imaginary future? Better to relinquish the straight-edged thoughts: drift into the diffuseness of dreams instead. Is it a surrender? Why, I wonder. Retrieving one's past; speculating; inventing a history.

The children seem to be feeling relaxed too. They're reading, of course. Floppily tumbled over the pillows. Wonder whether I shouldn't light a fire for them in the sitting-room. One of the cafés up the road sells coal. And firewood – usually rooikrans that's green still with sap. I think I could make a fire quite easily. Never done it, but I remember helping François. Crumpling up newspaper and breaking up the thin twigs into kindling. You make a kind of stook with the wood, thickest branches on top; and pack the coals around it? When we were children, Frans and I would lie near the fire in our pyjamas, reading our library books; with the brass fender gleaming and burning across our pages. But you have to tend a fire, I think. Break away the ash from the shiny coal; encourage the air to pierce the burning interstices. Constance must have done that, lifting the poker from time to time and leaning forward. Frans and I with our faces puckered, lost in stories. But I think that Observatory is a smoke-free zone. Or going to be one. Wonder about the factories then. You can see at least three charred, brick smoke-stacks from the front garden, and the hospital keeps a furnace going constantly too.

Wish I had Papa's self-discipline. While I dressed for school, as a child, shivering – struggling to pull on my spencer under my pyjama jacket – Papa would be already at his desk. And in the afternoons, when I came home hot and irritable after compulsory games on the playing fields, he'd be back already from the university, and working in the study. Lectures and seminars he had to prepare, I suppose. And assignments from his students that he had to mark. I know he spent a lot of his time reading as well, and perhaps just thinking.

I was perfectly comfortable by then with the knowledge that Papa was also Anton Rossouw. The only thing that still disconcerted me was that special tone of voice our Afrikaans teacher would use for me – hushed and silky; almost contrite. I suppose that every tiny child believes its father to be some magnificently famous, universal hero. You imagine that even his name is peculiarly rich in its rustling sibilance and the roll that begins it. But normally. . . . What happens normally? I suppose the myth must slowly die as you learn to understand your father's real status. And then you begin to see your family as part of a class. Or a neighbourhood, at any rate? I wonder how things would have been if Papa's numinous aura had gradually dimmed and then faded. Perhaps I'd have been able to get free of him? I don't know. Experience only taught me that he *was* someone intensely admired, and by thousands of other people.

Well, he was well known at any rate. I remember the information I got from Sarah Ravenscroft when I was about nine. She went to a private school where they wore neat, dusty-pink uniforms; and her parents had forbidden her to come out into the road. Swinging blithely on their front gate, she told us that she wasn't allowed to play with Mark Greenberg or the Jacobsons or Helen or Rachel or the Rossouws: we were all gutter children. Fascinated by her none-theless, we used to stand patiently outside her house, hoping for interviews. She and I had a tête-à-tête once. Not strictly; since she'd positioned herself carefully behind the bricked gate-pillar. Both of us vaguely aware that Mr Ravenscroft was present in the back-ground. A warm, silvery rustling from a hosepipe in amongst the shadowiness of shrubs, earth and prune trees. Everything about their garden was dark: reflections from the maroon brickwork of the house, perhaps; or from the beds of zinnia and dahlia. 'My daddy says your father is a poet,' she said. Staring at me curiously. She had a broad face, and a dense mass of wavy, golden-orange blonde hair down her back. 'He writes in Ofrikaans.' And suddenly she skipped away, rushing to her father, whose cardigan sleeve she clutched at. From the shadows, from behind the sheen of the water, she was giggling into heather mix and knotted leather buttons: al-most sick with glee.

Until then I'd never thought consciously of Papa as a poet. It wasn't until we moved to the bigger house that I became consis-tently aware of the fact that he wrote. Suppose because there were enough rooms then for him to have a study – emphasized his wor-king habits. I'm sure that if he found it possible to contemplate the idea of steadily decaying order in the universe – and he must have – it was probably only because so much of his life was rigidly pat-terned. Fixed habits permit a greater freedom?

Well, in Papa's case it was habit and Constance.

Maybe my feelings there are still those of a fourteen-year-old. I don't know. I'm still bewildered by it. That parents can get di-vorced? DIVORCE IS A SUBURBAN INSTITUTION. Saw that written on a lavatory door once, on campus. Not sure whether it was cynical or religious or political.

But Constance was the one, after all, who made the light-brown, geometrically sliced toast and the soft-boiled egg for me to take in to Papa at his desk every morning. Special dark blue raffia runner we always put on his tray. And for all those years that we lived in the rented house, with Papa finishing his doctoral thesis, Constance never employed a servant. She was the one who stood for hours in the afternoons at the ironing board, with its scorched linen cover. Smell of Papa's warm shirts. Pale colours they had then; and the sleeve cuffs with button holes, for Papa to put the links through – shiny, black stones I remember. She used to do sewing. And typing – for Papa, and charities. Washing: some days the bathroom was crowded with the noise of the machine thumping and slopping and spinning our clothes; and there would be a reek of soap-suds and perished rubber tubing.

Who said: objects the common people put into their houses are the mass-reproduced copies of precious things you used to find in the mansions of the nobility? Those people had chamber-maids and scullery-maids to polish the brass and clean the grates and scrape the grease from the dishes and rinse the crystalware; and cooks; and laundry-maids to tidy the velvets and swirl the cottons in the stream, against the stones; and seamstresses, nurse-maids, valets, butlers. While the modern bourgeois has only a wife. Maybe a reason why? Why she has to wax the furniture, brasso the scuttle, vacuum-clean the carpets, polish the floors, shine the doorknobs, soap and rinse the dishes, feed the children, rub at the windowpanes with a squeaking rag soaked in meths, dust the pelmets, scrub the lavatory, sweep under the beds, air the bedspreads, beat the rugs, soak the washing in Biotex, devise the suppers and cook them and serve them.

Constance had a servant later on, though. It used to embarrass me. That a grown woman should shift her bulk awkwardly when I passed her in the passage, and not speak – as though I were meant not to distinguish her from the gleaming oak bureau that she oiled and buffed with her duster. To have a child's name; and a gauche-ness more savagely painful than my own? I know that Mom tried to be a decent employer. She paid 'Lizzie' more than anybody else in the neighbourhood paid their servants; gave her a hot meat lunch every day and groceries to take home; drove her down to the railway station if Papa was home from university in time; bought her a tin of paraffin each month, from the local hardware shop. 'Well, it really doesn't cost *me* much, but in the townships you know, those African shopkeepers really rob their own kind.' But I'd feel a tight bar of tension between my shoulder blades every time I came home from school to find the polishing machine still roaring drearily in the sitting-room, and the kitchen chairs put into the pantry, with mats draped over them. To have to step past Lizzie and smile at her while she fumbled tiredly through the gestures of pretended complaisance, pretended humility, pretended dullness. You can't ask someone to stop being a stranger to you when she has learnt to be alien to herself even.

By then, though, Mom seemed to have abandoned all interests of her own, apart from reading and gardening. Think she was exhausted by marriage, but perhaps the brightness died out of her so slowly, so gradually, that it seemed to be nothing more than the natural process of ageing.

Whereas Papa by the time he reached forty was beginning to be a celebrity, in a modest way. I suppose it was a kind of rejuvenescence; and maybe he wanted everything around him to reflect richness and praise and delight. But there was Constance, grown dull, and me – a difficult child. He began going out on his own, in the evenings and over week-ends. Those notorious gatherings with his coterie of friends in Stellenbosch. Sestigers. Although I don't know how accurate it is when people group him with them. Papa was slightly older than most of them. Also, in retrospect it's difficult to see how that surge of Euro-centric modernism affected his style in any fundamental way: that brittle, intellectual quality of his was already there in the poetry he was writing during the fifties.

I remember. We went once with Papa to a farm outside Stellenbosch. Frans and I hated it, though – being overawed by the lithe Afrikaans children who approached us politely and spoke in superior English. They brought us sticky cake, which we humbly accepted. They themselves scorned food, however, and ran down nimbly instead to the white-washed stables we could see amidst the oak trees, blue-gums and a maverick bougainvillaea strung through with jasmine. Must have been spring then. Still remember the dustiness, and the rich smell of manure. Frans and I were stilled by our fear – trembling when the horses came heavily thudding, racing past us. There were women who wore dresses made from shining purple-blue stuff: when they bent forward to be kind to you, their pendants would swing free – large coppery or silver ornaments, with veined blue stones in them. Something about these people made me wince: the ampleness of their attentions; or simply perhaps their perfume. You couldn't ask to go home, though, or even stand and talk to Mom, because she was sitting hedged in on an antique bench on the veranda, drinking coffee with two women who were effusively at pains to re-assure her with their elegant English. I remember noticing with an extraordinary rage how the home-made beskuit was crumbling all over Mom's blouse and skirt. And she was awkward, maybe too warm. All that white-wash intensified the heat of the sun, and the leafy fig tree in front of the stoep, far from offering shade merely added its profound scent and lime-coloured tints to the light.

I think Mom was really too worn-out to enjoy company like that – probably preferring to stay at home, comfortable in an armchair with her latest library book.

I wasn't . . . I'm afraid I wasn't very helpful, especially straight after the divorce. Tempers of weeping and accusation. Why? Sulking in my room; hating poor Mom for her broad cheekbones and that dense, chestnut hair of hers, swept up in wings at the sides of her face; hating her for the vehemence of her opinions; for the old-fashioned chiffon scarves she knotted at her throat, when she should have preferred Oriental or Russian necklaces. I whispered all those tearful insults into my pillows – unaware that what I resented most of all was my own freckled pallor; my thin, straight hair.

I used to be afraid of Mommy. Fearful imaginings that were merged with uncertain images from dreams. And for some reason I used to believe that she shouted, or at least spoke loudly always, and roughly. Can't think why. Because her features are firmly expressive? She'll purse up her mouth when she's doubtful; grimace energetically when she's dumbfounded by something. Maybe because of that nightmare I had. I was about four years old, I think. Being killed in my sleep, suffocated with a hideous slowness, while Mommy's voice echoed colossally around me, disembodied, and uttering commands for the dense, heavy pillows to be sent down one after the other, slow as sand, on top of my face.

There's a photograph of me at about two years: I'd been dressed up in one of the dainty little smocks Constance sewed for me, and they'd put a hairbrush in my hand – for me to play with, perhaps. It seems I was a wooden sort of baby though – staring sullenly at the brush, almost as though I were miserable in that helpless role of 'infant'. Wish I'd been the kind of child that purses up its mouth and then twinkles helplessly into smiles, or knows how to stroke its father's cheek contemplatively.

I think I never quite lost that obstinately glowering look. Remember the humiliation of the kindergarten. There was a game we played, with flashcards. The teacher spread the printed words out across the floor: supposed to be stepping stones. And we'd tip-toe from one to the other. Chair at the end you were supposed to reach, and then you were king. King? Or frog. Something. Horrible brat I was, stumping rudely across the silly cards. Someone should have taught me how to teeter uncertainly and stammer and blush and pull funny little fey faces of self-doubt. Instead I stared out through the classroom windows from the trestle-chair throne, stared out at the grey sand that skimmed across the asphalted playing ground, stared at the broken, wind-bowed eucalyptus trees.

Later I was allowed to take out books from the Big Children's library. I remember the teacher who led me along the unfamiliar length of the concrete stoep, past all the prefab classrooms. I'd always thought she was rather stern – but she held my hand then. Her voice was husky; slow and quite soft. She showed me the issuing desk, all the books. Said I could go there whenever I liked. It was a cramped, dingy room – converted toolshed, really, that still smelled, in my imagination, of the caretaker's spades and rakes and mop buckets; and the windows were barred, meshed over with a fine diamond pattern of rusted, heavy-duty wire. Against burglars?

Once I overheard Papa attacking Mom about me: 'Constance, for heaven's sake, can't you do something with Anna? I don't know who she thinks she is, scowling at everything and everybody all the time. Willem was saying. . . .' The rest of his words were lost as a swarming, singing sound filled my skull. I was about twelve then. Of course, I can see now that his anger was probably a reflection of some other irritation. But for weeks after that, when anyone spoke to me at school I'd feel nauseous and light-headed, while tiny points of sweat came prickling out on my upper lip. Wonder why that desperate desire to escape always takes the form of a raging thirst. Eventually I got back enough courage to engineer some sort of stiff smile for myself, and whenever any of Papa's friends came to the house I'd use it, or else fluster desolately into giggles that meant nothing, certainly not mirth.

And Frans. It's odd that he should have been the one to break down in the end: he was always charming and easy, even as a small boy. When Constance told us about the divorce, he behaved so much better than I did. It was a hopeless, stifling occasion: the three of us sitting on the old, rattan-backed settee that none of us ever chose normally, because it seemed so formal. (Well, when we were very tiny, Frans and I used to fatten it out with the pillows off our beds, and huddle there, squabbling and crowding each other, while Mom read us stories about the dinosaurs or meteorites and comets.) Both of us knew in advance what she was going to tell us. François used to pad into my room in his pyjamas sometimes, when Mom's bedroom door was ominously closed and Papa was talking to her in strong, ceaseless whispers. 'Do you think Mommy and Papa are going to get divorced?' he said one day, pretending to be nonchalant over that word, but terrified, secretly. I was speechless, and could only stare at him, amazed by the daring of his thought. He was just a little kid then: I remember how the sun used to burn his ragged, cow-licked hair into uneven patches of straw and honey. I knew the word as well, but had never dreamed it could have meanings that touched on one's own most deeply buried fears. When Mom drew us down on to the settee, with her arms comfortingly around us – Frans and I knew that he'd been right. My shoulder was uncomfortable where Mom was hugging me, and I didn't know how we were supposed to react. With tears? I fidgeted through Constance's reassurances. It was François who spoke up, choking slightly from nervousness: 'You mustn't worry, Mom; I'll look after you now.'

Afterwards Frans came quietly into my bedroom and stood there – fiddling with books, staring at the pastel print of my curtains. Finally he looked directly at me. His straw-coloured hair seemed to be fussing across his face; and the usual deep clarity of his eyes was broken up by a rapid, dark flickering of his eyelashes. 'You know, he can't do this,' he said. And I, being afraid of the heavy truth of Frans's words, felt painfully embarrassed; and couldn't help him.

94

For a few years after that he hardly mentioned Papa at all. Then when he was about sixteen he began referring to him again, but always as 'the old man'. The phrase was affectionately off-hand, but at the same time sounded cryptically insulting. Yet he'd enjoyed Papa's company so much as a small boy.

I remember the walks Papa used to take us on – along the beaches at Muizenberg or Strandfontein, on Saturday afternoons. Suppose those were Constance's times for herself. We rolling down the car windows to wave goodbye to her: and she'd be stalking off already to the veranda, with a book under her arm. She had an old, greying wicker chair there, that had sagged into comfortable contours over the years. Hanging baskets of maidenhair held the light above her; and there were bleached perlemoen shells arranged on a makeshift shelf. Dark, dusty leaves of her unsuccessful African violets. But at the beach, at the parking lot, Frans and I would tumble out of the car to escape our headaches and squabbling, and the smell of warm rubber.

There was one dull afternoon when the three of us strode along the damp, unending stretch of long beach. Or rather, Frans and Papa strode, long-legged and wirily fit. Vying, I think. I'd alternate between running after them, stumbling in the sand, and lingering behind, to stare out instead at the white horses and the thick tangles of kelp that rolled in the foam at the water's edge. Frans and I used to take turns riding the slippery gold heads – one of us clutching the thick, sticky bole and the other tugging valiantly. The blue-black mussel shells would get churned up, tumbling in that wake of coarse white sand. But that afternoon there was only fine sand stinging at the backs of my knees. Frans and Papa were far ahead of me when they began their great outcry of discovery. Heard Papa calling, 'Frans, Fransie, kom kyk gou, dis 'n . . .' The blown, salty sand in my mouth smothered the rest of his words from me. The two of them moved closer together; both gazing down at something that lay in the debris of wrack strands, gull feathers and the dark strings of bluebottles. I rushed up across the sand; thinking that I might steal a way into that companionship. But my insistent questions were either too cloying in their false ignorance, or else too loudly demanding, I suspect.

'Ag, Antjie.' Papa murmured. Impatiently. I looked down at their find, hatred for it burning white inside me. It was an odd

95

thing, bristling all over with stiff spines, and with its little whitish belly enormously puffed out. 'It's a blaasoppie, Frans,' Papa said, earnestly pedagogic. And next to me Frans gurgled, offended, and pretended to punch Papa in the belly. 'What do you think I am, a total *idiot* . . .' Papa looked straight at Frans, his face utterly expressionless for an instant – and then broke into one of his rare, rather brilliant grins and pretended to shrug his shoulders apologetically. It amazed me that Frans didn't even need to watch Papa's gestures of concession. He was bent down, carefully lifting the fish by its tail. Solemnly he showed it to me, and then, with his small chin quivering and his eyes seriously grey, he explained it to me and Papa. 'In English they call it a porcupine fish. I mean, I think. But there is another thing. Must be a kind of cousin: called a puffer fish.'

They moved on, and I was left feeling stranded, my face burning in the wind. I tried staring down at the dead fish in the same way that Frans had done. But I couldn't see what it had meant to him or Papa. The sharp cold gnawed at the back of my skull and the wind that was darkening whipped at my clothes and hair. I saw the edges of the dunes, with the sparse, pale grasses flailing and dipping. Sometimes broken glass in that sand. And I was terrified – only for a moment or two, and perhaps only in a minor way: sensing that the strong south-easter was ruining something. Ripping into chaos all the peace of my customary landscapes.

That evening I was flustered, with an ache in my chest, and had to have an aspirin crushed for me in a teaspoon of jam.

François always knew the names of things. He would stoop on the beach, seize up a bleached shell with a lilac-coloured inner whorl and then, after squinting at it in the sea-bright light, instantly understand it. Words had a special way of meaning for him: a way that's been lost to me from the beginning. Although I can make surmises. I think, I do think that it must be possible to grasp at words the way you can scrape up a handful of pebbles and dry grass from the ground, bruising you knuckles and with the powdery dust drifting into your nostrils.

And that field next to our first house – thick with vivid kikuyu grass, snail-bitten weeds, tadpoles in the ditches, and rain, and in the winter, arums: Frans was virtually lord of it. Once he found some larvae in the ditch near the broken-backed mimosa tree. The

96

gang came to help: or to guard their admiration with grudging scepticism, that is. 'Gants, gants,' I remember Frans crying out, obscurely, since his mouth was muffled in the neck of his pullover, and the creatures were obstinately refusing to be rocked along on the surface of the water into his peanut-butter bottle. 'What,' said Bruce Jacobson solidly. That large boy with shiny, creased knees. Hotly scornful I rounded on him: 'They're gants. Don't you *know*.'

And I was amazedly proud of François. He and I had both read about gnats and aquatic larvae in a book that Constance gave us, but Frans's miracle lay in crossing the gap between those doubtful sketches on the page and the unexpectedly tiny creatures that clung beneath the stagnant film of water in reality. I'd never guessed that such words might be pronounced, far less exchanged with other people.

Constance used to bring us home books as though they were toffees, or packets of charms. Wedged down inside her old string shopping bag, along with the bread and toothpaste. Little Golden books: I still remember the inky smell of that fine gilt tracery down their spines. And Dr Zim's books. About the stars and the world and the universe, mostly.

I suppose I should confess that I was jealous of François. Because of the secret he shared with Constance. At bed-time, I remember, he would reach up and put his ear near her face, giggling but imperious: and the song would be chanted to him in their hushed, private language. It was only some nonsense rhyme that we'd heard in a film, but all the same I wept desolately: because I couldn't remember the words. One of those family films that we'd been taken to see at a crowded, looming place that smelled of candied popcorn, the dried dullness of late afternoon, and faintly acrid perfume. So much noise there was from the screen: a chaos of light and ochre-coloured shadows and such huge, swollen faces of glistening mirth. When the song came it seemed to me to be lost almost instantly in a mass of other dark, flickering sounds. And there was something quick and sharp: the cantering of horses, perhaps, along a cobbled street.

I preferred books: where the story was permanently imprinted in one form – where the words of songs or rhymes could not be changed or, worse, become inexplicably lost or rubbed at the edges. Suppose I felt that Frans must know a way of holding on to the

97

shapes of sound. But perhaps it wasn't really the lost words that I hated him for owning. It was that other language I envied him. The language of wordless delight that they shared as they rested close together, as Frans's arm slid with a small boy's unconscious tenderness around Mom's shoulders.

But even that gift of his – that knowing how words can lay their fingers on the skin of the world – didn't help him. In the end. I think it was silence then that he went out to try and get back from the country. The farmer thought that he was dead: lying so deathly still on the hot earth, with the ants crawling unperturbed over him.

I think that I can almost understand it. I can imagine the immense peace that comes from gazing, hour upon hour, at the creatures in the sand; while you keep the burning strength of the sun fixed steadily between your shoulder blades in a balance that nothing, not even the wind or other people's shouting, can shake. It comes near to my own idea of paradise.

He never seemed to want to leave home – not with that same storming insistence I felt. Although it's possible I've misunderstood something there. While he was studying at Stellenbosch he'd stay in his residence in the town during the week; sometimes coming back home to Rondebosch on his motorbike for the Saturdays and Sundays. Most of his week-ends, though, he spent out in the country. Used to go off with his primus cooker in his rucksack; take his sweater, perhaps a book, and his entomological kit. That didn't change much after he'd dropped out of university and begun to work at the museum here in the city. At least, as far as I knew then. One reason for not needing to move out of the flat was always: 'Ja well, but I spend so little time here anyway. Just a pozzie where I can sleep. Seems silly to take a place of my own when I'm not even around most of the time.' Or another reason would be that his motorbike was temporarily in a thousand, gold-greased pieces on the floor of his room – impossible to pack up and transport that. But Constance confessed to me last year, after the first breakdown, that in fact he'd used to suffer from bleak, agonized moods of unhappiness, that haunted her own dreams in turn. Mostly during the winter months. He'd stay in his room for the entire week-end sometimes; unspeaking, too listless to eat. Ashamed that people would guess from his drained, pale face that he'd been sobbing into his pillow.

Constance told me this as we were walking away from the ward one afternoon: she had dark glasses on, to hide the shadows under her eyes; and as she spoke her voice kept catching painfully, as though something were smouldering in her chest. I'm not certain whether she reproached herself. Partly I should think she was bitter about Anton's living so many thousands of miles away in Paris, from where he sent uselessly consoling postcards and letters. The doctors would only tell us that Frans was suffering from 'belated adolescent turmoil'. I think Constance was afraid that the phrase was merely a euphemism meant to protect her.

Remembering something he told me. About that time – during his first spell in hospital – when he wouldn't speak for two weeks. Outwardly he seemed to be absorbed in some profound distress – and Constance and I were scared by the way his mouth had slackened. But he said afterwards that it had been the most exquisitely peaceful period of his life. Everyone else's words receded, till the world became unutterably remote, and yet there was something still very near to him, something that seemed to lie just beyond the reef of solid silence that encircled him. He felt protected: the sounds of our voices no more than brushing against him, softer than already melting hail. Inside himself he was hearing Mozart; or when he ran out of remembered music, new themes and orchestral textures simply floated into his mind.

Frans said that the longer he stayed inside that refuge, the more difficult it became to contemplate breaking back out. After a week it was physically painful even to experiment with speech. He did it finally, but the wrench was far worse than any anguish of the body: more a sense of infinite loss. François became embarrassed as he tried to express this; a quizzical, self-deprecating wryness creeping into his words. For a long time afterwards, he muttered, it seemed to him that speaking was the most laborious, physically breaking act imaginable. Like battling to swim a long distance back to shore once the tide has turned aquamarine, begun to swirl with cloudy sand, and the cold, crisply ruffled currents are streaming outward, to sea.

It's after eleven. The children have gone out again. And it seems such madness to me. The night is streaming with rain, relentlessly icy-black. What can they possibly hope to achieve in it.

Sounding a bit sharp – I'm sorry. I feel on edge.

At least they ate something for lunch – pilchards out of a tin that I'd warmed up with thyme and origanum. Can I really be consoled by absurd details like this. Wilson brought the Memmi to the table again. Think he must be reading it a second time. I asked him how he liked the book, and had a grudging concession from him: 'Actually it's very . . . interesting.' He used an oddly pointed tone: as though the real meaning of that verdict would certainly escape me. I said, 'You can keep it if you like.' He didn't blush: if anything his face became less revealing even than it is usually. 'Thanks,' he said; curtly – as if to cancel any sense of indebtedness.

I wish the rain would end now, and the winter. The old neurotic aching is beginning to stir crustily in my ankles. It's the cold, I'm sure. Perhaps there is even snow on the mountains, in the Hottentots' Holland. It's difficult to believe tonight that there will ever be September again, with the pale spring warmth falling lightly on one's shoulders, and garden hedges dripping, streaked with jasmine flowers. Feel too frozen for the moment to admit that the planet's tethered wanderings around the sun make certain kinds of delight unavoidable. Or perhaps I'm bitter. Because thinking that the changing seasons don't after all magically induce similar changes in societies. And our annual nostalgia of syringa, pittosporum, the dry heat of the berg wind, honeysuckle, dust and sweet-peas – perhaps it's the memories of things that ought to have been.

School again the day after tomorrow. Time has gone so quickly. I must be going back after all then. Too inert to struggle for a different future. I've picked over my dozens of little doubts, but they always seem to skitter away in the end, fine and swift as sand-grains slipping over glass. Perhaps I ought to stay back until I've reached a conscious decision. It's true that I don't feel ready; although in a trivial sense I'm perfectly prepared, with two terms' lessons planned. But if I am to carry on teaching, it ought to be deliberately. Isn't that right? Self-abasing not to accept my freedom, my control over my own mind and life.

Went and made myself some coffee. Water from the tap is icy. And even the kettle: my fingers touching the blackened aluminium. If I go out tomorrow I could look out across the Flats – try to see beyond the factories with their own dismal miasma, and through the drizzle. See if there is snow.

I don't care if I never sleep again. Tea, coffee – caffeine's the same. Supposed to be.

Snow in the mountains, at Ceres. People will be driving out on Sunday so that their kiddies can throw snowballs at each other. The grown-ups sighing rapturously over the muddied, crystalline frostiness: 'Imagine living in England.'

What else? What else? There's the rain, I suppose, still to listen to: its faint susurrus of reminiscences that drift through my skull. And that's another thing. People saying that it prospers you only to look to the present, material conditions of history. Sometimes that's hard, though. Especially living in this city: seems that wherever you walk you kick over the scantily buried traces of a most ancient past. They say that before the acacias spread across the dunes at Milnerton you could walk there and find arrow-heads, bones, shaped bits of mother-of-pearl, beads. Sometimes under the melkbos you might find a decayed, porous blade of a hip-bone, with a still ochreous mail-work of strung eggshell beads draped over it, welded against it by grains of the chalky sand. One of the richest sites is closed off now to the public, because they're building the nuclear power plant on top of it. The labourers who work there earn pin-money, some of them, selling occasional finds as curios. You find fossilised teeth there too, of sharks and whales. After storms, if you stroll along the tide-mark. Cowrie shells too, Frans told me: trading items from the hold of a wrecked ship in the bay.

And people find swords. Or is that only a story. A chased bronze and silver sabre that the wind discovered in the sand, under driftwood and burnt twig, in the vygies. From one of those numberless battles that the Europeans fought on African terrain.

Frans and I made a trip once to Cape Point. I remember how we turned off down a dust track inside the reserve and jolted along it on the bike till we came to a stretch of wild beach. We set off then, walking along the heavy, sliding, shimmering sand of the dunes. That was when Frans pointed out to me the bleached surface scatter lying almost everywhere around us. There must be a few hundred square kilometres of unconsolidated midden in the peninsula alone – the cast-aside shells of alikreukel, limpet, perlemoen, mussel. I went up to a bank where a slow trickle of powdery sand seemed to be slipping away, streaming off the dune – to leave behind a harder core of compressed earth that was shored up by a reticulation of fine roots, tendrils, pebbles and shells. Saw some small bulbs suspended from the fibrous mass: loosely clothed in flimsy gold-brown skins. Or what is the name? Do you say corms. I broke one off and pinched it between my fingernails. Shiny white on the inside. Tried squeezing out some of the whey-like juice into my palm.

What do I know about vegetation – about the edible and medicinal plants. Perhaps it's another reason for dreaming about the Khoi–San with such sentimental, belated regret: that they found out ways of subsisting in the desert.

But why should they have had to. When this demi-island was thronged with game and bird-life, sea-foods, roots, tubers, bulbs and water. Ja I know. What may have been; what could have been: these are the modalities of futile speculation, aren't they. And yet it's true that when the Company's garden was designed – to save the sailors from scurvy and to tame a metaphysical wilderness – the mountain was still densely forested, with yellow-woods and stink-woods. Van Riebeeck noting that every tree was straight enough timber for a ship's mast. They must have built busily, to raise up the walls of civilization: hewn stone for the fortress, and dense almond for the hedge to keep the wild people at bay. Those merchant fleets that grew on the mountain's slopes were steadily toppled, though: after blue flashes of an axe-blade, a groaning of wood and then the catastrophic splintering of branches, birds and undergrowth.

I tasted the warm liquid that was seeping over my knuckles: and winced, of course, at the bitter taste of my own ignorance.

What haunts me sometimes is the awareness that every last thing I know about the San comes out of other people's fictions. Different stories too: some about barbarism, others about innocence. In the seventeenth century the visitors most feared by the Capemen were the Sonkwa, who would arrive across the plain from the north by night, from Saldanha Bay and Elandsbaai – unstoppable and armed with frail but fatal arrows. That man they called Harry went to the

Dutch newcomers with frantic warnings about the approaching winter months – stories of plains that would be lit for two to three nights running by the distant, scattered campfires of the merciless raiders who were coming. But in other people's versions the San had some peaceful contract with nature, and their lifestyle was pre-lapsarian almost in its dignity and grace.

I know. The wistful ogling at other societies is yet another deluded form of quest. The San themselves simply existed. So do you think it's wrong? To be interested. And those different stories are only the obverse and reverse of a single myth, aren't they.

But then: I suppose 'Harry' would be unlikely to have had a Romantic mythology. Maybe he was simply a brilliant pragmatist, willing to play off the Dutch against the San. Wondering suddenly whether even the Dutch had a Romantic tradition then. Later, I know, in the eighteenth and nineteenth centuries, the textual basis of their beliefs was the Old Testament, rather than the myths of Christian redemption. It's possible that my desire to understand these things, to understand the constant system of patterning in the under-tow of a world myth, along with the cultural inheritance of realized, unique patterns at the breaking surface of that myth – this desire may be hopelessly steeped in romance itself.

Stared around me again at the shell-strewn earth. Millennia of former feasts now turned to sharp, small pieces of worm-eaten shell . . . eerily faded mother-of-pearl. How can those colours die, then. Is it the thin layers in the nacre slowly collapsing inward? Those layers that trap the frequencies of light: collapsing, dissolving the spectrum. I had a sudden yearning to stay there and search for something else. A bead, I suppose, or an arrow-head. A smell of vegetable decay came from the sandy bank; and blown, crumbled hints of ash. Suppose it was the burial place of a hundred thousand bush-fires over time: whose acrid devastation would have been mourned by wind, sand – and people, perhaps. Idly I scraped up handfuls of the sand; and watched the bits of twig and tiny, bleached snail shells drift down through my filtering fingers.

François grew bored and wandered off further along the dunes, through crystallina and patches of sour-fig – probing the ground with a twig. Suppose he was looking out for those primitive ants with stings: ponerines, I think.

I still hankered to find a bead, or even a fragment of one: just

103

as François said he'd found them sometimes, with traces of red ochre still clinging to them.

The people that had left behind such vast, scattered ruins of a culture: I crouched there in the sand wondering helplessly whether they'd been Capemen, or the people from Hout Bay, or those people who once owned the rights to the Fish Hoek coast. They say there were people here at Kommetjie, Cape Hangklip, all along the coast – using stone tools hundreds of thousands of years ago.

Weren't there even epochs of glaciers in all that time? Suppose if more of the sea is frozen then the water shrinks away, receding from the edges of the landmass. Maybe there were the vestiges of history out there, buried under the sea, on the continental shelf. Inter-glacial now. Find tide-marks inland, too: ancient beaches beneath the grey scrub and pebbles of the veld. I was beginning to get a headache from the sound of the sea nearby, smashing and re-breaking endlessly upon itself. The light in my eyes. Wild daisies; sprawled, untidy sour-figs.

All that is on a different time-scale, though, isn't it. What François used to say about his ants, although it was incomprehensible to me. About durations and continuums. He tried to explain, but I couldn't . . . couldn't see. Trying to determine significant periods, because of arbitrary divisions. François would also swear that he could see the mountains slowly crumbling to dust and splinters of quartz crystal. In earnest, I think. Once he pointed out to me a reddish cliff-face on the mountain. 'Rockfall: you see, recent.'

Papa has a similar theme, I think, in *Glas het g'n Kristalstruk-tuur*. I haven't understood the full complexity of that long cycle yet. Partly because the language is difficult – highly colloquial in parts but tightly elided and also richly, dazzlingly packed with neologisms from Dutch, German, Malay and French. Characteristically too, there are ironies whose presence I can only be wary of in the Afrikaans. But mostly it's the concepts that are strange to me still. Well, I know about the fact that, despite its apparent rigidity, glass is really a liquid. Think Papa must have seen somewhere in Europe those old window panes you read about, where the glass has sagged with time and now stands thicker at the base. One poem is a kind of fantasy about a single consciousness watching a sheet of glass over a thousand years: how it would appear as something rippling and falling away, and useless as material to stop up the spaces in a

104

dwelling structure. Although the *envoi* contains a kind of riposte in its dry observation that people only live for a few seasonally quickened, flickering years of small rains, drought, heavy storms, mellow light, then frost, then a desert winter. So that glass is nonetheless solid enough for human purposes.

Another poem I remember now is even drier, perhaps. A sceptical observation that the European explorers of the fifteenth, sixteenth, seventeenth centuries seem consistently to have stumbled on other cultures at 'critical' moments in their history. Suppose it's possible that Papa's thinking is becoming more Marxian. Because he seems to be suggesting that no human society is ever static.

Ja, and here too. So many thousands of years of societies changing: shaping tools, domesticating animals, building stone fish-traps in the estuaries. While the Portuguese achieved their periplus of Africa a mere five centuries ago; using caravels; leaving crosses carved in stone along the sketchy coastline of geography. Only three centuries ago that the Dutch dared their outflung navigations along the Trades, and then put the surgeon Van Riebeeck down at the Cape, to grow them vegetables. Perhaps it's useless to think about the lost past? When so much has changed in three hundred years. In fifty, even. What Marianne would say: 'Mmm ja, maar. What you want to transform –' Frowning slightly over the amount of roll to put into the word. 'Ja: what you work with, what you change – can only be this present, now. It doesn't *help* to think about what came before.' And a worried, helpless glance at me. 'But isn't that so now?'

There was something hard, some small thing tumbling over in the grains of the sand.

Marianne has little patience with tyro liberals who found their frenzied protestations on the fact that there were civilizations here for tens of hundreds of years before the Westerners arrived. 'Ag,' she'll murmur: 'Isn't that irrelevant now?' And then she'll grow rather irritated, 'Anna, you're being unhistorical: it's static, staties, kan jy nie sien nie. Wat wil jy hê? Dat ons nou almal terug moet trek na die oorspronklike paradystuin toe?' She laughs hugely at my mistakes sometimes: and it's good for me, of course.

It was a fragment of weathered bone. Thin and porous; weighing almost nothing in the palm of my hand. There was a curious tracery all over it of delicate, faintly purplish veins. From a field-mouse or a dassie, perhaps.

Frans came ambling back then. He patted his shirt pocket where he kept a few vials always. 'Got a bee,' he said. 'For Dr De Wet.' He was in a tranquil mood, I think. Rather silent. Probably wanting to get back to a spot out of the wind, where he could light up his pipe.

I showed him my find. 'Ja,' he said, glancing down at it. 'You're probably right: but it's old, hey.' He meant because of that patterning all over it. Softly he told me how he'd seen the same thing often on the bones in the archaeology department. They were stains – left by the creeping, hair-thin explorations of capillary roots in the earth. 'You know, once I was with them on a trip when they excavated a burial site . . . two skeletons really, a mother and child. And all the bones had this: everything so tiny, and thin, you know, paper-thin little ribs and shoulder blades, everything – all stained a kind of puce colour, and covered with these miniature veins.'

Frans was bored again quickly, though. His thoughts returning to whatever it was he'd found amongst the dunes. Reddish pebbles, sand, ants, a small bee, grasses and silver-greyish succulents. . . .

I was beginning to shiver, although the sun still burned at my face and arms.

There was a tang of sea in the air as a breeze came up, and Frans seemed to be exhilarated suddenly. Seizing me by the elbow, he forced me to run with him, roaring and breathless, till we'd scaled the dune ahead of us. The skin at the back of my heels was blistering, I could feel. Triumphantly we stared out from the crest of the dune, though: and there were endless sculptures, we saw, of further dunes receding and framing still further ones. And in the ultimate, distant crescent of sand we glimpsed something – something out of our earliest storybooks, lying just beyond the sheer, sweeping curve of the dune: the rusted, enormous hulk of a wrecked ship. Then we were racing again, on towards the bright sea: leaping, we ran down, leaping, almost flying down across the dunes till we ended up sprawled on the level sand below – and then sprinting on again to the edge of the water, to reach that metal ruin.

I suppose it was an old trawler. Anchored there immovably by some storm in sand that was burning with light and mica. The waves – heavy tides – had long since smashed it into two: one part lay half-way up the beach, dragged there by a colossal power of the sea, sand smothered in sand; the other part was wedged into the coastline, against boulders, where the water was surging into the angled wheelhouse and amplified by the hollow iron bulwarks into a mockery of sighs and flooding. We picked our way across the pale, slippery weed on the rocks till we found a place where the riveted plates of the careened hull had burst apart and we could peer through into the echoing cavern of dark water. We saw a set of rungs – but the metal had turned to black and brown flakes.

Frans wanted to stay there, gazing into the rock pools, crouched down with his hands dangling over his knees. He looked blissful, with the water still drying at the neck of his shirt and at his elbows, where the cuffs were rolled up.

I scrambled back up to the beach to investigate the stranded, dry part of the wreck. There were bars of solid iron clad with metal plates that had rusted to the thinness of paper. Mostly, though, the meanings of the different structures eluded me. Ducking my head to avoid the sharp, brittle sheets of rust, I climbed through and stooped under fallen beams till I reached an interior space where I could stand erect. It was all shored up with sand in there, and littered with kelp and collapsed metal. And then for a moment, despite myself and despite the absurd frailness of that perforated hull, just for a moment I was seized with a kind of choking panic. Though I could see the sky still, and touch the sand. I crawled out hurriedly, heedless of blows to my elbows and skull. It was only for a moment that I lost myself like that. Recovering, I grinned; and began a wary tour of the ship's outside. Saw iron bolts altered almost out of recognition by slow oxidation. There was one that I found lying loose in the sand, striated by corrosion into vivid flakes and orange-yellow splinters, so that it looked like a vygie flower cast in metal. I tossed it away.

I walked for a while along the beach after that, kicking at the damp sand; with the smell of iron still on my fingers. Too familiar – that slight, lingering smell of blood. Women never escape it completely, I think.

A clutter along the beach marked the most recent tides: blackened, dry kelp that was seething with flies, smooth grey driftwood, tangled fishing line, fragments of bleached net and cork floats, stinking red-bait, gull-pecked cuttlebones. Birds stalked over the detritus, searching for scarps of fish or insects, maybe. Gulls and sandpipers. Saw an old rusted canister that looked like an aerosol spray. From a ship at sea, I suppose. Toss out their junk into the ocean.

I was thinking about commerce. About the *Cabo de Boa Esperanza*. And about prosperity in the fifteenth and sixteenth centuries being both a religious and a mercantile enterprise. All the great trading cities of Europe had cathedrals, slums and sea-ports. In Shakespeare you see how the mediaeval mystic's ship of faith became the merchant's cargo ship, hazarding everything for hope of reward – in the face of tempests; pirates; and the ever-present risk of a ruined freight. A leaky hold and the nutmeg and mace and cloves would go to ruin, or the silks turn black with the mildew. Defoe wrote about that – forging truthful histories of the thievery of gold, ivory, territory and human beings from Africa. Do you know the moment in *Captain Singleton* when that abandoned ship looms up with its sails rigged meaninglessly, part collapsed. And the pirates found slaves on board, hundreds of people chained in the holds. I never got free of that passage until I read Césaire. That the slaves should have managed to destroy their masters, only to remain the prisoners of a strange technology: freely drifting on Defoe's unruffled, literary seas – powerless to control the topsails, mainsails, even the wheeling rudder.

There was a swarm of tiny flies hovering near me, nudging and dipping and settling on my arms. Suppose they were after salt. I was beginning to get a headache and there was darkness behind my eyes because of the sunlight breaking up constantly in the surf. Larger flies kept darting up from the kelp at my feet. Defoe had some of his pirates sneak into Table Bay for fresh water. There really was a spring. Meeting place for the European traders. Sometimes even today when they're excavating in the city for an office block, a workman's spade will ring against the stonework of an old conduit. Real: ja, not a city of fictions. I had to slap fiercely at the little flies. Beginning to feel thirsty: and resentful of Frans's serene delight in crustacea and sea grass.

Suddenly I was choking on the dryness in my mouth, on temper; and I wanted to start going back. Frans was still trailing his graceful, bony hands in the water, out there on the rocks below the wreck.

Only Defoe and Conrad acknowledged it, but at the heart of any European novel, isn't there always secretly the erased, astonished memory of the slave trade. There was capital being stored up in the cities – a new class rising, a squalid poverty and suffering beginning – but the left hand of capital was always in the colonies: the factories, workhouses, glory and literature of an England were founded on the stolen wealth of Africa, on the millions of African dead.

Frans came away from the rocks and we began the journey back, following the coastline. Teasing me for being fretful, he made me pull off my shoes and socks and walk in the clear, riffling shallows. Felt better then, and soon we were running again, racing across the film of the receding water. There were more rocks, thick with mussel, clustered half-way along that beach. Remember we found a part of a ship's life-belt, with most of the paint weathered away from the decaying cork. But those rocks, I saw suddenly, teemed with rustling, scurrying insects – mottled, transparent things that came scattering over our insteps. Frans laughed at me. Crustaceans, he explained – scavengers: if it weren't for them the beaches would be stinking with the carcasses of other creatures. And successful, because they had no predators. He stooped to admire them. I saw one moulting: even in the sloughed skin you could still see all the legs – a pair to every segment. But then a few more of them came scuttling over my feet and I jumped down from the rocks, nervous, and yearning to wade in the cool sea again. Felt as though there were flies at my face. But that was sheer imagination.

We found driftwood, pumice stones – from molten rock, Frans said, that had landed, still frothing, on the surface of the sea. And there was an entire beach draped with sea-weeds – kelp, lilac and mauve and white lacy weed, klokkiesgras, and long, gleaming bands. Frans showed me the sand-fleas – scraping a swathe of the surface sand away. And there was the putrid reek of decaying plants, and stagnant sea. Little pellets we found too, gritty in the sand: from a ship, he said. Polymerized ethylene, on its way to factories.

We were slowly heading back to the bike, while that western sea steadily dinned and came surging up on to the sand. I was trying to think of the meaning of two fragile, interlocked skeletons. Mother and infant, both dead in childbirth. The bones weren't the meaning of death, because those are material relics only, like chalk or sea-shells. And death means where something once was living. Perhaps there were hollows in the embankment; sand and roots and shells

109

compacted across the curves where flesh was once. Natural sand-casts of death. Frans may have been thinking similar things. Once he was astride the bike he reached for his helmet, and grimaced involuntarily as he tightened the chin-strap. Murmuring almost inaudibly: 'The baby's rib-bones, from that Bushman grave . . . you know, even the biggest one was smaller than a wish-bone.'

On the ride home through the reserve we saw sewejaartjies, the sheen on their papery flowers. Clusters of them growing all across the veld, shimmering and riposting at the sunlight: a burning white snow, miraculous in that heat, lying amongst the heath and the sweetreed.

How can the children still be out in this night. Madness. It's madness. There's nothing outside but raining in the darkness, and disintegration: a smashing down on to cold iron, smashing and trickling in the iron gutters, while the darkness shivers in spangles of small, watery beads.

It isn't true that François went mad. I know that he never meant to kill himself. People want to think that, because he was found unconscious in the hospital grounds, under a hedge. He took all those tablets, but it was an accident, I'm certain: he was feeling bad and just wanted to drift; to stare at leaves and the husks of moths in a spider-web. I feel convinced of it, because of something he told me afterwards when he was staying here. 'I trust in the future, Anna, because I want to. Otherwise I'd have blown my brains out long ago.'

Sometimes wonder whether part of his unhappiness didn't come from being caught in between two trends in zoology. By the time he was in his teens he'd already acquired an astonishing knowledge of that old-world, purely taxonomic approach, so that the sort of thing they studied at university, even in second year, was tediously familiar to him. And by the age of sixteen he'd begun to find a different direction for himself, picking up ideas from *Scientific American* and *New Scientist* as he went; but also relying on his own intuitions. I remember how he used to spend Saturday mornings in the reading room at the library, paging through the latest copies of the journals. Of course, there was nothing to stop him in his spare time studying organisms as part of living, intricately interdependent systems. I think he lived for the week-ends when he was at Stellenbosch. But his formal studies must have depressed him.

He and I dropped out of university at almost the same time in 1976. At least he enjoyed his work at the museum, I thought – with that emphasis on field-work. And the tolerant company: everyone's idiosyncracies were humoured there, and no one thought it was odd of François to keep a nest of ants. People from other departments would sometimes bring in a worm or a dead moth to put on to the foraging tray: just to see the worker ants flurrying. Or else they'd want to peer at the little cache of larvae and pupae under the glass. Also, I think Frans was deeply proud of working under Dr De Wet. He told me he'd been looking up a reference once in the museum's library, and found out purely by chance that there were a dozen monographs by J. P. de Wet, just on the formicine species of southern Africa.

He was lucky to be given fairly skilled work, for a technical assistant. Those drawings he was doing, with notes. But even that may have begun to weary him. Day after day spent staring down a microscope at sections of almost imperceptibly different species. Mouthparts of weevil larvae. It was important work: but then Frans was always so fond of sweeping theories, and to someone who yearned for nothing less than a single grand hypothesis that would account for every last thing in the universe – the number of bristles on a larva's mandible must have begun to seem more and more ridiculously inconsequential.

What does it matter if on one particular day he puttered out into the country on his motorbike; and didn't come back. It was – predictable, maybe. After all, bush country is where he feels most free, most himself. I should think he was looking for a sort of no man's land, where he would belong to nobody else – not Constance, or Anton, or even Dr De Wet. The doctor said that he had lost touch with reality. Just because he was reduced to telling himself stories out loud? There was no one else for company. And what if he stole a few greenish, sun-burnt potatoes that the farmer had left behind in the sandy furrows for beetles to eat, or wasps. Or if he begged a tinful of water and the heel of a loaf from passing labourers. He wanted to survive, that's all. No one who wants that could be called insane. Even if the price of survival is the haun-

111

ting, indelible knowledge of one's own guilt.

Suppose there are other criteria, though. Saw a man one afternoon when I was walking through the grounds of the hospital. He was grinning and nodding his head, sputtering something. Then I saw that he'd uprooted a fistful of marigolds and was holding them out to me. Wilted, earthy, richly-scented offerings to add to his frantic assertions. François explained afterwards. He was found by a social worker in a yard, huddled at the back of a hok and smeared with the lime and dirt and feathers of the chickens he'd grown up amongst. Now he lives at the hospital – because he can only gibber and bluster. Not being able to speak, having no language in common with other people – does that make one a lunatic? That gesture with the flowers – surely that was speaking. There was a vocative there and really, deixis was inherent in the setting. Who can say that the marigolds were not his word for 'desire'. Or it may be that the gesture had significance, while the flowers were only some inflection or accent.

I was glad when François left that place. What he said: 'You're insane while you live in an asylum. It's simple.'

There were other things François told me during his stay here. He'd sit opposite me – his bony weight fully relaxed into the cushions and his long legs stretched out in front of him – working at something with his hands. He was busy constantly, mending things in preparation for his journey, or rubbing that orange, waxy stuff into his boots. What do you call it? Strong, sweetish smell, and afterwards the shoes have to be stood outside in the sunlight for the wax to work its way into the leather. Tough cotton he bought too, proper cobbler's thread, for repairs. I sprawled on my cushion, watching the sunlight on the carpet. Think François's thoughts were drifting too, peaceful as dust. He began to speak about the delusions he'd had, coming round after that accident, with the tablets. Mostly he remembered nothing, but once or twice he'd discovered himself just below the surface of waking, in some area that seemed to be an enormous, dazzlingly white room with no clearly defined planes or angles anywhere. His only real awareness amounted to the physical knowledge that his own body was locked into vicious, backward-arching spasms. I was afraid that Frans would get himself upset, remembering. But his voice was even and his hands continued to work away calmly at suppling the heels of his

112

boots.

'I couldn't stop myself, Anna. My back just kept on kind of yearning, stretching itself, like a fish, leaping. I thought, oh God, I thought my spinal cord would snap, and yet I had to go on, arching and arching like that. There was . . . it wasn't in words, Anna . . . an incredible conviction that each time I completed one of those arcs . . .' He broke off for a moment. Scooped some more of the wax from the tin. 'Ag, you'll laugh, but I really thought at the time – each arc I managed was somehow guaranteeing the existence of another entire universe someday in the future. In eternity. I was, I thought I was making up an endless store of eternities. For humanity.' He glanced at me furtively, trying to make out whether I was stifling laughter. He seemed acutely embarrassed, and kneaded at the leather for several long minutes before continuing.

'That was why I couldn't die, you know. I just had to survive and create as many of those future universes as I could, before my strength ran out finally.'

We sipped at our tea, both of us. Silently. I feeling ashamed for fancies I'd had myself, as a child, and never dared to confess.

I stood up to refill the kettle. Ambling barefoot into the kitchen.

When I came back the light had shifted its column already to a new patch of carpet. Frans had taken up the leather sheath he was making for his hunting knife.

'When they were giving me that shock treatment, Anna: I was too sick to understand anything. I was hardly even conscious most of the time, you know. So I . . .' He had a lump of opaque, scored beeswax that he picked up every now and then to draw his cotton thread across. He reached for it then. 'I knew that there were rows of us, all waiting; but somehow I imagined that we were all inside huge white cylinders, Anna. You know, I thought that people were being incinerated, in these long cylinders.' He concentrated on drawing the waxed thread through a stiff fold of the leather. Saw his mouth flicker briefly in a way that didn't seem to signify anything. Perhaps he was trying to smile – to reassure me that he was quite calm.

'I heard the voices of the doctors as they came nearer and nearer, and one of them said, "We'll do these two straight." I thought, Anna, I thought it meant that they were going to incinerate those two alive, and the only thing is, the only thing: I thought they

113

meant the people in the cylinders next to me, you see.' Slowly then he forced himself to tell the truth: 'I mean . . . what I mean is, I was praying that it would be somebody else.' As he paused to catch back his breath, he reached out for the beeswax again; touched the cotton to it uncertainly. 'The last thing was when I . . . they touched my head. And I knew that it *was* me they were going to do, to do . . . straight.' I was watching François's hands as he spoke. He has Papa's hands - big-boned; powerful; and yet not clumsy. He was clutching the beeswax firmly when he finished speaking. What do you say? I knew he would not want to meet my gaze. Think he'd have hated me violently if I'd offered any mumblings of sympathy. There was a brief fragment of a second when his grip on the lump of wax slackened - and I saw that his hand was trembling. But he renewed his stern grasp almost immediately.

What can it be like when people have that. ECT, they say. Sounds less crude than shock treatment. Do they lose consciousness, I wonder. Black out? And afterwards: feel confused; forget things. That part didn't bother him, Frans said. Some things he was glad he couldn't remember.

But it was the world losing its colours. There is some beetle you find on morning glory creepers: a tortoise beetle. Can that be right? But it's golden - a vivid, metallic, greeny-yellow jewel against the dark leaves; with part of the elytra transparent as perspex. Only when you kill it, the colour fades. Dull brown beetle then. François says the whole world seems to have been dying slowly around him, ever since that time in hospital. Once he could walk along pavements and be thrilled by the wind shimmering in the common weeds - wild oats, tremor grass, clocks and chinese lanterns. Now they all seem like straw to him; and dangerous - dry and brittle in the summer, they're tinder to the bush-fires.

Summer: when the mountain will blaze at least once, with the south-easter driving the flames up into the kloofs.

CHAPTER 4

Heard Felicia tapping at the front door at about six o'clock this morning. It was drizzling outside still: as we stood there, speechless for a moment, facing one another across the threshold, there were peaceful scents of the dawn stirring in the garden – fresh mint, and a faint, paraffin-like smell of geraniums, earth, snails and damp bricks. She was alone.

Panic-stricken, I reached out without thinking and almost dragged her indoors, into my arms. Collected myself, though. Realizing that I would have to help her gently, as calmly as possible.

She said nothing, as though speech had frozen up inside her. And my own thoughts were still partly gripped by bad dreams.

What in the world are we going to do now.

I hardly knew what to do for the sick-looking, exhausted child stumbling at my side. I kept up a murmuring at any rate, of absurd reassurances. Keeping my voice low because of the neighbours on the other side of the passage wall – in the small hours you hear their breathing almost, the rustlings of their mattress. Still hushing her, whispering, I sat her down on the edge of the bed. Wanted to take the rug out from the chest of drawers.

She just sat there, rigidly upright.

I mumbled on, speaking more in cadences than words; too frightened to let up. 'We could have some strong tea, would you like that, let's go into the kitchen, let's just get you warm, wrap you up a bit in this blanket, there honey, perhaps you, do you know how cold . . .' She let me carry on, resisting nothing, not even the rug draped lightly around her shoulders and over her arms.

I wondered whether I shouldn't let her simply get to sleep: but her hands felt icy, and there was something; something in her eyes.

While I kept up my discreet, monotonous agitations. 'It was

bitterly cold,' I said. And noticed a faint iridescence in her hair, where the mist of the rain still clung to it. Hurried to the wardrobe then, to fetch that thick polo-neck sweater of mine. The rug fell away as she struggled out of the clammy, useless anorak and her dark-coloured sweater. The way her wrists and elbows flexed for her – stiffly reluctant, I saw. 'Would you like to come through to the kitchen,' I said. 'I'm sure you need that tea.' There are uses for inanities, I was finding.

I followed her along the passage, carrying the rug.

She settled herself on one of the chairs and listlessly accepted the burden of that tasselled mohair. And a few minutes later, still mute, she consented to take the mug of strong, sweet tea that I put into her hands. Softly I continued speculating aloud – whether it had snowed in the mountains, and wondering about the effects of caffeine, tannin, sugar. . . . The frantic, voiceless questions were singing and singing in my ears, nonetheless. While she nestled the warm china in her hands I went and fetched a towel from the bathroom, and a pair of socks that had been drying there on the rail.

When I asked her if she'd like more tea she shook her head and roughly whispered a refusal. But she didn't protest when I eased off the sodden shoes from her feet and stripped away the socks. Eventually she took the towel from me and finished drying her own feet. I'd felt how cold they were, though, and limp. Her insteps are high and bony, the kind that's prone to make the ankles buckle.

After that I was briefly at a loss. What to do. What does one do?

She hadn't eaten, I suddenly thought, not for hours. Deliberately not asking her first, I took down jars of milk powder and Pro-nutro. Used warm water to mix it up; and tracked down a small, folded packet that still had sunflower seeds in it. I half expected her to reject it – but she took the spoon I offered her and began to eat.

And for as long as she continued to chew the stuff fastidiously and swallow, I was able to believe that nothing unrescuable could have happened. Watching the dull light that gleamed from her spoon. The curtains were slightly parted – the window panes behind them were shadowy mirrors still. Winter: dark until about seven in the morning these days; and the rain, of course, makes it seem much darker.

She pushed away the empty bowl then and asked, 'Have you got

116

a cigarette for me?' I hadn't, naturally, but she seemed indifferent even to her own disappointment; while I was the one left smothered by trivial feelings of inadequacy. The best I could do, feeling suddenly sick with uneasiness, was to offer her more tea. Or coffee. Stood up to re-fill the kettle, just to move around, to run the tap at the sink – anything to suppress the intense, rising thirst of panic. I suggested as well, trying still to sound gentle, that she ought to get some sleep. Could feel an aching between my shoulder blades.

It was plain, though, that there were still things on her mind. She sat forward slightly and stated, urgently, 'School starts again on Tuesday – I . . . tomorrow.' I saw the silky folds of the mohair slip, forgotten, to the floor. 'Please,' she said, 'do you think you could take a message for me. Ivan Hendrickse. In ten B?' I stood there at the kettle, uselessly stirring at sugar that had long since dissolved itself into the coffee. 'Yes,' I said, finally passing her the mug. 'But yes of course.' Instantly, all that seemed to matter was that she should find me reliable. I kept my gaze fastened on her face; timid even to ask for further details, in case she thought that I was hedging. Yet I must have looked expectant, as though some unguessable sentence had still to be uttered. What? 'You just have to tell him that I need to know what has happened,' she said, cautiously. Her eyes were dull, I saw; and there was a hint of sallowness below the glinting bronze of her cheekbones.

I heard the rain stir more strongly outside, streaming in a noisy rushing across the roof, as if to tear a swathe through the stormy cloud and the last of the morning stars. Felicia hadn't touched the coffee. Surely she'll go to bed now, I was thinking, almost angrily.

There was more that she wanted to say. 'We got separated, you see. It was all a mess . . . at the roadblock.' She wasn't looking at me as she spoke. Staring at her pinched face, I wondered fleetingly whether she was really addressing anyone. 'We made mistakes; people went off in the wrong . . . just, people got lost, I mean.'

The nausea came back. I picked up the rug hurriedly and began trying forcibly to coax Felicia. Touching her upper arms; urging her to stand up. And she allowed herself to be helped; even accepting my arm around her waist. As we walked along the passage, I felt how weak she was, and heavy with tiredness. Deliberately I resumed that role again of the one who whispers and hums all the small, fragile sentences of chit-chat.

117

At about mid-day I glanced in at the bedroom door, but she hadn't begun to stir. It's three o'clock now, and she's still drowsing. That smoky hair of hers streaming out in dull, knotted tangles across the pillow. I'm glad she's resting.

I've just had a long, soaking bath. To try and quieten myself. Forcing myself to lie back in the tub and let my shoulders sink into the warmth. Hostility of that smooth enamel, though: rejecting my vertebrae and scapulae. The more I tried to make myself calm down, the more rigidly I found myself gripped by my muscles. Something just underneath my ribs was seething, and I could feel the darkness gathering behind my eyes. I think that too much slow, sustained control becomes a nightmare in turn – a worse one than disintegration itself. And as I stood there on the tiles afterwards, making myself linger, rubbing the towel dreamily through my hair – I was conscious of a thin-walled core of disaster in my chest. Looked into the bathroom mirror, and there was the flecked skin, the dull-lashed eyes. The same; the same features that I've seen in mirrors for ten, twenty years. My tongue felt the molars crowding at the back of my jaw. The same too. Been rooted there for two decades. Sometimes I feel myself beginning to choke on the fear that the world – the physical, real world – is going to stay looking exactly the same for as long as I live. The sweat was beginning to break out on my upper lip. Steaminess still in the bathroom.

There's no point in giving in to panic yet. We don't know what has really happened.

That's something I learned from the conversations with François. How dangerous it is to be suspended, I mean, in a drifting equilibrium where the feelings and those familiar stories that surge up from the individual psyche have coalesced with multiple, equally profound myths of a nation. Because then you have a dyad composed only of fear and fear, with no hope of deliverance from it all. And in reality they're not equi-poised, are they? That's one thing. But the other is that you need some severing agent – some intermediary? People go crazy without that. Maybe why those myths of redemption are so passionately clung to by people in totalitarian societies. Why the legends of transcendence depend for their dynamism on the concept of a trinity.

While he was in that coma Frans's mind would sometimes break open and he'd hear speech from somewhere outside himself. 'One time I actually thought, Anna, do you know, I really thought that my body had died and that . . .' He paused frequently, telling me that story. 'Do you know, I thought they'd transplanted my brain somehow into another person's body. I . . .' He glanced up at me, then quickly looked away; silent for another moment. 'I couldn't feel anything, anything like my own skin, my hands, my ribs – just my own flesh, you know, it was all dead. And only my mind was left alive.' He paused again. I could see the tautness of his jaw as he bit down on some private anguish. 'I could hear the voices of the doctors around me,' he went on eventually. 'I tried to speak to them, you know, I was trying to force out the words with this tongue, with these lips, all this . . . it wasn't my own flesh, Anna. But I thought that it must be some experiment, and I just wanted to tell them that it had worked out. I mean, that I had survived.'

Maybe it was his psyche that had died. Do you think that's possible. To be born with your soul already fatally smothered? Because no one came to save you. Or there was no sacrifice; not even the smallest surrender. It would be like being born into slavery, perhaps.

François was deluded. You could say that, couldn't you. Although it only means that he tried to tell the absolute truth about himself. Workable truths – the social ones – are always shifting, relative, I suppose.

What happened to him. What really happened to him. I wonder if there is ever a finite number of answers to that question.

And Wilson? It's difficult to make sense of the things Felicia said this morning, in the small hours. There was a meeting at someone's house – a dozen of the student leaders. And afterwards as they were coming away the shrubbery at the front gate and the shadows behind a parked van moved into life – and the police were there suddenly, waiting for them. Felicia said something about a boy called Taliep who fell back with Wilson. The rest of them froze, agonized for a second, till Taliep screamed and screamed at them hoarsely to run for it.

Seems likely that the two have been detained. But perhaps we'll hear tomorrow, from Ivan. Ivan Hendrickse. Think I've been trying too hard to memorize that name – it keeps slipping away from me, and then I have to claw at my own thoughts to try and get it back again.

Need to concentrate on practical things, to keep out spectres.

How to get to school tomorrow - that's something. The bus boycott must still be on. . . . I've tried listening to the radio once or twice, but they don't seem to report anything that matters. Could walk. Wonder how far it is from here to Athlone - maybe five kilometres? Maybe more. Suppose two hours is ample time to allow. One and a half, even.

I was caught out on the first day of the boycott, through not thinking ahead. Hadn't arranged a lift with anyone, and by the time I reached Mowbray there was no choice but to take the bus if I wanted to be at school on time. The long shelters at each destination sign were deserted, of course, except for groups of inspectors self-consciously huddled together, pretending indifference, while their walkie-talkie sets bleeped aleatoric music. There were hundreds of people coming away from the railway station, on their way to work. Where. Factories, I suppose; garages, shops, private houses, banks, the university. I doubt that any of them noticed me huddling guiltily at the Athlone bus-stop. The children that sell newspapers were there as usual - the crowd came streaming past their pitch on the pavement. And the fruit sellers. Busy setting up their barrows with pyramids of purple tissue paper, apples, white styrofoam, bananas, pineapples, litchis, paw-paws. People came threading through the crowd on bicycles, jingling those little domed bells. And there were a few cars trying to make headway. Out-of-date, dented models, with shark fins and trailing, rusted exhaust pipes. About ten people crushed inside one car. I blanched instantly when someone behind me hawked aggressively and then spat on to the pavement. But it was an old man's habit, of course: presumptuous of me to want the whole world to validate my own sense of guilt. I picked up my basketful of exercise books and put it down again nearer to my feet. Hide my scuffed shoes from that man's accusing gaze. Hiding something, at any rate. Something imaginary.

It's a fiction, isn't it - the grammatical concept of the third person. Really there's only you and I, who hold one another warily, rigidly at bay; while taking for granted the existence of a world out there. That's the third domain: things as they are. Great lie it is too - only once they called it *verismo*: when novelists recreated reality through a kind of literary extensionalism. Papa seems to speak about that quite often in *Glas*: about the world of prose - about realism. He was fascinated to read once about a process that gives glass a crystalline structure, with true intermolecular bondings – so that it becomes a far less fragile material. Suppose what appealed to him was the idea of greater order producing greater strength. And it evidently amuses him to relate that to the notion of cohesion in poetry. The corollary being that realism has the least possible symmetry. I don't believe that. I mean, that the two functions are so crudely separable. . . . If we understand one another – you and I – it must be because of the patterns, the system to my utterances. And if I manage to tell you anything it must be because of the randomness and all the contingent detail in my speech? I'm confused by Papa's poetry: because, in a way, he seems to be saying that as well. When he invokes this ambivalent status of glass, he's partly suggesting a much more complex and fluid relation, I think, between the individual and society. Suggesting perhaps that the third person – the common vision of the world – exists more accurately somewhere between us, in some gap that you and I have translated into words.

That narrow-backed man with his chronic cough: would it have been more honest not to tell you about him? I don't know anymore. In that trivial sequence of actions there were both real and unreal things, although I can't say now which were which: that man walking slowly, doggedly frail, along the pavement; that moment when I stooped to shift the basket, and saw how the wicker around the handle was beginning to unravel.

The school siren was already wailing when the bus let me down near the school. Remember how the pale, wiry grass brushed at the backs of my calves as I rushed clumsily across a vacant field to the school gate. And the membranes in my skull were beginning to burn. Felt for the rest of the day that I had been stung, somehow. At lunch-time I spoke to Marianne, hesitantly, trying to make a joke out of the stupid headache, and out of my own inevitable liberal anguish.

She understood, though, I know. Nicholas was flushed and crowing, hugely proud of himself for having cycled to school, in under twenty minutes. 'Heeeey man I feel tremendous, it really is fantastic, you should try it, you know. Hey Anna, why don't you get a bike too.' Listening to him, Marianne and I both became subdued. I don't know what she was thinking, but I was baffled and I suppose a little jealous that a twenty-three-year-old who lived on hamburgers and sandwiches, and whose body was no more developed than a child's should have such reserves of physical strength. 'You know what, I think I'm going to keep on cycling after this boycott's over. It's so fantastic.'

Started taking a lift with Marianne after that, meeting her each morning at the foot of the railway bridge in Mowbray. Having someone to share petrol money may have helped her a bit, but I still felt awkward about the arrangement – despite Marianne's cheerful insistence. It's a long way out of her usual route; and she seems to spend so much of her time doing things for other people. Chrisjan apparently becomes engrossed in the newspaper or a book in the evening – anything to stop himself from seeing that Marianne is sweeping up the crumbs from under his feet, or scraping at the threadbare rug with a stiff brush. And Marianne's response to that indifference is to get up at five in the morning, to dust and clean in a curious, sick sort of franzy – soaking Chrisjan's jeans in the bathtub and pummeling them in the hot suds; boiling up tripe for the dogs; cooking breakfast for Chrisjan and Benjamin.

What is that in Hegel about the slave and his labour? Becoming free through work. But what happens when someone like Chrisjan despises the work that Marianne does – claims he can't see why she makes such a fuss over unnecessary things. And when he won't even concede that it *is* labour?

A couple of years ago I came across her after school, still sitting in the staffroom. It was winter, but the cold had a dry, sharp edge to it that year, with the drought: she was trying to chafe her thin hands warm in the cotton folds of her summer skirt. I could see how stiff the tendons were at the back of her neck – headache she had, I think. She was waiting for her car to be returned, she explained. Some of the matric boys had borrowed it at lunch-time for a joy-ride, and were still not back. 'Now I suppose they've had an accident,' she said bleakly. 'And it will be my fault.'

The kids drove back into the parking lot a few minutes later, of course, and came trailing into the staffroom. Solicitously they apologized, soothing her and deeply contrite until they'd coaxed her into forgiving them. Marianne yielded in the end, with a would-be stern, 'Orright. Maar volgende keer, hoor . . .' I don't think the kids picked up the tired residue of panic that underlay her kindly chuckle.

122

She told me once about her parents' home, out on a farm near Bredasdorp. Called *Oorvloed*. And the dining-room table becomes the setting every day for pageants of superabundance, she said. There will be roast chicken, freshly shelled peas in cream sauce, little fritters made from sweetcorn and served with honey, crisp new potatoes, beetroot salad, sousboontjies, onion sauce, geelrys, baked tomatoes – all of it in potential hospitality towards unexpected guests. And on the sideboard the garish Victorian porcelain is always filled to overflowing with the orchard's windfalls of quinces, apples, peaches, gooseberries, guavas. Once I went to supper at Marianne's and the meal she gave us was almost as elaborate as the feasts she'd told me about. Speaking to her in the kitchen I couldn't help – as she placed a dish of custard in the oven – couldn't help telling her how amazed I was. She straightened up, flushed; tried to brush back her hair from her face with hands still cumbered by the oven gloves. 'Ja,' she said, uncertainly. 'Ja, but it is just the way I was brought up.' And she puffed out her thin cheeks for an instant before she began to chuckle, perplexed. Yet Marianne hardly ever eats enough for herself. Why she's always cold in the winters. And her chest seems so narrow and collapsed – as though she refuses even to breathe in enough air for herself. Afraid to take up someone else's share, maybe.

Think it must be her generosity that also softens and rounds out the meagreness of her shoulders and collar bones. Capacity she has for self-surrender. I've always been afraid to expose myself by using languages whose principles I don't fully understand. Maybe Marianne lacks that fear. Ja. I know that she loves Chrisjan, despite all her exasperation and anger. I imagine she'd be brave enough to risk anything, even to try out utterances of her own in some enigmatic, tender language of desire.

But this isn't what I want to talk about at all.

It began raining again about half an hour ago, with a determined amount of sound and greyness to it. If it keeps up until tomorrow morning, will I be able to walk to school, I wonder.

Maybe it's not possible for women to find a mid-way – between freedom and death, I mean. Lacking any surrogate for ourselves we have to surrender everything or nothing.

Made us some supper. Mostly out of tins, I'm afraid; although I did use up the last of the greenish, near to sprouting potatoes, and there were freshly ground peppercorns at least, to sprinkle over it all, and a tiny bit of parsley and chopped chives that I ventured out into the backyard to retrieve from under the morning glory leaves. Why do I relay each of my ingenious recipes to you? Maybe just to affirm that even if my resources are minimal, there's almost no end to the variety I can make them yield. We can hold out still. They say that to survive you need stored grain, powdered milk, salt and honey: that's all.

Felicia seemed to be looking less tired. There was even an insouciant, happy light glinting once again in her eyes. Perhaps I was only fooling myself. But it was comforting to see her push back from the table with the palms of her hands and lean in the chair as it teetered on two legs. The way François used to, to incense Constance. She inclined her head slightly, pretending vaguely to listen while I made conversation about potatoes and beans, and theories of their edibility.

Felt heartened enough, as we were eating, to ask her something outright. It's been bothering me, ever since she asked me to deliver the message to the kid at school. Why she can't go to him herself. Predictably, though, her face simply tightened. I persisted – clinging to a vain belief that I had some right to know. And she answered eventually, resentfully.

It seems absolutely set that she won't go back to school now. I can understand it. Partly. Suppose there's a certain critical stage of dissent: once you reach it, the decisions you take about your future have to be irreversible. And yet it's a massive pity. Teachers are often stingy with that word 'gifted'; but I'd use it about Felicia.

I had my back to her as I was thinking those things to myself. Taking out the skim milk from the fridge; poking at the thin disc of ice across the surface in the jug. Wish I knew how to adjust the wiring of the thermostat. Range should be wider, I think: easier to gauge the settings then. I felt angry. As I straightened up, some of the milk spilled, dipping from underneath the frozen surface. I was beginning to feel a failure because I couldn't provide alternatives for a child like Felicia.

What will become of her. I tried to goad her into thinking about that. Reminding her, 'Felicia, with a matric, with your ability – you would easily get into university. You'd have no problem getting bursaries. . . .' She didn't even answer, but went on sipping her tea, leaning back dangerously in her chair and staring abstractedly at the curtain rail.

There had been nervous, sparse falls of rain against the windows throughout the supper; and the last of the light withdrew rather quickly into a blankness that wasn't truly night but a merging of the sporadic drizzle with the air's dull coldness.

I stood up again for a moment, to switch on the light. Another thing I needed to ask Felicia. About her mother, who may have become one of the parents that telephone Mr Naidoo at home, tearfully imploring him to save their children. I'd even go and see her if Felicia wanted me to.

It's frustrating trying to get anything out of the kid. She keeps her own meanings locked away, deliberately obscure within the privacy of her thinking – and I'm left to reveal myself constantly in the act of assaulting that silence. She never speaks to me in any casual way, either. Well: I suppose I belong to a world that she no longer values. I'm a part of some faintly ludicrous enterprise involving the chalk-thick atmosphere of classrooms, and those Romantic reveries contained in certain poems about childhood, nature, solitude. . . .

Too angry suddenly to care whether I upset her, I repeated my questions. She let her eyes sweep slowly over me; then fixed her gaze on the curtains again. And muttered furiously that her mother was fine.

Was I being totally unreasonable? Felicia's an only child – as far as I know. And if Mr Moodie is away at sea at the moment, the mother will be on her own in that house of theirs, all the way out at the coast. In the damn sand dunes. She could be sick, half crazy with worry.

Once I took it for granted that I understood the phrase *in loco parentis*. Feel chagrined to find out that I don't really know after all whether I am answerable first to Felicia or to her mother.

I went on beating dully at the child with my own doubts. 'Will you get a job then?' I asked her, and simultaneously wondered, heavily, what sort of work she could find. Junior certicificate – that's all she has. Might get a job as a clerk. Receptionist. Shop assistant. And her intellect and her sense of self would steadily be ground down, crushed into dust. It's possible she'd qualify for

125

entrance to a training college? Not sure. They may have pushed up the standard. Thinking of that, though, I felt faintly, fleetingly cheered.

Felicia answered me steadily, however: 'It's joining the system, isn't it?'

Defeated, I returned to the idea of university. 'Felicia, don't you still want to go on to drama school?' I noticed again how the subtle lustre seems to have dried from her cheeks; hints in her complexion of sallowness, perhaps even illness. I think that my futile harping must have angered her – she breathed in sharply before answering fiercely. 'Listen, I'm not interested in bourgeois theatre. Can't you understand that.' She paused for a second, speechlessly blazing at me. 'And in any case I don't believe any more in acting in made-up stories on stages. There's the real world, okay, and and . . . that's where . . . you have to live in it, okay, and fight in it.' She stood up, agitated by her own emotion. Clasping the back of the chair she added, 'That's the only kind of acting I believe in now. It's the struggle for a future; it's acting *really*.'

Silent then, she picked up our supper plates from the table and took them to the sink. Stood there rinsing them carefully, with her back to me. Idly I registered that she still had my sweater on. I hope she keeps it. Hope she keeps that tee-shirt too. She ought to have more, more of everything, I mean. I saw, even through that thick sweater I could see, that her shoulder blades are standing out, bonily.

The rain has let up, but it's left a thin veneer of coldness over everything. There's light flooding into the sitting-room through the window, almost fluorescent in its whiteness. Starlight? I suppose so. But it seems outrageously bright. Perhaps there's a massive banking-up of cloud left behind, after the rain. Trapping the diffuse, scattering light from the suburban streets and reflecting it back. Turns the wake of the rainstorm into soundless carnival. I heard the fragile, timid chime of the Conradies' clock as I came back from the bathroom. Never hear it in the daytime. One o'clock, it was intimating, delicately.

Stood for a moment outside the bedroom, listening to Felicia's faint, rhythmic breathing. And it occurred to me then for the first time to wonder whether she and Wilson weren't lovers.

Was it stupidly insensitive of me to put them in the same bed? But at the time – that first time they came here – I didn't think for a moment, they were simply two of my kids, on the point of collapse: the major thing seemed to be to get them under some blankets, cuddled up into the warmth, as quickly as possible. How many things am I supposed to take account of.

We'll know soon, at least. Ivan Hendrickse: that's the boy's name. What is it that I keep trying to remember? What is it that I'm trying to forget, I also wonder.

He's been detained, I feel fairly certain. I wish that I'd been more generous towards him. Why did I dislike him, after all. Because he seemed to sneer at me? For a too feverish light in his brown eyes?

It's difficult to go on remembering. It's too cold; my fingers keep stumbling on to the wrong keys. Please don't be angry, but I think it is possible that you are becoming an epistolary fiction. You can't answer me, after all, and so our conversation keeps winding back on itself – becoming internally sufficient, like the language of music, or insanity, maybe.

Yet I don't believe that I'm mad. Frans is the one who went away. And I sound normal, don't I? That's because of the practising. I'd be afraid to try and calculate honestly how much time I've ever spent really speaking to anyone, outside the classroom I mean, or maybe to you. And Marianne. Think I've spent the greater part of my life in silence. I know that I transmuted my childhood into stillness, using a leaky fountain pen that would sneak its way blotchily across the pages of my secret journals. As for my adolescence – that was filled with charming brilliant conversations that all took place between figures in mirrors, mostly in Afrikaans. Interminable dialogues I'd script – talking to imaginary characters: invented lovers, Michael, Papa, famous writers. Letters I'd write too.

I know that I ought to lie down, try and get some rest before I set out. In a few hours' time.

Sometimes I have a childish fantasy, thinking how perfect it would be if we could sleep without losing consciousness: if it were possible to sprawl on the silky sheets, wide awake, listening to stories with all the lights still burning; and instead of falling asleep, to eat something that provided peace – huge, milky-white roses melting inside us, in place of dreams.

127

Feeling a bit brittle again.

Would you believe it if I told you that as a young girl I saw the world as a miracle of beauty. Always slightly feverish, I could glance upward at a mass of papery, blighted oak leaves against the sun and think that there was a singing, golden outburst of light. Or there would be mired feathers in the grass, and the half of a small, broken eggshell; or the thin, suspended arc of a stalk, with the wild oats dipping from it, blonde and weightless, dry in the panicles. I think there were feelings that I could not imagine how to contain within my own clumsily boned frame, and perhaps I transferred them to the impartial, cool stones that fitted in my hand, and those dark flakes of resin-scented tree bark. A wistful magic.

At my sedate girls' school we'd sit on the grass at tea-time, debating, or swotting, or gossiping; idly picking over the sorrel at our ankles, and the light flowers of the oxalis. There was a summer, I remember, when one or two girls brought star-shaped looms to school and wove us all sandals out of bright raffia. Hardly sandals: a daisy that rested on your instep, with two flimsy, glistening strands to tie it by. We were thrilled to slip off our heavy school shoes and socks, stretching out our bare feet in flowers instead. Towards the end of the sixties that was, when we were thirteen, fourteen, going on fifteen. And had heard about the artless spontaneity of the hippies in San Francisco. Sometimes the most daring girls would twine jasmine or honeysuckle in their hair: but they'd only have to disentangle it hurriedly, tearing the stamens and calyces, when the bell rang for class again. To avoid the rebuke of prefects.

It withered away slowly, though – that faith in loveliness. Very slowly, over the years, beginning perhaps in my first year at university. In the early seventies. Now, in the aftermath, it seems strange to me that we'd known about the Flower Children at school, but not about the student rebellions in Germany and France, nor even about events on the university campuses in our own country. When I did find out, though, it was devastating.

I think that something went wrong when they drove their way into us, armed with those clubs. The din; our banners slowly collapsing and tangling with our panicked bodies. The noise of fright and disaster that seemed to come from all around us, from the city itself, and yet was in our own ears. We shouldn't have been driven backward like that, not into that stonily walled, silent, light-filled

128

place. Some kind of involuted, stifled explosion. Perhaps for a moment or two we really were in paradise then? Daring to think for an instant, 'The Revolution has begun at last.' As we huddled, crouching on our knees, or cross-legged on the floor of the nave, listening to the slow fall of the painted light and dust on to the wooden beams; the strange hush – perhaps the finite world had truly ended and left us pure spirit, in some eternal, ideal domain. Maybe the chill on our skins, that sensation of exquisite brightness inside us – maybe that was hope. I doubt it. And if hope really does require a combination of granite and sandstone, wet steps, stained glass, tear-gas, disciplined brutality, carved marble and shocked, surging crowds – I think I'd much rather die in despair.

Afterwards, when we crept out from that place, numbed, under the escort of politicians, it was to find that nothing in the city had changed at all. There was a slight drizzle in the twilight: the flowers in the church garden drooped dazedly under the steady trickling of the water, and pigeons shuffled mournfully on their ledges. But that was all. In the streets there was still traffic, as late workers left their offices finally for home in the suburbs, and the delivery vans set out on their last rounds of the day. Papers were beginning to stir in the gutters and there was a smell of exhaust fumes that the damp air intensified.

It was only a few years later that I learned. That the whole episode had been meaningless, historically. Because at the time there was unrest smouldering right across the country, especially on the black campuses. And our peaceful demonstration, ja – our assault, those pictures of us in the newspapers, all those direly worded, forceful editorials in the English Press – all of it was merely liberal self-indulgence, for white students only. So it meant nothing, they say.

But it still happened, didn't it.

I know that it really happened. Because ever since I saw the lustre fading slowly from the light that came streaming, narrow and roseate through those lancet windows in the grey stone – ever since then the colours of the living world have continued to die down in my memory, where now there are only shades of powdered ash, and tints of chalk.

It was encounters, I suppose, immediate experience slowly changing into symbol, language . . . knowledge. And one of the dreams that got broken apart, smashed up till it buckled inward on itself was the high Romance of the Christian myths: although I'll confess I hardly knew that till now – hardly knowing what those myths meant then.

Shortly afterwards I left home to begin my years of wandering from one student household to the next. Looking for something. Community, perhaps? Strange, though, how assiduously I struggled to lose myself in books. I was a hard-working student, it's true: so much so that lecturers would sometimes suggest I take a break. Only they couldn't know, you see, what monstrous dreams I was battling to free myself from. Even during the day there would be a sudden sense that the walls of the lecture-theatre were living, quietly respiring; or at home in my bedroom I'd have the lingering impression that the crumpled blanket on the floor was a sprawled, gigantic rose of living flesh. I seldom slept easily, but when I did allow myself to yield and fall into that state of unreason, my sleep would be thick with nausea: nightmares that were either nothing but the pure, intolerable presence of some suffocating incubus, or else some crazy dream of Papa standing over me, jeering as he slowly raised the heavy baton in his right hand.

Once there was a much longer, more intricate dream. I remember that I watched it come from a tiny, determined corner of consciousness: watched the dream come, the figure slowly advancing along a track that held a meaning of dustiness to itself. A sort of farmer: Agricola, his name was, only it meant a poet or a sage in the dream; and the words for his clothes came from the stories about Oupa. Corduroys, maybe, and a jacket and hat, perhaps a beard: I never saw them, just knew them to be there in the dream; clipped together in a sheaf of sounds and forgotten words. There was a sickly-sweet miasma of love filling the dream – for that ancient figure of the learned man. And then from the peripheries of language a horde of people in thick, huddled cloaks drew round him. Disciples? They were almost a part of him, fused into him; and then was the worst, because I was amongst them, stifled by the overpowering sweetness of the group's adoration: that was when I tore myself out of their pressing circle, dragging my way out through dry air, through the choking stillness of dreams, back into the thin screaming of consciousness. Knowing in the final instant of escape and waking that it was Papa, and that someone had raised a knife over him; knowing that it wasn't Papa over whose head the steely light was quivering, but me; knowing that the one who held that knife was also me.

Someone came racing into my room, frightened, patting the air with soft demands to know what was wrong. Confusedly, I pulled my jeans on, and a musty tee-shirt, and followed her into the kitchen where the electric light was off, and candles instead were tilting in enamelled candlesticks. I remember all the trivial, burning detail of that night. The faces turning towards me as people stared, curious for a second or two before returning to their debate. A skinny honours student was arguing about the role of intellectuals. Organize the working classes. We were all in our early twenties, and none of us had ever worked except Rick. Who'd spent a vacation working for the mines as a foreman. There was a kettle of bush tea simmering on the stove, and Marie poured me out a mugful for the creamy, rich-coloured alkaline comfort of it. And someone was spreading thick wedges of bread with salt and butter – ravenous after smoking grass, I think. Sopping up the cold supper vegetables with his slice, and sending the rest around the circle on a bread-board. Still involved in the ritual of smoking: take for yourself, and pass on. I felt peaceful suddenly, eating that clumsily buttered, gritty bread. But it was boring listening to Rick. Maliciously I stared at his caved-in chest and stringy limbs; thinking how he hated having to wash the dishes and flatly refused to scrub the lavatory. When the bread-board was put into his pale hands he passed it on swiftly, with a lightly interpolated insult. There were no curtains in the window-case, and I remember seeing the darkness outside, beyond the light-gilded mirrors of the glass panes.

When was that night, I wonder. What year. 1973? They say one hundred thousand workers were involved in strikes that year. And the police killed more than a hundred and seventy miners. There were protests on university campuses, right across the country, right throughout the year. Or 1974, was it? When Caetano was overthrown in Portugal, and people knew, they could feel that soon the empire in Africa would fall. Safe so long as my thoughts were centred on paper – on the fleshless, the non-real. Was it 1975. My honours year. And the year Papa was given that prize by the Akademie, for *Sprakeloos*. 'This prestigious award', the newspapers

131

said.

Sometimes on a Sunday afternoon I'd walk to Rondebosch, to visit Mom at the flat. We'd gossip a bit, she'd tell me about Frans; and then, after we'd refilled our mugs with tea, she'd begin to draw me out. So that she could get around to the conventional reproaches: 'Oh, Anna – all work and no play: I know you'll tell me that's a cliché, but it's true, you know. . . .' There would be a faint hint of suspicion to her tone; and she'd settle herself more comfortably in the armchair, heavily self-assured and choking with the kind of irritation that's only permitted within a family. 'Why can't you just go out and have fun like other young people: just be *normal*. . . . Don't they have parties and things? Why don't you go to the cinema sometimes. Or the beach. Isn't that what the other girls do, in your class, I mean?'

There was a beach-party that I went to once with everyone else from English III: one summery afternoon on Llandudno beach. A few people came with wet-suits and surfboards, and rather brilliantly they shattered all literature and speech to a million shards of sunlight on the racing, vivid, trembling waves. Others wrote gigantic words in the sand, or else helped to shape prostrate human forms out of mud. And a few of us wandered away towards the colossal boulders at the end of the beach: to pick our way barefoot up the narrow tracks of sand, eroded granite, crumbled salt and the low, sprawling, succulent scrub.

As we scrambled up, sometimes dawdling, sometimes leaping, and all of us contentedly silent – we'd startle a hopping, green-breasted bird into flight, or else transform a tiny, basking skink into a silvery streak of speed. The winds of a thousand years, or perhaps the surf of a more ancient ocean had worn out caves under some of the huge, rearing rocks: we saw burnt twigs and ashes there, from campfires, with rusted tin cans and charred fish bones in amongst the refuse. The sunlight set itself into our hair; and once we'd tugged our tee-shirts off over our heads, it traced languid patterns over our shoulders, and across our collar bones. Up there on the windy heights of the rocks, one or two people went prowling further: but I simply loosened the tie of the print skirt I wore and flung myself down to lie spread-eagled on that warm stone with its harsh crystals of fluorspar and mica. Staring up at the domed rocks, where the granite was coming away in thin sheets; staring at the

132

colours of the lichen. A blue-headed lizard clung warily to his rock, and underlying the smell of the seaspray there was the musky scent of the dassies who huddled in the shadows, I suppose.

I remember reaching out to play with the glittering leaves of a succulent plant. The roots could have clung to little more than a sprinkling of dust and salt in the rock crevice: live off dew, those plants, or sea-mists and winter rain, or the water they store in those glistening storage cells. The surge and the steady unrest of the sea was echoing everywhere, distorted, rebounding from and amplified by the deep hollows in the stones. If I turned my head I could see the water way below us, dark and only faintly ruffled in the small bay. And a few kilometres away there was the low, featureless mass of the prison island. Where they kept the country's greatest leader. Turned my face away again, shocked by the hazy ordinariness of the view; and stared up instead at the mountain's endless series of buttresses. It's a privilege in prison to read books and study, isn't it. The grace, the grace of our mountain flowers is not in their veined translucence, but in that robustness that enables them to last out storms and drought and the berg winds and south-easters of the summer, and the north-westerly gales of the winter. It's a privilege in this country to be literate at all.

The sun's distilled warmth was sinking into my vertebrae and shoulder blades. I lay there, very still, with one hand loosely clenched near my face. The mountain vegetation seems to find an uppermost level: beyond which there's only the sheer rock rising in those folds and outcrops of ochre-coloured sandstone. Stupefied I lay there gazing upward at the rocky faces; and then another image interposed itself, substanceless and floating – a trick of the peripheral vision. While I was thinking about the textures set into amber light by shadows and lichen, crystals, burnt twigs and the dried debris of abandoned birds' nests – a dead fist raised itself slowly, transparent and emblematic between me and the quietly burning colours of stone.

And once those nightmares had come to an end, there were worse visions – more austere, and more reasoned.

I'd used to delight in the walk up to campus, along those steep, winding little streets, some cobbled and some that turn out to be cul-de-sacs. The gardens there are overgrown with trailing nasturtiums, plumbago, wistaria, hibiscus, jasmine, honeysuckle, morning

133

glory, vygie, privet, tecoma: and yet their real abundance is in lassitude and warm sunlight settled on the stones, drowsy cats, untrimmed hedges, the tranquil neglect of flaking rust on an iron gate. I used to bask in something of that peace as I walked up in the mornings, or ambled home more slowly, late in the afternoons, slightly headachy from reading. Over the years, though, I wondered more and more bleakly about the lives of the academics who lived in those houses. Seeing a man wander out into a courtyard sometimes, dressed in a kind of uniform of white shorts and an ill-fitting white top – carrying a plastic basin full of greyed, soapy water. Or seeing the women who leave those houses at five in the afternoon: huge, maroon-coloured, vinyl carry-alls balanced on their heads. The women walking slowly, careful of swollen feet in second-hand, down-at-heel shoes; and burdened often by a child on the back, secured by a towel or a tasselled rug.

Think that I slowly came to understand the privileged quality of my own childhood. Everything I was beginning to reject was tangled inextricably with memories of the jacaranda tree on our front lawn, and the keurboom that the carpenter bees loved. Memories of the fern plants on the veranda: the wire baskets that simultaneously overflowed with a trembling, light-coloured foliage and held back the limp, brown strands of decayed fronds. Memories of the linen cushions whose pastel floral patterns could be guiltlessly ruined – tossed down on to the grass for a visitor, or offered comfortingly to one of François's stray cats.

Steadily the gardens that I passed every day came to have the absent colours for me of words, of philosophy. The low stone walls were no longer bright with the breeze-flustered alyssum and lobelia, but grey instead, in the evening shadows; while the decrepit hawthorn in the corner was turned to a confused, yellow-green glimmering of darkness under the streetlight. I felt unhappily compelled – to distrust the sweetish, lilac scent of syringa: every suave assertion of civil peace. Idleness I came to hate too. Glimpsing people sometimes, sun-flushed, puffy-armed, reaching up without real physical purpose to admire the blowsy, pallid rose on a trellis. Suspecting, you see, that it must mean the existence, somewhere, of slaves.

There were a few other parties that I went to, in search of normality, perhaps. I remember music being played very loudly –

driving music with electric guitars and mouth-organs that turned the lyrics into noise. People would sit around on the floor, drinking Tassenberg wine from paper cups, smoking cigarettes, and hunched forward in the intensity of their conversations. Stunned by the din, by the light in everyone's eyes, they'd let the ash fall from their cigarettes and then dust it silently into the muted rusts and indigos of a Kelim rug. There was a girl who sat next to me once: confused, crimson-cheeked and secretly, painfully miserable about the sumptuousness of her own flesh, you could tell. All the same, she wore her hair in tousled, rich screeds hanging down around her cheekbones, and darkened her lashes with some crumbly paste. Offering me sips of that metallic-edged wine; as well as other intimacies, confessions. She just lived for poetry, didn't I? For the arts, anything to do with – she paused before pronouncing it – culture. I accepted her wine in silence; studied the flowing kaftan she wore, closely embroidered and thick with appliqué. The people in the department were so sensitive, didn't I think? It was their Englishness, somehow . . . oh. Her eyes were dazzled with love as she spoke. I watched her fumbling for another cigarette: and that inchoate enthusiasm, and the mass of her dark hair seemed to confuse her further. Blushing and tossing back the gleaming strands, she murmured, 'I know, I suppose I'm talking nonsense really, I'm a bietjie dronk, you see.' There was an archness underlying that language switch, something conveyed by emphasis and the deliberately inept pronunciation. As if to say, This is not my own behaviour, but a fleeting state borrowed from others who are truly debased. I was driven then to excuse myself in thick, uncertain words.

Outside on the veranda I could stare directly at least into the dark shadows of the garden, haunted by those vestiges of light that still lay along the leaves of an old silver-tree. There were couples out there, teasing and wittily laughing behind the clusters of fuchsia bushes: faintly, remotely I could see the small flowers tossing as the wind caught and bruised them up against their own leaves. And there was a rhythmic squeaking from the rusty frame of an old garden swing-chair. I used the same words, the same idiom, the same accent as these people: yet theirs was not a language that I wanted to share. From the creeper near me there was a sudden drift of scent and dust. The fathers of these students were the ones who managed banks and insurance companies, who owned depart-

135

ment stores, who bought and sold shares in every industry that rested upon and exploited black labour. I have always lacked words for pride, I know, and for power, but the lacunae they left were suddenly filled with a shameful vindictiveness: that young people so finely dressed and fat could dare to blame Afrikaners even for the grossness of their own ennui. Seeing themselves as the oppressed. I reached out, I remember, and touched the woody stem of the wistaria. Tracing the fibrous curves and the leaf-stalks and the fragile showers of its blossom. Forcing myself to hold on. To push back the shouts of rage in my throat.

It might have been better for me if I'd involved myself in student politics – but those were the days of the strangely racist interregnum. The black students had abandoned NUSAS: and the white students on being left to re-examine themselves could come up with little more than an imported counter-culture of 'grass' and rock music. And a hatred for the people they called 'boere'. That particular kind of racism persisted long after the people in SASO had altered their analysis of the struggle; persists even now, as far as I can tell.

I remember once hearing students chatting after a seminar – someone making a remark, lightly sneering, about boere. I walked on past them and out of the building; going across to the library, to my usual working place. But I couldn't concentrate for the rest of the morning; and that poem of Papa's about his father kept going through my head, incessantly, until I thought that I would be sick from the clamour of it. The title poem of *Sprakeloos*. It isn't mentioned anywhere that the man in it is Zak Rossouw; but I know, because of hearing the story so often from Papa when we were children. How Oupa came home from Ceylon where he'd been interned by the English to find his farmland changed into acres and acres, as far as the horizon, of blackened, still acrid, powdery stubble and charred wood. He walked across that landscape, alone: encountering the skeletons occasionally of sheep that must have scattered – fragments of the wool and hide left stuck to the bones, stinking, and coming away where beetles and ants were eating. Finding the old homestead too – the site, at any rate, marked by strewn stones and the darkened sand where burnt wood had slowly disintegrated with time, under the wind. And as he tramped across those ashes, listening to the crackling of the brittle charcoal under his boots – he still wondered soundlessly, wordless with grief, why his wife

136

and their two small sons should have died in the care of the English, in a concentration camp.

There were other chapters to the story too.

What Oupa did to build himself up again. Someone gave him a pair of disused, rusted shears which he sharpened and scoured, and then took with him from farm to farm; walking across the country to shear other men's sheep. From the Transvaal down through the Orange Free State, sometimes even into the northern Cape. He bartered himself a horse after the first year, and six years later bought back his old farm. Went in for horse-breeding; gradually accumulating wealth, and more land. Married again, and had eight children, perhaps in the bitter memory of his two dead heirs or his own destroyed youth.

Papa was the laatlammetjie. He told us once that his father had always seemed to him to be an old man, too short-tempered ever to stoop and prattle to his children or teach them games. And when the village teacher came and solemnly asked permission to speak to his father, Papa says he doubted that Oupa felt even a trace of reluctance – to send his youngest child away to school in the Cape.

I must keep on; yet everything in my head seems to be drifting and sinking – starlight trapped in the clouds, or the drizzle, or dreaming, perhaps. No, but I know that I am awake: I can feel small fibulae of cold piercing the spindly bones in my feet. And my fingers fall stiffly against the keys, in stupid configurations that keep jamming the keyboard.

Michael worked hard for NUSAS, especially for its welfare division – because his faith was irrepressible, I think: brimming and restless in its ardour. He chaired several committees on campus and kept up his work for the youth wing of the Progressive Party as well. He even kept up ties with Youth Action, although he wasn't a schoolkid anymore, of course: I've heard that the constitution was largely drawn up by him.

While I was at school still I tried a few more times to join in. I remember one Saturday afternoon going out with a gang of other kids – because Michael had phoned to ask me, chattering and teasing, crowing with enthusiasm. It took half an hour's crazy, complicated conversation, to explain to me: no one in Youth Action could legally handle the donations that were flowing in, so they'd had to

137

hand over the funds to some grown-ups who regularly organized bursaries for black kids. And one of the things this group did was to collect old textbooks from the schools for white children and redistribute them amongst black pupils.

Sometimes Michael would burst out giggling. And I would wonder – stupefied, withdrawn teenager that I was – what one did with a plastic handset that crackled and hissed with such exuberance. Think Michael found it farcical that Youth Action was being turned into a glorified charity. In one of his long letters to me he confided once that the Afrikaans Press had probably analyzed the original protest meeting most accurately with that caption, 'Skoolkinders wil sakgeld gee om Bantoes te help'. The English papers reported the occasion with urgent, emotional fanfares of approval: even editorial comment. And yet I don't know. Michael had no choice but to be a liberal.

We were invited, anyway, to help sort through thousands of tattered, dog-eared readers and maths primers.

I remember that we went out in the back of a combi-van, about a dozen of us, to a school that seemed to be miles away from any of the suburbs that I knew. Travelling through a semi-industrial area – a wasteland, almost: hundreds of square kilometres that were overgrown by acacias, with shanties leaned up in the densest parts, that you could sometimes glimpse. In the cleared parts there were warehouses and factory buildings. Why are they roofed like that? Repeated, rearing pyramids. Sky-lighting, maybe. Also sometimes saw those three-tiered tenement blocks, council housing, I think, with the rickety-looking spiral iron staircases on the outside: there were children playing under the lines of washing in the concrete yards. The road was edged along some stretches by listing, rusted wire fences, or stands of eucalyptus with their papery bark peeling away. Once we glimpsed the wreck of an old car lying in a ditch. And we saw farms: open land, with large sheds at one end and dozens of small hutches set up across the fields. Poultry maybe, we were wondering.

We being jolted around in the back of the van. I didn't know many of the other kids. That girl from my school, of course. Felt too shy to talk to her, though. She was more friendly with the other kids who'd spoken at the protest meeting: a girl whose surname was familiar because her uncle was the political leader of the die-hard English right wing; and the chairman of Youth Action – a boy with a dashing, outrageous grin, who charmed everyone with his rhetoric. His father was managing director in South Africa of an American multi-national company. Michael joked with everyone, but spoke to me quietly in between, telling me about the boy who was driving the combi. The only member who was old enough to have a driver's licence. His eyes glimmering behind his lenses, Michael explained to me in whispers, 'Dave is a hell of a nice guy. You know, we needed a lift one night at eleven o'clock and so we phoned him. And you know, he came round straight away. When he says it's no problem, he *means* it, Anna.' A packet of potato chips came skating across the floor and there were suddenly salty flakes over everything. We giggled and there was a general roaring of mirth. Almost anything anyone said was liable to be given a ribald re-interpretation, and most of the small, scattered conversations kept breaking down in yells of laughter.

The school itself was deserted: we were there on a Saturday afternoon, or it may have been during school holidays, I forget. And the building lay in the lee of some roadworks and shored-up dunes, so that the restless, tiring noise of the south-easter was lulled. The desks had been pushed aside and stacked one on top of the other in the classrooms. There was a smell of disinfectant; suppose the caretakers had been scrubbing the floors. We saw a cardboard box in a corner, I remember, with a tangled mass of multi-coloured sashes inside it: girdles to be worn in team games.

The books we'd come to sort were stacked in one of the bigger classrooms, along the walls and in free-standing piles on the dusty wooden floor-boards. I remember the sleepy peacefulness of that afternoon. Sunlight streamed in through the windows, warming the limp backs of the books we paged through, warming the floor where we kneeled or sat cross-legged. So much dust you get in books; and fish-moths came scuttling away from some of the boxes. Michael and I worked together, with cardboard boxes all around us, each for a different category of subject or standard.

It's strange to rediscover your own earliest lessons. Janet and John at the toy-shop. Those animal fables in Afrikaans. African stories really, aren't they – learned centuries ago from a slave of the imperial masters. There were history books too – well used, of course, with caricatures and remarks scribbled in the margins by bored children.

Our throats got drier and drier from all that dust and from tossing around ridiculous jokes. I remember: after a couple of hours Michael began to crawl around on the floor like a desert survivor in a cartoon sketch, clutching at his throat. 'Oh man,' he groaned, 'I need a Coke.'

I went to a meeting once as well, that they held in an anteroom at the civic hall in Mowbray. Another of those dusty suburban centres with an adjacent public library, a brass-barred counter where people went to pay their electricity bills and buy dog licences, and a hall where they had a dance-band for teenagers on Friday nights. I was bored though. There were so many stencilled documents, with numbered resolutions, questions of procedure – that sort of thing. Maybe because they were powerless to do anything real? Energy all dissipated into debate and the politics of organization. Suppose it may have been good training for some people. In what, though.

I heard that the movement became more powerful a few years later, after some kids from Cape Flats schools took over the leadership. They were more intelligent, from a political point of view. I don't know much about it, but I think they channelled that endless, futile discussion into more soberly thought-out programmes of reading and study. The odd thing was that they stayed nonracial – just at the time of the Black Consciousness Movement. The new leaders rejected that word 'coloured' for themselves, I think – in solidarity with black students; but almost simultaneously they took up the more progressive philosophy of history as class war. I wonder what happened to most of those kids. That girl from my school was chairman for one year, but she's supposed to have had a string of nervous breakdowns afterwards. And Michael mentioned to me once that the person who was chairman after her was also unstable: slightly paranoid and prone to fits of profound distress when he'd sometimes try deliberately to smash his car on the freeway. He fled the country eventually in terror, convinced that he was being pursued. It's quite likely, though, that he was utterly sane. A few other people went overseas to study; usually to the London School of Economics, where they wrote theses on trade unionism or the role of black women in resisting oppression in South Africa. Chrisjan was involved with Youth Action at one time, apparently. And he went on to university here. Works now for one of the radical church movements, helping communities to organize themselves.

Michael dropped out of university. Think he only scraped through one of his courses at the end of 1972, after that cathedral rout. Doing too many other things. Also I know he never stopped being tormented by thoughts of the army. Think he couldn't stand it that his exemption had come on purely physical grounds. His eyesight, of course. Being undersized as well, and slightly overweight, maybe. He went on working full-time at NUSAS head office for a while after scrapping university, and then made his way up to Johannesburg, to work for a left-wing Christian publisher. Haven't heard from him for years now, although someone did tell me that he took on the Christian faith eventually: went into a seminary to train for the Anglican priesthood.

I remember visiting him once or twice at his mother's flat when I was still at school. In a high-rise building in Sea Point; their flat was on the tenth floor, looking over the sea. Felt a bit out of place there, tip-toeing across the thick carpets, and overwhelmed by the smell in the sitting-room of furniture polish, perfume and food. Michael's room was a kind of cubicle, mostly taken up with books, a desk, box-files, scattered papers . . . and an immense poster of John F. Kennedy on one wall. We sat on the rug, looking at pictures and magazines that his sister had sent him from America. Tapes she'd sent him too, of Martin Luther King's speeches: we listened to those, getting goose-flesh and trying to comprehend what had once been their powerful immediacy for massed audiences of roused, fervent, living people.

Michael's heroes were all victims, in a sense – victims of sacred or political murder.

Our conversations, like our letters, were almost always about questions of violence, the concept of a just war. With his chin in his hands, he said once, 'You know that saying – that your life isn't worth living unless there's something you'd be prepared to die for?' Blinking at me, he went on, 'I've thought about it, and I'd be prepared to die to end apartheid. I really do mean that.' When I asked, though, miserably, 'But Michael, could you kill for that?' – he winced, desolate, and said nothing. Knowing that my words had no questioning intent: we'd agreed long before that we had no answers. A little later he repeated unhappily something that

141

he'd told me once before. 'You know what Kennedy said. That the means determines the end – it's not the other way around. Can you ... can you see, though? If you use violence, then you end up with a violent regime.

Think I dozed off for a while. Know that I must lie down now, just for a couple of hours. There's a clammy, ashy feeling to the air. Not raining. Heard the neighbours' Alsatian barking. Must have been what woke me.

There's something I keep thinking, images that won't go away. . . . Someone is struggling desperately to run, but stumbles, borne to the ground with his flesh heavily bruised, grazed from the fall on to asphalt and splintered glass. A burnt-out petrol drum keeps on rolling endlessly through a clattering, senseless arc; and there are cars, trucks and vans as well; some stuck siren; and the persistent, flickering amber of warning lamps.

CHAPTER 5

i

When she left on Tuesday night she still hadn't told me what was in that note. As we stood outside on the stoep, in the darkness, I lingered helplessly near her, struggling to interrogate her with – who knows what – my paleness, the myriad anxieties in my eyes. I suppose I was irritating her; but tiredness had left me bleakly sceptical that ordinary speech could still phrase the questions in my heart. Eventually she turned to me, coldly, and hissed at me point-blank: 'Look, you know he is.'

I know. But do I? All I seem to know now is fantasy. There was an accident: I know that there was an accident somewhere in the flickering, musky shadows. A barricade of hauled-up tyres, crates, oil drums, iron sheets and dead branches; but all of it up in flames, with the puckering rubber giving off an acrid stench. There were sirens blaring as trucks and fast cars drove up; and overhead a helicopter was hovering, with its rotor blade chuttering and killing out all other noise of commands or screams. The sirens kept up a continuous howling. While green sap was sighing in the burning wood and a faint, persistent drumming rose, remote as a storm: a shimmer in the burning air, and then a sudden staggering intake as the petrol can unfolded into flying metal and a towering of liquid, fiery, reverberating din.

Somehow there are other things I know as well. An uneven concrete floor somewhere – rough-cast and clammy, with insects scuttling over it. And a bucket in the corner, reeking of ammonia. The single grey blanket is too rough and unyielding to offer any solace; although it's frequently claimed that despairing individuals, those whose faces have once too often been left stained with tears and blood – discover of their own accord how to change the dull folds of cloth to a noose.

Nobody seems to know what is going to happen. Mr Naidoo gave his usual start-of-term speech, but the kids were no more impressed than they ever are. And at the staff meeting later he told us to assume that classes would be running as normal. Offering us gruff parentheses about the troublesome and trying period we've all been through, and the need for us to make every effort now to make up for lost time. . . . People were shuffling pointedly long before he finished.

Passed a shoe-shop in Mowbray on my way to the bus-stop that morning: next to a row of smart schoolshoes there was a small blackboard mounted on an easel, with the chalked exclamation, 'Back to School!'. Perhaps the gaping doubtfulness of the slogan simply hadn't occurred to the small-time entrepreneur.

I had to take the bus in the end, after waking up at half past seven and having to scramble into my neatly waiting clothes. There was just time to brush my teeth and rinse my face before I had to grab the basket from my desk and flee the house. And then I raced rather than walked to Mowbray, half skipping, sometimes jogging for a little way until my breath gave out. I felt sick about breaking the boycott, but I was still too flustered by the time I reached the terminus to go through the absorbing ritual of guilt with a proper slowness.

The fruit-sellers were there with their goods packed out on barrows; and the side-streets and stone gutters of the suburb were thronged with workers. Women in scuffed, trodden-over shoes plodding rigidly past the little slate stoeps with their window tubs full of lobelias and wintry, flowerless alyssum. I stumbling, clumsily racing in the opposite direction. Some of the shabby clothing shops are already advertising winter sales, with bright, urgent posters in the windows. And there were butcher shops with the usual smeared messages white in their shopfronts: 'All our food is halaal' and 'Chikens special lowest prices'. One had garlands of flecked sausage draped behind the glass and a sheet of cardboard next to them had pictures of holly on it, with the command, 'Lay-bye now for Christmas'.

The red-meat boycott is still on, I've found out. And also the boycott of pasta products, because the manufacturers are refusing to take back those workers who were dismissed after the strike.

I saw the children who sell newspapers again: two small kids who

144

were squabbling, cursing briskly and laying into one another with their fists. Absurd not to know any Xhosa: the only word I could make out was 'imali' – it was money they were quarrelling over. One child leapt away deftly then and cupped his hand triumphantly over the coins that had been ranked carefully in piles on top of a bundle of the papers. His private system of accounting, maybe. And the violent bickering petered out into hostile mutterings. The two of them looked about eight or nine – maybe ten, but undersized. All the newspaper sellers wear bright orange Sam Browns buckled across their chests now, because the decent citizens of Cape Town were beginning to be mildly shocked by the number of fatal accidents: the little kids often dart through heavy traffic to get a paper to a motorist who's beckoning from a rolled-down window, impatiently jingling the silver.

Maybe one should boycott the newspapers? But they're innocent. They claim. It's not them but the distribution agencies to blame. And in any case those children are bread-winners. That's the other argument: you can't deprive their poor families of that badly needed money.

Usually it leaves me dizzy with anger to recall these things. But that morning I was too tired to feel much outrage. Instead I felt passive; and strangely transparent, stung by the texture and light and human clamour of the world around me.

The bus-driver looked ill: dry-skinned and sallow. He couldn't understand me at first, when I offered him my fare – and his eyes narrowed in frustration. Suppose it must be a difficult job: the driver's cabin is wired in, but there's no grade of diamond mesh that can ward off a bullet or a flaming sheet of petrol. There was a letter in the newspaper from a mother in Elsies River: 'Please remember next time you throw bricks, my son is one of the drivers.'

There were half a dozen broken windows and you could see some of the shattered debris lying under the seats still, neglected in the hurry to sweep out the bus and have it running again. Felt slightly nauseous as I stepped down the ringing aisle of the empty bus. Some of the vinyl seat coverings were ripped. Couldn't think whether it would be safer to sit away from the broken windows or next to them. Thinking that stones would smash the still intact panes. Too shaky to decide, I finally sat down abruptly on the

nearest seat. Wishing I had a tissue to wipe my upper lip. I began
to wonder whether I shouldn't get off the bus and walk back home;
and I think I would have, too – if the driver hadn't started up the
engine then.

I wasn't, in the end, the only one to defy the boycott that morning. The bus route passes the children's hospital opposite Rondebosch common with its wild grass and weeds and sundews: there
are almost always a few women waiting at the side gate with babies
in their arms, cuddled into the silky fringes of shawls and home-
knitted rugs. The road's being widened there, so there's no sheltered
bus-stop, only rows of white-washed drums and temporary road
markers. As soon as people see the bus coming into sight they cross
over the busy road to flag it down, and wait in the dust for it to
pull over. And on Tuesday morning it wasn't any different: about
half a dozen people climbed on, jostling and complaining in high-
pitched voices, trying to shelter themselves and their soft bundles
from the sudden spattering drizzle that was coming down.

Why? So early in the morning. Maybe when their babies are sick,
the women spend the night with them at the hospital? Then they'd
go home first thing the next day. Ja. You couldn't walk four or
five kilometres in the drizzling cold with a feverish baby fretting
in your arms.

Then, as I crossed the empty field behind the school, trudging
through the dull, heavy sand, staring at the wind-blown rain and
the dampened tufts of sparse yellow grass, I admitted to myself
that I had no child to put before all principles. The wind hollowed
my dress against the sharp bones of my hips, and I was anguished
for a minute, thinking that cold thought: no child.

I've walked every morning since then, although I usually manage
to hitch a lift in the afternoons – as far as the common. It's tiring,
of course, but if other people can do it. . . .

Marianne hasn't come back. Whole of Tuesday I thought she
might be coming in late: kept expecting, hoping to catch a glimpse
of her swinging in through the doorway, with the thin tufts of her
hair flying, and that troubled, myopic look in her eyes. But it's
been two days now. Beverley isn't at work either. And it seems
that Nicholas has left also.

Think that some of the staff really believed everything would
be back to normal. We went to sit with our own classes after the

146

staff meeting, supposedly to hand out books. There still aren't enough copies of *Julius Caesar* to go around. And there's a book of short stories that simply hasn't arrived at all – for the standard nines who take English as a second language. It was futile trying to argue with the department at the beginning of the year, and then the boycott started. . . .

It's possible that there was some inexplicable, mountainous rage buried deep inside me, but thinking about those textbooks I was suddenly goaded into fury, on behalf of the kids. Mr Korsten was taken aback, I think, when I confronted him in the dusty store-room. He was half-way up a stepladder when I stormed in, busy lifting down a heavy column of exercise books. 'What, Miss,' he said absently, arms encumbered and his head turned away awk-wardly from the jutting corners of the books near his face. Smell of rubbers and pencil lead in that room. 'You want a pen?' After I'd explained he came slowly down the ladder, backwards: and put down his burden. I staring at the veined, thick-skinned backs of his hands. 'Well,' he said finally, almost bemused, 'if you want to phone the department yourself?' It may have been doubt in his voice.

I phoned from the secretary's office: discovering how brittle I can be. Feel as though I'm growing old, sometimes; exhausted by a fever of struggle and panic. Somewhere in that unreal void of elec-tronic communication there were clicks and buzzings. Outmoded system we have, with the lines clumsily overloaded. For handing over someday, I suppose. Newly independent African states usually seem to inherit burnt-out, dilapidated infra-structures. Along with a wasted environment, and pillaged resources, and millions of near-starving, semi-literate, haunted people. As though decades of a ghastly, bitter war had come to an end. Waiting quietly there in the office I could feel a burning soreness beginning at the back of my throat. I had to force myself to smother those bleak thoughts. The cynical vision is seldom accurate. Ja, and usually lacks authen-ticity in the other sense as well. To understand, rather; try to un-derstand. My thoughts were wrangling silently with themselves when a voice came through the receiver finally, amiably terse: 'Ja, kan ek help?' I could have responded in Afrikaans, except that I don't know how to be icily patient and insistent in Papa's language. I was put through to another clerk; then to someone else; finally

147

to a chief clerk.

It was all assurances in the end, soothing promises. They're going to send the school new requisition forms, since our original ones 'got lost' apparently. Can't help remembering that Mr Korsten specially sent the forms in early last year because he knows, wearied by experience, that textbooks can take up to six months to reach us.

I went and sat with Fayrooza and Natalie in the staffroom afterwards and marked out a private zone for myself between them with pages of manuscript notes, opened texts in front of me and irritably discarded pages lying crushed under my forearms. I was trying to draft swot notes for my standard nines. It's partly a challenge, I suppose; to see whether I can get the kids through their exams at this stage. But partly also it just makes me feel miserably incensed. They didn't want to hear what I had to say earlier, about the bourgeois revolution in England, about trade and colonization, about individualism, about divinely ordained stasis; about nature, about nurture; about Aristotle, Plato, Bacon, Hobbes, Macchiavelli; about kingship; about Christianity, about the Middle Ages, about Italian humanism. . . . And now none of them will really think about any of it: cram a few garbled details into their heads, that's all.

I mustn't blame the kids for my own frustration, though. Know why I feel disappointed: I was wanting to try out some ideas about fiction. About novels where the lonely heroes doggedly refuse to share the dreams of the dominant class: and yet can't accept the consequences of commitment to some steady dream of a different future. Seems their only recourse is to Romanticism? Protestations about the value of self-realization.

Ja, and I wanted to talk about ambiguous heroes. About characters existing in some impossible region where they see the conflicting dreams of their society. As though myths were sheets of some transparent, rigid substance that through clashes reveals itself in visible cracks, and the trickle of white, semi-crystalline powder.

My kids. There are nineteen of them at the moment. That's by this morning's roll call. On Tuesday I had twenty-three, and even that was eleven children missing. Most of those who stay away are attending sit-ins in the hall; though some may be absent from school, I suppose. And some may have dropped out altogether.

Those who came to sit diligently at their desks this week didn't

148

really seem happy either. Some of the girls bring handwork, but you can see that they're not lulled any more by the soft clicks and chattering of the needles. Not satisfied any more to watch the flimsy strands of yarn steadily knitted up into fabric and garment simultaneously. Yasmin reads most of the time, with her chin propped in her hands, and her skinny elbows uncomfortably rested on the wooden desk-top. Fretting to start catching up the missed work, I suppose. Maybe they're wishing I would come to their rescue with some assumption of authority: wanting me to be the thoroughly competent, respectable, sternly demanding teacher.

I still have Michael in the class – that slow, troubled, kindly boy. William Perreira. And Melanie: that spindly, shy child, who seems to feel constrained to be her usual helpful, eager self – still leaping up each time the blackboard needs dusting or there are papers to be handed out. Except that something in her has been dimmed by a new, troubling doubt. There's Willie Peters, Omar and Shafiek. And Salie, who'd probably do far better at his schoolwork if he moved to the Afrikaans stream – but who'd also probably be destroyed by the humiliation if he were forced to change.

Gavin came to the classroom door on Wednesday morning and hovered there with his hand on the doorknob, glancing fiercely around the room. Saw a flickering behind him; a slim, nervous figure. The two of them entered then; warily crossed the room to my desk. Cynthie I saw – fiddling with the dangling button of her blazer. Something at the top of my chest was feeling sore. 'It's all right,' I think I said, huskily uncertain whether I was whispering or speaking out loud. 'Rather go back to the hall if you want to.' They stared back at me. 'I'm not teaching anything now and there'll be swot notes for you later.' Suddenly I sensed that I must sound ridiculous with my naively encouraging tone. 'If you want them, I mean,' I felt I had to add.

I can't help thinking about Cynthia's background. Is it wrong? I can't *un*hear the staffroom gossip. About her unmarried mother; about the steady stream of new 'uncles'. About Cynthia's father, a 'white' who occasionally still sends money, it seems – each time rekindling the mother's compulsive aspirations for Cynthia. That tormented, goaded kid has to take ballet lessons, extra maths. And dare not fail her school exams, if she's to avoid the ugly scenes when her mother begins to drink belligerently, and then rounds on the child, weeping and screaming abuse at her. Sometimes, apparently, Cynthie is 'white trash': other times she's 'too bladdy stupid to make it for white'.

Usually after tea-break the kids don't come back to the classroom. And the schoolday dissolves into a blur of dust, tiredness and headache. I sit drinking tea, trying to write helpful notes. And thinking, for some reason, about the chalkiness and the grey skin of death that seem to have settled over the succulent plants on the window ledges of my classroom.

I went and chatted to Mr Jeffries on Tuesday, pretending not to be offended by the smoke that kept wafting across to me, setting its reek in my hair and on my clothes. And casually I brought up Wilson's name. He seemed not quite suspicious, just astonished, perhaps. I was flustered, and added hurriedly, 'I just thought . . . well, wasn't he one of the student leaders?' He struck a match aimlessly and then watched it slowly burn itself out in the nicotine-stained saucer. 'Ja,' he said, relaxing a little, 'ja he is.' And then he told me what he knew of Wilson's background. His father is permanently out of work now, it seems. He used to be foreman at some factory that makes plastic mouldings for industry, but he would persistently come to work with the warm scent of alcohol still on his breath – and belligerent, either because of the savage pain in his skull or because the liquor had cured him of gentility. Once he beat up a machine operator, or went as far as pinning him down, Mr Jeffries murmured. When someone else tried to intervene, William Fransman threatened to kill him, apparently. It seems he was fired several times, only to be taken on again after a few days – because he was an excellent foreman. The factory's best production runs were ones that he had overseen entirely on his own, taking critical decisions when the boss was out at dinner or playing golf. 'I tell you something, he's probably brilliant in his own way, you know. It's just that the drink gets him every time.' One morning finally, with his breath seeming almost to blaze in fumes of brandy, he cursed the manager in a vicious outburst that lasted nearly five minutes. 'That was his last chance. I mean, they *couldn't* take him back.'

Mrs Fransman works as a cutter at a clothing factory, and keeps a hand-lettered card in her window at home to say that she takes in dress-making and alterations. Seems she also has a small week-end business selling seedlings, bulbs, cut flowers and fresh vegetables from the front stoep of their house. Produce from the makeshift greenhouse in the backyard – a one-time hobby of her husband's. There are several other children, although the two eldest are married already, with families of their own to support. Mr Fransman is reduced now to being a scrounger – wheedling small loans from his friends; dependent on his wife for Friday night's bottle of cheap, colourless liquor. 'Ja, they don't have it easy, you know. And as for Wilson, how he manages to study in that place with all those small kids around . . .' Mr Jeffries picked up the charred matchstick from the saucer; and absently snapped it. 'Ja, I think he's quite a boy.'

For some time after that conversation I kept remembering something. About a child who could sprawl on a carpet with cushions under his belly – reading, reading and thinking; softly turning over his own calm thoughts as though they were crystals spread out, silent and rough, in front of him.

At lunch-time I wandered out of the staffroom, glad to escape on to the concrete verandas. Trailing my fingers idly over the maroon glaze of the bricks in the wall. I wanted to find the ten B classroom, to see if there were any students there. One thing I've missed this year is time spent talking to kids. Think it's only when I'm in a classroom speaking that I ever feel honest. Freedom your pupils give you not to pretend false ignorance, false compassion, false politeness.

But there was something as soon as I walked into the room: unlocatable, fractured – but definitely hisses and murmured subaudible comments that it would have been self-insult to try and interpret. It was too late for me to retreat, though. Debbie Johnson was in there, I saw; sitting up on a desk with her guitar across her knees – bent earnestly over it, so that she could see the strings. She glanced up and waved to me, spontaneously. 'Hullo, Miss.' Ingenuously affable, she chimed out also, 'Did you have a nice holiday, Miss.' Seems to be a faint nasal resonance that makes her voice carry with the bright clarity of song. A friend must have nudged her; or perhaps she suddenly glimpsed the steely set of someone's jaw. Because she fell abruptly silent, and hunched herself more intently over her guitar. Pretending in her agitation to be working out a chord.

Nobody confronted me: the kids were clustered in small groups

151

around the room, and most of them seemed to have their backs to me. Yet the corrosive, furtive comments were kept up. Unhappily I asked the child nearest me whether Ivan Hendrickse was in the room. 'Yes, Miss,' he said pertly; and then was nudging his shoulder with his chin, trying nervously to make out whether his friends had understood the rudeness in his tone. He seemed to be looking most fixedly at a group of kids in the corner. I stalked over to them, chafing furiously to counter the voiceless innuendos I heard behind my back.

Marianne would have sighed, I think, and resigned herself. 'Ja, but you see I can understand it. Black consciousness, it is now a, ag, I can't say it. Kyk, dit is mos 'n tydelike beweging. En miskien is dit rassisties. Nou ja. Maar dis ook noodsaaklik – onvermydelik, eintlik, op hierdie huidige stadium. Dit help nie om die kinders te blameer nie. Kan jy dit nie aanvaar nie? You, you see? You have to understand it.'

I suppose she's right. I have to understand that for the present it's inevitable.

I had to pick my way past a few desks, and occasionally there was a child standing, obstinately unhelpful, in my path. Freshly scrubbed wood of the floor I was smelling, and the rag-rinsed blackboard. Most of the children were in clean clothes – shirts whitened in bleach and gaberdine that still smelled of the dry-cleaners. A fragrance of innocence on all of them: the mint flavour of toothpaste, the faint astringence of soap and deodorant and cheap colognes. Glances and shrugs guided me towards a tall boy at the centre of that group. 'Are you Ivan?' He seemed to grudge me even that confirmation and, finally losing my patience, I whispered bitterly, 'Felicia needs information. Felicia Moodie: she wants to know what has happened.' His face didn't lose its disdain: but perhaps he didn't know how to respond then. I asked him to let me have a message. And walked out of the classroom.

Outside in the corridor once again I felt the cold lay its thin, glistening film on my cheeks and hands.

A spasm of hunger took me by surprise. Crossed the quadrangle and then stepped gingerly over the mud that lies between the brick buildings and the prefab section. The tuckshop was still selling things. Had enough small change at the bottom of my handbag to buy a couple of samoosas – last two that were left on the grease-

152

stained paper, golden fried, with lentils and peppers under the folded pastry.

A child came up to me as I was heading reluctantly back to the staffroom. Rather a little kid – in standard six, I suppose; with matted, dark-bronze curls and the peeping, mischievous look some children wear perpetually once they know they're regarded as 'naughty'. 'Miss, is Miss Rossouw?' he asked me, befuddled by the number of Misses. When I said 'Ja,' he went on quickly, without taking a breath: 'This is for Miss.' Handing me a minutely scrolled piece of paper. And I was hankering to draw out the conversation, partly out of shame at not knowing his name. Mr Naidoo would have known the child. 'Er dankie,' I said, guessing that he must be Afrikaans-speaking. And I tried to ask him, 'Die . . . die boodskap, kom dit van . . .?'

But the Afrikaans kids at our school seem to have a stubborn system of politeness: they'll always speak to teachers in the language they think is their own. And so he went on doggedly in English: 'Miss, it's from the other boy. By the ten B room. He told me I must bring it to Miss.' He looked embarrassed and was beginning to fidget with the buttons of his blazer. Ducking his head suddenly, as if to excuse himself, he slipped away. Though not before I'd seen the impish sparkle come back into his hazel eyes – self-confidence returning.

If Fayrooza hadn't given me a lift part of the way I think I might have given in after all and taken a bus. Even the walk from the common seemed interminable. Know there was an unhealthy, greyish glistening across my blanched cheeks. My body seemed almost unreal – could have believed I was incorporeal, or made of glass perhaps, blown glass, if the smouldering in my knees and ankles hadn't proved to me my fleshly state. Ja, the last thing I want is to be invisible; without history; unresisting. I'm opaque to you, aren't I? Aren't I?

I watched the suburbs drifting past me, through me as I walked. Children coming home from school; clambering out of their mothers' cars, trailing rucksacks, or swinging hats on broken tails of elastic. Windows were discreetly protected by wrought-iron burglar bars; and behind the glass panes there would be the comfortable form of a slinky, dozing cat on the sill. Once I'd passed the old fountain there was heavy traffic constantly passing me. In the fumes – lead, isn't there? Carbon dioxide, monoxide; sulphur? Even the buildings along that stretch of road seem dingy – stained by smoke and dust. Derelict place. But the Victorians used to turn their carriages there, smartly, and water their horses at the drinking fountain. I remember passing a bus-stop shelter where graffiti were scratched on to the galvanized iron. Names of gangs, with the esses made into dollar signs. One motto, 'Devil Kids', with a small sketch of a dripping knife blade under it. And scribbled in koki pen: 'Billie cam here loking for his gole.'

Felicia was waiting for me when I came in. There was a tightness to her jawline: maybe she'd been expecting me earlier. I fetched out the note for her, fumbling with the loaf of bread in its tissue paper and the paper packets in my arms. I left her with the message, and came into the study to lie down – dumping my basket and raincoat and the groceries on the floor. Once I was prone on the mattress I found that I was trembling. But I slept, almost instantly falling into a heavy, turbulent sleep.

I'm afraid I'm a bit tired tonight. And there's some work I still want to do. Typing a few more study notes on to stencils.

ii

School closed early today. Well, things have been unsettled ever since we came back, with the kids spending most of their time milling in the hall, trying to re-organize. They seem to be having rallies: concerts of songs and protest poems. But today there was mosque; and also, we were paid. Mr Naidoo came into the staffroom briefly, harassed-looking – and muttered huskily that we would probably like to get to our banks.

Fayrooza came to me, upset and apologetic that she couldn't offer me a lift. I'm slightly in awe of her, even though she's younger than me. She has an almost translucent skin, pale as jasmine, and a fine-boned aquilinity – yet she seems unaware of her loveliness: self-humorous and competent at everything, she's almost down-to-earth. And too generous, I suspect, to judge me for my tongue-tied gaucheness.

I walked home through the downbeat districts of Athlone, passing small cafés on almost every street corner: neglected whitewash

154

flaked off the outer walls to reveal earlier coats of blue paint, and ultimately the red clay of the crumbling bricks themselves. Usually there were a few kids lounging on the steps, with bottles of brightly coloured cooldrink in their hands. Recognized some of them as students from our school. Inside those shops there would be crates propped up to display apples and pears in straw or tissue paper; and sisal strings running overhead from wall to wall – hung with cheap toys, comics, magazines and advertisements for cigarettes and fruit. Smells of curry powder and incense; sound of Indian music from a record-player somewhere at the back. There would be little bottles of patent medicine displayed under the glass-topped counters; plastic-beaded purses; a card holding a dozen nail-clippers; 'crystal' vials full of cheap, synthetic perfumes.

It was difficult to work out boundaries. Of class within class, I mean. But some of the houses were recently built: double-storied, with ornate chimney stacks and front doors that gleamed with walnut stain and varnish. These ones had flower beds laid out in neat grids and lawns of straggling new grass that was just beginning to grip the ancient dune-sand. Others, though, were built of iron sheets and painted powder-blue or green or pink. A yard of grey sand there'd be, strewn with the silvery, sawn-off hulks of dead trees, old tins, dented hubcaps, discarded bottles and the brown, spiky nuts of the bluegums. Saw some coppery-coloured bantams huddling under a dripping bush, and a scruffy donkey outside one house where a hawker's cart was drawn up in the sandy driveway.

I walked past a stand of bluegums – relics from the first farms – and there was that resiny scent in the wet air. Saw the clay-white trunks, and the way the telephone wires were whipping and swaying in amongst the drab clutter of leaves. It was raining softly, briefly when a bakkie came slowly up the road and passed me: laden with snoek, whose silver-yellow tails hung over the board, glistening. A man held one up to me, trying to point at it invitingly and hold an oilskin over his head at the same time; while a child crouched behind him and drew out a bleating, wailing sound from a copper horn. They went on ahead of me, travelling so slowly that the engine kept stalling and the sellers would be jolted, with that supple, reeking cargo of fish slithering over their rubber boots.

Some of the cottages had gardens overgrown with morning glory, convolvulus, plumbago, tecoma, honeysuckle. A pot-of-gold trained

155

up over the trellised veranda, or grape vines, or bougainvillaea. There'd be bricked paths with herbs sprouting in the crevices; perhaps a dark-patinaed tap leaning at an angle out of the ground. One house had a fallen, rusted fence tangled up with dead sunflowers and wistaria. Someone had hooped a length of iron into a heart shape and put it up over the front gate: it was black with rust, but the creeper had reached out and claimed it with tendrils. People had been living there for years, for generations, you could tell.

But none of this seemed real in the world. It didn't hurt me, any of it, being only dreaming, perhaps, and botanical solecisms – the things I use like cottonwool to pack into the real wounds.

No, but I mustn't wander. I was walking steadily, silently through Athlone. And came out eventually on to the concrete freeway, where a section was cordoned off with drums and detour signs. Through swathes of the drizzle I saw the massive steel armature of struts for a new bridge; parts of it already formed in concrete, but dulled for the present by rain. There was a group of prefab sheds at the edge of the road – latrines and shacks for the site workers. On the doorstep of one there was a glowing brazier: sticks, maybe grass and charcoal, lit inside an old, pierced tin. A worker was sitting on an up-ended crate nearby, huddling over its warmth; drinking something from an enamelled mug. He had a heavy-duty plastic rain-cape, draped over his head and shoulders.

Saw the mud running where the rain spattered down on to the earthworks, forming tiny channels. Ochreous colour. Yet you think of the Cape flats sand as grey, usually – lifeless. Because the plain was covered once by sea: that what they say? Sometimes people unearth the bleached fossils of sea-shells in their gardens.

Why are they building roads? Into the townships; up to the borders, to Namibia. Some people say it's because of progress. This lift in the economy, because of gold getting costly: means growth, busier commerce – heavier traffic. Other people say it's a symptom of decline: as capitalism cracks apart, so it has to bolt itself together with more and more massive techniques. Ja, the bitter-enders still want imperial roads: sturdy ones to carry jeeps, armoured cars, missile-trucks.

I miss Marianne and Nicholas, angrily almost. They know the answers to these things. They set me right, usually.

Couldn't get to the bank, of course. Arrived home feeling translucent, and cool as glass; with my shoes sodden, soaked through, and my dress clinging to my body. But I'm getting stronger, I think. Felt far less tired today than I did yesterday, or the day before. And I've been jolted to realize how many things I've let slip. The rent is due in a few days' time, and the last electricity bill is still tacked up in the kitchen, unpaid. Tomorrow. Tomorrow I'm going to go into Mowbray to sort things out.

On Tuesday evening I woke up suddenly, uneasy, and with a pulsing headache.

Felicia was standing in the doorway, hesitant. Looked relieved when I sat up. 'Anna?' she said. I stared back at her, trying to smile, to seem calm. 'I must go now,' she said. 'We can't use this place any more.' Trying to push aside the aching confusion in my skull, I whispered, 'Right now? No look, honey, we're . . . I'm going to start the supper in a minute, it won't take long. Then we'll see after that?'

There was a tiny puckering of her upper lip, and she shook her head slightly, thinking to herself. 'Okay,' she said finally. 'But look, I'm not hungry. Haven't you got some bread there?' She was glancing over the few parcels on the rug. 'We can have bread and cheese. Just something quick, man.'

She slipped the canvas rucksack off her shoulder and hung it over the back of a chair in the kitchen. Pushing up the sleeves of her sweater, she began to slice the bread. In a hurry to leave.

I reached for a packet of powdered soup and tried to rip it open with my fingers: but struggled with tough layers of foil and plastic. Couldn't light the gas properly either, but burnt down match after match until the blue flame finally flared.

She hadn't mentioned the note. And - obscurely - I was afraid to ask.

So we talked about other things, over supper. Or at least, I spoke - in between playing with the crusts of my bread or dabbling my spoon unwillingly in the gelatinous, onion-fragrant soup.

Stung at last, though, she cried out, 'Well, it has to be like this. How do you think guerrilla fighting works? One thing the boers taught us.' Her voice petered out for a few seconds; but then she added: 'It has to go on for years, you've got to keep up fighting, keep the little sparks alive, to encourage people. Otherwise they just get ground down, with poverty and suffering, man.'

157

As she was speaking, the stiffness of her face dissolved and she was alive, suddenly; giving. Speaking is a radical act, maybe: it's a miracle how people change when they venture into breaking words, yielding up the frozen state of solitude. I came near to acquiescence, listening to Felicia's glittering riskiness.

'Haven't you ever seen a river-bed,' she blazed at me, 'that's cut away in solid rock? That's just from the water, you know, like grinding over it for millions of years, with little stones tumbling – and it carves out, the water, millions of drops of water streaming – they carve out river-beds and canyons and cathedrals of gullies, in the solid rock.' She paused for a moment, dazed with feeling. But readying herself to speak again, in a rush. And there was something – not the line of her jawbone, or the vivid light in her eyes – something about her that stabbed at me sharply, catching my breath away. 'If, if I need to be part of the stream,' she carried on, 'if I'm just one of those tiny pebbles, then that's the real drama: that's what I want to be, it's my role.'

I sat very still, trying to breathe; bruised by the physical impact that she made on me. Waiting patiently till I could visualize a single branch from a pear tree. I tried thinking of the flimsy, tasselled blossoms that cluster along the purplish length of the knobbed twigs. But I was too tired: flowers eluded me. There was nothing but a faint trace of textures. White petals crushed in the hand; tiny grains crumbling away to powder.

The drizzle outside pattered steadily down on to concrete; on to the leaves of mint, geranium and dormant marigold; on to the knotted plastic bags full of rubbish in the alleyway.

When there was finally a stillness in my heart again, I tried to speak. 'But Felicia, isn't the struggle the workers' own fight; isn't change finding its way right now through strikes and boycotts and demonstrations, and . . . and . . . non-collaboration?' I wanted to add, 'Isn't this vision of a bloody tide only the white person's impotent fantasy, Felicia: why do you want to make it real?' But I choked back that wishful assertion, unwilling to hear her answers.

She looked at me with her suave, impatient eyes: 'Of course, man, of course it's a popular struggle; but do you think there's no place for me, just because I . . . well, because.' She was angry, suddenly. 'I tell you, I tell you, you need the inspiration too, like victories, sometimes.'

158

She stood up swiftly, gaunt for an instant as she gathered up her plates and cutlery: went into the scullery and crashed the things under running water for a moment or two. When she turned back to me she was already briskly pushing down her sleeves, and searching for her rucksack.

'Felicia?' I muttered; and she glanced at me, irritably. I couldn't continue, and she looked away, dismissing me with a brief tightening of her lips. Softly she moved out of the kitchen, heading for the passage, after a pause only to say, 'Listen, thanks.' I followed her to the front door – reluctance stiffening each step.

That was where we waited, unfamiliar with the language of cold farewells. Under the painted iron lace with its rustling, faded capsules of the dead morning-glory flowers; each of us lit by the streaky shadows of the mercury vapour lamp. That was when she told me, 'You know he is.'

And she was gone then. The damp geranium leaves near the gate shivering as she brushed past them.

I was left feeling feverish, stupefied by my own ignorance. I went into the bedroom, and lay face down on the mattress, on the tumbled blankets: my face on the damp linen of the pillowcase and my hands burning, my hands were burning with the scented, smoky richness of her hair that I have never touched.

CHAPTER 6

I've been trying to read, but somehow I can't seem to concentrate.

In Mowbray this morning there were so many people all around me, pedestrians picking their way, with umbrellas bumping and knocking. Rainwater was dripping from the shops' canvas awnings; and in a gutter, where the metal grate was blocked by litter and dead leaves from the rubber tree, I saw a miniature torrent of sculptured, iron-coloured water, seething. Women getting their stockings splashed; students, young people – in love with the bright wetness and the rich feeling of boots, corduroys, Aran-knit sweaters. But most of the people looked worn-out – too burdened to revel in the wintriness. I passed an old man huddled into an ex-army greatcoat that reeked mustily of pipe tobacco. He was coming out of the cobbler's, with a brown paper packet under his arm, crumpled to the shape of his mended shoes. Holding a plastic shopping-bag over his head, and staring straight ahead of him with cataracted, canny eyes. Around him, women were trudging stolidly along the pavement on painful feet. Dressed in sagging, second-hand clothes too drab to signify anything more than decency. The older women wore turbans, berets, cloches to cover their hair, but some women of my own age had delicately braided patterns and combed partings in hair that was soft as smoke.

Passing the pub on the corner I heard the ugly clamour of people getting drunk at eleven o'clock in the morning; suppose it's cane they drink, or gin: a choking stench came from behind the high wooden shutters. You could hear the people inside groaning out fragments of songs and jeers and laughter. There was a scrawny-looking woman, not old, hovering on the red-polished stoep of the place, waiting for someone to come out, maybe. Her own breath blazing too; and a fixed, viciously sad smile of deference on her

160

face.

There used to be a block of condemned buildings – old shops and warehouses – opposite the bottlestore. They're beginning to demolish them now, though, and it's strange to look up and suddenly see a buttress of the mountain, dark with wind and cloud, where there used to be brick façades with boarded-up windows, dusty panes of glass. A few walls are still standing, but it's mostly all rubble now: with the swaying iron rods sticking out of the ruined masonry – metal grids with huge clots of stone, concrete still stuck to them. One of the big chain stores is setting up a new branch.

Had a couple of books to take back to the library. There was the usual business at the issue desk, of apologizing for their lateness and trying to find small change, while the librarian sorted through the cards in her tray. And afterwards I couldn't think of anything to take out: found myself vacantly gazing at the shelf of recommended books, with the fluorescent light gleaming off their plastic covers. Thrillers; romances; science fiction; historical romances; biography. There was a smell of dust in the building, and floor wax. I stood next to one of the book-cases, pretending to be browsing; occasionally lifting down a book and riffling through it. As I hovered there, I heard the talk of two women in the foyer who were waiting, like me, for the drizzle to lighten. They'd packed their library books in with the tumble of blankets and toys in their babies' prams. And there was a tiny girl clutching a fistful of her mother's skirt. 'Mm, mm,' one kept agreeing with the other, absent-mindedly humming a kind of accompaniment. 'Yes, after all; that's true, I think.' Her friend was saying, 'Children are very resilient, basically, you know: they do adjust, I mean?' The other woman hummed, with her eyes wandering elsewhere – over the librarian's notice-board: poster for a variety concert; the city orchestra's programme for the season; dustjackets of new books. 'And when you think, it's not as though she hasn't got a father at all: you know she spends the week-ends with him, and er, I think she's come to terms with it. Don't you think?'

I looked at the little kid. Clinging to the gathered fold of her mother's skirt.

The novel in my hands was only paper and ink, I suddenly knew. A hot surge rose in my throat and I was wanting – I almost lost myself, almost strode over to that woman – wanting to shout out a blazing refutation.

But I didn't; luckily I didn't make a fool of myself. I'd only have ended in a fit of stormy, racking wordlessness, I know, and have had to be led away while people stood watching, shaking their heads.

I rushed out of the library then, striding past those troubled, uncertain women with their children; racing, because I wanted to be blinded, to be stunned by the rain on my skin. I still had to go to the chemist and the supermarket – couple of things I needed. Should have taken Disprins before I left, perhaps. Fierce cramp I had. Maybe what was secretly goading me. Just that?

Crossed the main road again, wary of traffic that veered too quickly over the fans of water on the tar. Clenching my jaw to hold down the words that roared in my mouth. It's not the way to change things. No, you must be calm, reasoned: people won't listen to you otherwise.

If you're really dedicated to a cause, you have to make yourself invincible, don't you. But how? Don't you fight back only when something is destroying you, when you're already half conquered. How? Have to pretend, maybe: that nothing hurts your flesh; nothing violates your dignity. A car came skidding past, startling me: but I was only splashed, and angered by my own irritability. I was out of temper with myself and other people, and even the cold air. Still wondering: to be invulnerable, must you pretend to have no flesh and no dignity? Might as well pretend you have no being, then. Be worse than conquered, worse than dead, in some permanent state of hysteria.

There were strings of buses travelling along the main road this morning, just about empty, most of them. One I saw was painted all over with labels – zany advertising for a French drink: 'le driver', 'le front wheel', 'le passengers' . . . things like that. So silly, you wanted to grin. But silliness alongside the hard, frosted edge of a smashed window-pane? It's difficult to think of commerce as witty when you remember the smell inside those deserted buses, of cold vinyl, stamped-out cigarette ash, and tainted iron.

There's a second chemist in Mowbray now. Crowded with people, I saw, peering beyond the flickering half shadow in the plate glass front. And remembering, I went in, jangling some electronic light beam with my shins as I entered. It's strange how one's mood can lift when the eyes are invaded by a bright haze and the multiple reflections of light from glassy surfaces. Walking slowly along the rows, gazing at the displays, searching for something, I could see why people liked to browse there. So many things – medicines, luxuries, trinkets. Little porcelain animals flecked with pinkish crystals: supposed to be weather predictors. Fancy harsh-smelling soaps in the shapes of cartoon characters. Creams to make your hair straight, or your skin lighter. There was a basket at the cosmetics counter, filled with bottles of nail varnish, eye shadow kits, tubes of mascara: special offers. Get something for Constance, I thought. But then – she never wears make-up.

Found myself glancing at bottles of hair-conditioning shampoo. And moved on quickly, in self-taught guilt. What I really needed was tampons, not luxuries. Walking up to the counter with the small box I wondered abut the women who earn maybe sixty rand a month. To spend more than a rand on these secret things – how can they manage? I was aware suddenly of the noise in the shop, from dozens of people chattering, from piped muzak, from a till that kept jingling and bleeping. I joined a queue and stood there furtively holding my purchase against my body. You don't let men see you buying them.

There were sweets on the counter – last-minute tempting reminders. I saw a jar filled with twisted sticks of amber-coloured barley sugar. Thinking how Mom used to buy it for us when we were tiny kids, vaguely believing that it was good for us. These were loosely wrapped in cellophane, as I remembered them. Except that they used to cost a penny, maybe tuppence – and these sticks were fifteen cents apiece.

Still waiting, I let my gaze wander. Saw a life-size cardboard cut-out of a woman in a bikini, holding a camera. Why, I wondered. And high up on the walls there were blown-up, back-lit transparencies, pictures of children, puppies, surfers, model girls – all emblazoned with the brand-name of a film. Miraculous images on that glowing paper, where people were given back the likenesses of themselves, except stripped of the dragging physicality of real existence. Is that what people really want to buy: exemption from struggle? A sudden taste of sweet, dissolving glucose flooded my mouth.

163

Near the ceiling a suspended mirror responded to my queries with the image of a woman staring up, trying to stare into the face of capitalism. I had to swallow down the sweet taste of my childhood then as I tried to think. Nothing is so simple and transparent? Somehow one emerges from that locked state. Somewhere was an I able to observe that woman observing.

Yet how is it possible. Unless somewhere in the mind there is an unreachable, encysted core of memory where the still-born twin of the soul lies trapped in permanent, living nightmare; so that *there* would be the hidden place necessary for transformations, dialectic, redemption. A world of spirits, or a Forest of Arden. I'm not going crazy, you know. I don't want to be insane. And I was saved once, like any other child - I must have been; from that speechless struggle between infant and parent: saved perhaps when I stumbled into the arena of humanness, where the common dreams of a society lie scattered underfoot, dry and powdery; as unremarked as grains of sand or the taste of words. It's a region we're encouraged to start finding at the age of five or six, in the kindergarten. I can remember kneeling on a seagrass mat and counting over those dyed wooden beads that I'd threaded on to string. Or using wax crayons to colour in the images of children and mothers and toys and fathers.

But then why do we need rescuing all over again, in our adolescence? Finding ourselves in deadly conflict for a second, or possibly a third time, as the buried dream threatens to wake and burst out from beneath the dead cells of memory. I remember that I peered into mirrors as a young girl of 14 or 15. Who does she think she is. I was Anton Rossouw's graceless daughter; and there were no answers for me in the Sixties, when the new Romantic artists were rejecting what they called society.

There was a half-page article in the newspaper on gang violence in the prisons and on the Cape Flats. It's topical, because there's been alarm amongst the suburbanites recently about rising crime statistics: people want more policemen, better pay for the cops - to beat the problem, they think. There were a couple of over-exposed, greyish photographs of those three-tiered council tenement blocks. Of a woman standing next to the cast-iron railing of a staircase, with a child heavy in her arms - a bleak, worried look on her face.

She was quoted, talking about the gangs that prey on the residents there. 'I can't even put out my plants, in the sunlight, because they come and steal them.' A group of a dozen men held her up early one morning as she was setting out for work: 'I gave them my watch and my handbag, my purse: and I was so scared because there wasn't much money in it, so I thought they might hurt me.' They only jostled her, though, and insulted her. Their breath stinking, she said, of dagga. 'And now I would really leave this place: I'm thinking of my child. But we don't have any money, so where else can we go?' In the background of the photograph, you saw the drab sand piled up over the concrete courtyards and mingled with the small black seeds of Port Jackson: blown there by the scouring wind of the marshy plains. She was a shop assistant, apparently.

And a man from Manenberg spoke angrily, helplessly, about the gang that entered his sitting-room one evening. 'They came before, you know. The time before, they took money and a watch and the radio.' There was no photograph of him, but the reporter wrote that the man looked harassed and ill. 'This time they raped my wife: in front of me; they tied me up, seven of them, and then they had a gun at my head and they took it in turns to rape her.' He said he joined the local vigilantes after that. Bitter, he felt, that the orthodox police didn't help them more, or allow them to be armed. 'All we want is to live a decent, peaceful life, and yet how can we? We're terrorized by these people, man, they're like packs, you know, packs of wild animals. And the police do nothing: too busy beating up children. Whatever they do. Arresting these poor people that haven't got passes.'

Seems that commerce and industry hardly need to fund this bourgeois revolution: there are enough people on the brink, struggling upwards - willing to share power with the whites. That man from Manenberg castigating the state for not being oppressive enough. . . .

What the gangs desire; what they attack. The reporter interviewed a gang member. Who said that he'd joined his gang while in prison. 'Now I feel like a man, djy ken? Because I'm a member of the Sexy Boys.' He wasn't a person who spoke eagerly. 'Ag ny man, they's my brothers. I know they will always be loyal for me, and I'm loyal for them. Before I was a member, I was just a nothing; but now I'm a man.'

Crime is a kind of political ritual? But peripheral, instead of all-pervading. I'm afraid of being reduced to scepticism. But I'm also afraid that any kind of social ethos – any kind at all – has to institute itself through a constant, iterative communion of violence. For any religion to have the status of a true faith it must be accompanied by inquisition and jihad; a massacre of St Bartholomew's day. Just as rebellions must inevitably be put down in any state or colony or empire. Because dissent by its simple existence seems to threaten the validity of our shared dreams and systems of signs – those things that make us human. Even though those systems can never be falsified, having no truth in themselves. And it's a curious thing: seems that violence in a modern state keeps people divided into castes, and unites them only within some system of power and economics. So that when dispossessed, frustrated individuals band together and redefine themselves through shared acts of violence, their sacraments have to be called illegal. Those medieval European notions of good and evil begin to turn slow cartwheels in my mind. Now it's possible for a policeman to act on caprice and pour methylated spirits over a sleeping vagrant before setting him alight and burning him to death. Or he can tear the clothes from, and insult and finally rape a frantic woman who has no permit to be in Cape Town. And he'll be cautioned in court, perhaps fined, perhaps given a suspended sentence. . . .

Marianne would never agree with me about these things. 'Nee, Anna. I don't know how you can say there is some reason for it? The whole thing is, it isn't reason at all. Nê? Religion is what drugs people, and . . . ag Anna, man.' It's an argument we've often had. She frowning at me, bewildered. 'It's the church that keeps the people oppressed, telling them it will all be fine – in heaven. Or God loves them. Something. "'n Christen aanvaar sy noodlot, want selfs lyding is God se plan."' Staring at me with her light-blue eyes fretfully narrowed. 'It's just a conspiracy, you know: a invention of the ruling classes to keep the masses sub –? Wat's die woord. Subdued? No. . . . But that's the only reason for it, I tell you, Anna.'

It's what you call teleological fallacy, isn't it. When a theory collapses cause, effect, reason and motive into one. And it's useless my trying to tell Marianne that I'm not justifying anything. That I simply want to understand; that I'm not content to invoke evil, or

166

wrong-headedness, or outright cynicism.

There's another story under the crime reporter's by-line. A dozen people appeared before a magistrate yesterday on a group charge of murder. This is the aftermath of that terrible incident where a man was stoned to death on a dilapidated old road in the semi-rural, semi-industrial outskirts of the city. It isn't easy to escape the fact that the man who sat there in the dust, staring back at the world with an already dying gaze, was 'white'. While the accused – people in their late teens, maybe students or workers, along with a couple of teachers – are 'black'. Perhaps no amount of periphrastic subtlety can completely conceal this: that on the popular level the revolution that is raging here now is a racist one.

And I'm beginning to use the quirkish quotation marks and parentheses of someone for whom language has been ripped out of its cultural context. . . .

It's because in our human world they murder all the heroes. That's why.

I'm not imagining that, you know: it's the truth. The people who reject racism and see history rather as war between classes – the progressive leaders get killed in hit-and-run car accidents; or disappear; or are discovered dead in their prison cells.

I can understand why those people are on trial, why they have to be. A worse thing, though, is that I understand why they will almost certainly be sentenced to death.

Couldn't really sleep last night with this wind raging – it was gale force, I'm certain. Stormy out at sea. They say that over the edge of the continental shelf the depth of the water is thousands of metres, utterly lightless, all shifting and heaving in masses as vast as mountains, shot through with the tiny, bright fishes. I was thinking of ships. While the wind kept lifting and falling, picking up slowly, steadily – before crashing down again in prolonged, massive waves of darkness and rain-cloud. And I was thinking of the people who have to sleep amongst the sand-dunes. For a few minutes there was hail. I could hear. Imagining the tiny, melting, stinging seeds of ice. I was thinking: they must have gone slurrying down over sacking and corrugated-iron sheets.

And Marianne has gone. I heard on Friday that she's gone, resigned.

167

It's raining still; it's been raining constantly. But at least that means that the wind dies down and there's a respite from all the noise; a kind of peace, muskily sweet as the sandalwood smoke that drifts from doorways in Athlone.

I keep thinking that I don't want to be here; not in Athlone or Observatory.

Thinking of the mountains in the Boland, those folded, lost ranges that lie between Franschhoek and Grabouw. I remember. Pelting rainstorms in those valleys, and everything scented with heath and reed and bitterwater. A scree of smooth white pebbles alongside a swollen, coppery-coloured, translucent stream where I dipped down once to drink, brushing aside damp branches of mimosa turned dark as iron in the rain. And buried in amongst the deep vegetation in the sloots I once saw the protea flowers, pearlescent and velvety against their broad, placid leaves.

There's another thing I can't put out of my mind. Mr Jeffries is still busy trying to revise the timetable – and he's beginning to look appallingly sick. His table in the staffroom is littered with large sheets of roughly pencilled drawing paper, and he keeps a half-empty cup of black coffee always at his elbow, with half-smoked cigarettes smouldering in the saucer as well as in the ash-tray. Deathly he looks, with his skin gone into tiny creases, and greyed. Smoking cuts down the peripheral circulation; he's gassing himself to death very, very slowly, taking in the slow, drifting smoke of the poison in tiny gulps each day. Makes me so angry I even went up to him, Wednesday, was it, or Thursday and tried bantering, jokily remonstrating with him. But even his sarcasm has been blunted – by exhaustion, it turned out. He hasn't slept properly since term began: keeps waking up with something nagging at him, and he'll have to light up a cigarette and draw at it furiously until he realizes finally what the problem is. That he's given Suleiman the seven B's for Geography when they're already scheduled to be at Woodwork or Domestic Science or Economics. Or else he'll have put down the Matrics for a Biology lesson when the six D's need the lab, because it's one of the few rooms large enough to hold forty-six kids. 'It's a hell of a job, man: why they can't use a computer. . . . Do it for us down at the department. You'd think, hey?'

He was striking a match as he spoke to me, but fumbled the movement, and the flimsy sliver of pine snapped. He cursed, reaching for another. And then, trying in turn to make a joke, he said, 'You're not also thinking of resigning, are you? Because I wish you'd just tell me now. If you don't want me to have a nervous breakdown, man.' The cigarette caught. Pungent, rich smell of quietly burning paper and the dark-gold, shredded tobacco.

I can't help feeling that my own desire for absolution is far less important than responsibility to my colleagues. And yet I also know that this sober, bourgeois dutifulness is part of the problem. Marianne was right to resign, I think. And Nicholas too.

I haven't told you. I called in at his house a few days ago. The front door was open, but I tapped at it uncertainly anyway. Waiting there on the dusty, trellised-in stoep: could see a kind of dresser in the passage-way, built from crates and covered with a tacked-up curtain of darkly woven cloth. Someone came to the door at last. Dull-faced, she looked. Or maybe I just couldn't understand: such impassive features. I tried to smile, introducing myself, but she looked all the more cold. Feel so tempted sometimes just to throw up my hands in a temper, and curse, and exclaim that I don't know how to read English-speaking people. But that'd be too simple, I'm sure. She gave out the information slowly, in small, grudging portions. Nick was in London, had been there for two weeks already. And I blurted out, 'Oh of course, I suppose his draft . . .?' But she was unwilling to give away any more. 'He's resigned from the school,' was all she said, flatly.

I stared for a minute at a poster on the wall behind her. Picture of Ché Guevara – glamorous revolutionary. With a last gathering of pride I thanked her, shortly, and turned away. It was drizzling again, softly. I walked blindly down the little pathway of grass-covered flagstones; catching a vague glimmering only of the stunted hawthorn that crowded in the gateway. A few partly blackened, sickly yellow berries still clinging to the branches.

I'd known all along that Nick was expecting his call-up papers, because of finishing university last year. But I think he was hoping to see his kids through to the end of their standard nine year. Very earnest, very eager: 'Naaa, hell, it's not really fair, I reckon, to just leave them in the middle. Then they've got to get used to a new teacher; the new person's got to get to know them, to find out the syllabus. . . . It would just be a bad scene.'

So now he's also gone into exile. There are supposed to be hundreds of South Africans in London, Amsterdam . . . those places. He was right to go, of course – had no choice. And now I'm beginning to see why it was right for Papa too. Perhaps it was necessary for him to abandon us. Any constancy in men here seems to lead to their permanent incarceration, or death. Or else it leads to enslavement, either to alcohol, insanity, other men – or to the brutal hysteria of manhood and soldiering. The women grow hardened too – burdened by the agonies of their children and the weaknesses of their husbands; except that their constancy has a kind of power to it: the strength of commitment.

In Anton's case also, it really was a return, I think: he with his intellectual and cultural rootedness in Europe. But then he was a part of his own generation, his own class, and that Sestiger ethos arose along with the emergence of the new Afrikaner *haute bourgeoisie*. With its super-sophisticated delight in contemporary art movements overseas, the full-blown decadence of *ars gratia artis*, and individualism glorified: die vreeslike lyding van die kunstenaar, en sy groot, oneindige soektog. . . .

I used to think in private that I hated Papa. Believed I was trapped forever by my own wistful sketches of him in air; light; silver-point. That I could never get away from the gentle, muscular leanness of his torso; from memories of his politely earnest face, memories of his voice – twilight-tinged, pedantic. 'Well, Anna, I'm glad to hear that your studies are progressing well. . . .'

But now I understand that he simply never taught me the words for hatred, any more than he taught me ones for love. And I also know when I should have learned that language from him. Aren't fathers supposed to feel intolerable stirrings when their daughters reach fifteen or sixteen and still want to be hugged, to be crushed against the cable-knit sweater; and leave kisses smothered in his beard, on the faintly dryish skin of his cheeks? I can only imagine this. But then: maybe some redisposition is worked out. And you learn some language of femininity in your nascent womanhood, some dialect that is foreign to the family, but well-known to a culture that demands you should tease and be coy. Be yourself; be a woman; be like your mother. Be an actress.

For me it would be a desertion, to leave my homeland now.

170

Oupa's ancestors arrived here almost three hundred years ago – Protestant fugitives from France, relocated by kindness of the Dutch, while Ouma's people settled even earlier – maybe fortune seekers. Muscular young adventurers, keen to leap up from an aspirant class to the prosperous one of self-made, fat-necked people: and something Calvinist also, wasn't it, to grapple with the world and win your pre-ordained destiny. Coming from a country where even God's sea needed to be held back by human inventiveness; while the deep-bellied, gilt-curlicued ships that creaked into port at Amsterdam would reveal, stuffed into their deep holds, the fragrant, rich, multi-coloured proof of enterprise and risk and reward. To enter a new world upon the earth: that was why Ouma's people came here in those wooden ships whose pilots knew how to chase down and ride the Trades; to be lifted down in the end into the longboats, clutching at the tar-brown ropes; and then to be rowed, choking, almost blinded with tears, rowed through the crackling, wind-spun surf in the bay: struggling to utter psalms, or to sing – only the salt in one's mouth, and the slight bleeding of the gums . . . De Goede Hoop; De Kaap de Goede Hoop.

And Constance's family. Gran's ancestors were some town-dwelling, maybe slightly shabby aristocrats who fled those revolutions of the nineteenth century in Europe. Could I go now to my great-great-great-grandmother's house in Bonn; or to Prussia, or Bavaria? When those countries don't exist anymore, I think. While Granpa was the son of a recent immigrant from Ireland, some young, mercurial cynic after the sort of fortune that you shook out of the damp river sand; curious, probably, about the legendary Zulus; and, with a war spoiling, willing to pick up a rifle and ride with the rebel Boers against the hated British imperialists.

Seems that my ancestors were always ones to escape, to head elsewhere, searching for something, yearning – and imagining that the answers could be found in literal quests across the seas. But since human beings have migrated right across the planet now, I can't help feeling that a phase has ended, and that now we have to stay put – to face our historical condition. Only autistic children, and mystics and Romantics struggle to hold on to a wholly self-enclosed unity. Maybe it's necessary, if you're realistically committed to a changed world – that you accept the taint that comes from existing in the present one.

I remember an early poem of Papa's, in *Stedelike Kuns*. Two people lie in bed in the late afternoon, with the dusk drawing fly-blown shadows across the wall; listening to the hectic sounds of teen-age children playing soccer in the street outside – those tall, languorous youths who recognize the glamour of their bodies. One of the lovers is thinking, or they're both thinking, about the decades of historical conscience that fence them in, barbing their privileged existence in one another's arms. And they comfort one another, not with lyricism, not with amnesia – but with unashamed banalities. Ek is lief vir jou. It would only be an impassioned adolescent who did not know that the phrase is already steeped in the sense of its own incompleteness – who would dare to withhold it on grounds that it did not express the absolute truth. Ek bemin jou hare; en jou arms, hier.

So we stand braced, then, with our backs to the wall.

And yet.

That is what we did, once. Although we weren't braced – since we never expected the police to storm us like that. The wide street just ahead of us, with its tarred traffic islands; the tall blocks of offices opposite. And behind us was the cool grey sandstone hewn out of the giant rough blocks off the mountain; darkened in the wet, because it was early winter then, and drizzling. The tar in the streets was black and you could smell – there was a faint scent rising – resin, maybe, bitumen. . . . We were standing on the steps outside the side-door from the transept; with a small arch overhead and water dripping down, seeping from the keystone. When that terror swept down over us and we were sent spilling, crashing into one another by that dense wall of solid-packed, flailing policemen: their boots they used, fists, and those truncheons and even their bodies, massively lunging into us. But the iron bar fell away from the door, and all of us were sinking back then, pushed, almost lifted up with the press of other people's thighs and chests, surging backward right through the gaping place into a sudden absence of movement, of sound – of anything living, it seemed.

That really happened. Even if it was nothing; nothing at all – it still really happened.

Sometimes I wonder whether these small, hard keys at my fingertips are real or merely the abstract code for some incorporeal

172

system. At times they seem to generate nothing but a sharp, incessant clatter. Also, I wonder more and more often now whether Memmi wasn't right. I've tried so hard to resist – believing, still believing that history cannot be deadlocked, that it's a contradiction in terms, absurd to speak of impasse. I've always felt a fierce, perhaps suspiciously vehement impatience with those English-speakers who lay claim so self-flatteringly to powerlessness. Years ago I rejected their bravely weak, sepia-tinged literature of regret. No one exists outside of history, I used to think, unless they've surrendered their humanness. Because we're not aerophagous after all – we feed, think, dream, trade, speak: we're not like those drab-leaved, spiky epiphytes that you sometimes see in people's gardens, suspended by a piece of grey string from the branches of a tree. Dull, slow-growing plants that only rarely put out a small, rustling showiness of bright flowers. We're human beings: survivors of floods, catastrophes and even our myths; ja, we're living and responsive; and answerable.

No survivor ever finally escapes the wordless, ghostly memories of others.

It must be late.

I peeped through the tiny square of glass in the bathroom window, and there's a vivid whiteness across the sky again. What is it making the clouds so bright? Saw the fig tree outlined against the dazzle – silhouette of its bare branches, moving in the wind.

I ought to go and visit Constance, I know. She must have been back for at least a week by now. And yet, if I'm truthful about my selfishness, I really don't want to. Feel reluctant to go out at all these days, and just thinking about conversations with Mom in particular leaves me feeling apprehensive.

The way she is these days I find upsetting: that aggressive intensity of hers; the unabashedly generous way she'll shape her mouth to form a groan or a cynical smile. And it's odd too that she's more emphatically extrovert now – she'll raise her whole arm or shrug heavily to make a point – yet also more withdrawn; with aspects of herself slumped broodingly inward.

Could take her a present, perhaps: a geranium in a small earthenware pot. Anyone else would like that. Or I could take her a few books to read, something better than the hotch-potch of mystical science and thrillers she allows herself to become absorbed in. But I know: she'd say, 'Ah thanks, Anna, that's nice of you,' and put them down on the rug at her feet, or even shove them carelessly under the easy-chair.

Maybe I'm just inventing excuses. It wouldn't be such an ordeal after all. She'd want to talk – about the train journey, about the family in Natal: and I could sit and listen softly, watching the way her features flickered. Mom must have been beautiful once, I think: that strong jaw, and those jutting, almost broad cheekbones. The deep-set hazel eyes. There are still the remnants about her of a stubbornly fiery youth. And she still wears her beloved scarves, silk or chiffon, casually knotted at her throat – where they stiffen and move uneasily now against her ageing, sunburnt skin.

What would I do, though, if she were to abandon her own story and begin a blunt interrogation of me. If she were to say unexpectedly, irritably almost, 'Don't you go out with people, Anna. I mean, aren't you interested in men at all?' I'd be left then having to think instantly of ways to flick aside the empty, unheard, weightless remark. What could anyone mean. To interfere so overbearingly. There must be a way to annihilate such questions – comments that are insubstantial in any case, if words are only the impact of air against the human tympanum; nothing at all, really, weightless as flies, as air. It's horrible, the way I can hear her words in my ears right now – exactly her intonations: that loudness, the callous self-confidence, dinning inside me, over and over. Well, of course, I don't mean to pry. Interfering woman. It isn't my business, but what on earth are you afraid of?

It'll rain soon again, I think. There's a brilliant clarity in the air – as though the whole world were on the threshold of exquisite brightness; of sadness.

In ten years' time, or twenty years, when Azania's come – the fig tree will probably still be there, feeding the starlings with its yellowed, bursting fruit in March. There might still be a dog-kennel in that concrete yard, and the roofs in the neighbourhood might still be made of metal sheets that come skidding, smashing down in the winter storms. Only there'll be differences. And maybe that's why the children now have no choice but to choose. They're the ones who have a future at stake, and they're the only ones coura-

174

geous enough, innocent enough to reject their parents' anxious conservatism. Suppose that's why they've hardened their faces and abandoned games of football played in the streets, and the dances at the discotheque. Why teenagers in Zimbabwe left their studies and put on battle-dress, living in camps in the bush for years – sleeping on the hard earth, digging out the pupae of ants under stones for a sweet and rich, if meagre food: to bring down a government. Wilson said one night with such a ravaged bitterness: 'We never fucken wanted violence. It's the last thing a person ever wants in the world: but we driven to it, man, by the fucken state. And that's the one thing, I tell you, in the end – that's the one thing I'm never going to forgive the bastards for.'

I just wish that our choices weren't broken down to such simple polarities of English or Afrikaans, black or white, liberal or radical. . . . For years now I've longed for a politics that would be more profound than revolution itself, yet still simple enough to explain the fate of my own brother to me.

It's there in *Glas* as well. That kind of longing, I mean. Seems that Papa yearns for a system of description more intricate even than the physics that accounts for the ambivalent status of vitreous substances. Of fused silica, limestone, and soda. Because there is no hard-edged, jagged break between the visions that resurrect themselves in the private mind – and the illusions of a state. The dream of the country. There's something more sinuous, more warmly flowing than the dark-edged gaping of nothingness. Some pattern, he meant; rather than any object.

Mr Bezuidenhout has none of these problems, it seems. I remember one morning last term. Marianne and I had the creased pages of the newspaper open in front of us; both staring silently at a report of two children shot dead in the Transvaal. Mr Bezuidenhout came up and stood behind us. Heard him clear his throat: 'Exciting times,' he murmured, 'don't you think these are exciting times all the same.' His voice had grown emphatic with delight by the end of the sentence. Marianne refused to look up, but I turned slightly and glanced at him. His face had a soft gleam to it: the same glow of genuine bliss it takes on when he watches the students practising their synchronized marching for the athletes' parade each year, to a blaring music of old war-time marches. I noted the way his trousers strained over the thighs where his flesh was heavy – and had

175

never been muscle. No one would expect such a well-fed, comfortable man to pick up a placard and go out on to the streets with others in the face of tear-gas, iron-hard fists, boots, unleashed dogs; and rifles. There was a taste in my mouth of bitterness, and I turned away to find some comfort in Marianne's steady gaze; the ironical set to her jaw.

What is it.

I know that the children are the only ones who can fight this war. And yet if they are to die, it seems impossible that there can be any recognizable meaning left to the word 'tomorrow'. I've toyed sometimes with the concept of tragedy; but this dry pedantry is only one more imitation of Papa. And if there is a dead child somewhere, then, no matter whether the dark wind is blowing across the Cape Flats, off the snow of the eastern mountains – if there is a child lying somewhere in a state mortuary, small body bleak and fractured in places, still spattered, almost deformed by congealed blood, then, whether there is another season of spring when the mountain slopes are littered in blowsily glistening daisies and the fine, translucent bells of the tulpies – if there is a dead child in those refrigerated rooms without windows, where the metal coffins are stacked like drawers to make place for more deaths – then, despite the sea's drifting, slow and grey beneath the mountain's chains of buttress after buttress, despite everything, there are no longer meanings to comedy or tragedy, and the brittle terms of literary theory take on instead the irreducible, momentary shapes of history.

There is such a noise all around me, something clamouring and racketing in my ears.

There was a lull in the staffroom on Friday. Chris was sitting with his shoulders slumped and his arms loosely flung out in front of him. Slow white veils of smoke floating from between his lips as he contemplated something fixedly; his eyes wide, unblinking.

Hennie leaned back in his chair suddenly, hands raised. With a story to tell us, that a friend had told him, a friend who taught in Elsies River. Chris pursed his lips briefly and Suleiman stirred, drawing back a shoulder. 'They had helicopters: the police were coming over the school, buzzing the place with helicopters.' Anger made his voice sound almost gay, and when he glared around our small group, his teeth showed. Suleiman stared back at him.

176

'I'm telling you,' Hennie went on. 'Half a dozen of those military copters over the school grounds, hovering – just over the kids' heads.' There were armed policemen crowded in the gaping part where a panel had been slid away. 'The kids could see the bastards mocking them up there, and they just went crazy, man, they started screaming.' There had been some mass demonstration in the school grounds, and close on fifteen hundred children were assembled, milling around on the sandy playing fields. 'You know what a racket those helicopters make, just *one* of them – but the kids were still shouting over it, in unison: "Jou moer! Jou moer!" Neville says he went dizzy from the noise: the sound, just the pure noise of it was like sparks, like little lights bursting inside his mind. He thought the kids would – I don't know, he said they were screaming themselves – just berserk.'

We all watched Hennie, stilled by his story. Each of us hearing faint, inward echoes of screaming.

'Why . . .' Chris tried to ask; but his mouth had gone dry and he choked sourly on cigarette smoke.

'You asking me?' said Hennie. 'Maybe they just felt like some fun: scare the hell out of the kids, you know.' He was trying to separate himself from his own narrative. Thin, weightless edge to his voice. 'Neville says he was certain someone was going to get killed. Some of the boere had their rifles up, I mean, you could see it all from the ground. They were pretending to take aim; and they were laughing, they were roaring themselves sick with laughter inside the helicopters. From behind the guns.' Hennie's voice was petering out. 'Kids were chucking stones, and then the helicopters would lift away. I don't know, I think maybe a few shots were fired; only into the sand, luckily.'

I heard Chris whisper to himself – some small curse; and then he slumped back, shirt-sleeves rustling as he dropped his head on his arms. His cigarette had slowly wasted itself away to ash in the brown-stained saucer; but he didn't light up another.

It was drizzling outside. Could see through the glassed doors of the staffroom. Bronze gleam of wetness on the concrete stoep, and faintly sketched, dim streaks of light, of the rain across the playing ground.

177

Something has happened, some sort of accident.

I feel uncertain. Why are there so many words swirling in my mouth, faintly sweet, washing across my tongue and my gums, my teeth.

I need to try and piece these broken things back together.

I don't know anymore what the time is. Towards evening, I think, from the sounds outside: hear papers being blown about, and tin cans rattling in the gutters – the wind must be rising for the night's rain. It was that cracked pane in the kitchen window, where there's a fragment missing in one corner, and the fine cracks radiating. Faint traces of light there: maybe the spectrum is fully rebuffed and falls back in whiteness out of the broken, powdered angles. What is that they say. Everything you can see of another person is already dead. Skin, corneas, hair, teeth, nails. I wasn't evading anything; standing there, staring. But a transparent reflection of myself kept intervening, floating somewhere between me and the glass – yet somewhere also beyond the ghostly colours of the faintly star-lit plants in the yard. It was drizzling faintly, skittishly – maybe that's what I was thinking; and I thought suddenly, idly, that I could probably pull away one of those triangular pieces between the cracks. Just to save it from being blown out in a gale, perhaps, and splintering. The window frame trembles sometimes in the beetle-hollowed wood of the Victorian casement. So stupid. I worked at it carefully, tugging; and it came away, but so quickly that I hardly knew I was falling backward, while my hand was suddenly stiff, unbearably stiff. From the centre of my fist, spreading over the knuckles, came a slow seeping of blood.

The minutes seemed to become paralysed: everything became distended, swollen with time, and a thousand impressions filled out each second. The sense of flowing time must be centred somewhere precariously in the chemistry of being. The windowframe and the kitchen chairs, even the salt cellar – all seemed to lose their stable shapes. Only that perception must have been within me, I know. In me the impulses were racing, ja; and the blood was dropping away from the brain. I was trying to remember something. What to do? Cold water – run the wound under cold water. One thing. Or press down on the artery. But I was already sagging: I tried to reach out for one of the lost, remote objects around, but then I was slumping downward; the back of a chair caught against my ribs as I fell, and there was a sickening sluggishness everywhere, as even blazing light grew full of darkness. My eyes were wide, but nothing reached the corneal film; and I was still fighting to remember, What does one do. There was something singing inside my skull, a shimmering sound of crickets; while there was no heat, no sunlight, no veld.

Who are you?

For a moment I thought there was someone very near me, someone alive, breathing, and close enough to reach out and touch me.

Wasn't unconscious for very long, I think. The singing swelled and became bewilderingly rich, as though the whole house were swarming with crickets and cicadas. It must be the blood? Rushing back through the numb, lifeness tissue of the mind. Or cherubim maybe, in their massed choirs. I seem to have dragged myself here to the bedroom, and then tumbled on to the bed; content to sprawl while the singing subsided to a low, serene chittering.

The first time that ever happened to me I was 11 years old. We were crowding round the teacher's table during a biology lesson, to learn about the circulation of the blood. The teacher had come with a horse's heart that he'd bought from the abattoir. Ja: coming into the classroom with the thing still wrapped in a dark-stained parcel of brown paper. He spread sheets of newspaper everywhere, and then, with his shirtsleeves rolled up, began flashing dextrously at that hard-to-see object with scissors – I saw the bright metal of the blade – and forceps. Do you see the ventricles: the left, and here, here the right? And these? The left atrium, and here the right? . . . Atrium, the right atrium. Lifting out words, the neat structures with hands that glistened with a dark, sluggish liquid, until everything in reality was obscured by that viscous stuff. The thickness of the aorta, see, see it: and these, a miracle, these tough valves. He breaking into that hollow, thick-walled muscle to show us: while we shoved and stood on tip-toe, craning to see what he could mean by hauling out that mass of bloody tissue in front of us. Then I was reeling backwards, as my classmates receded into some remote distance, and all sound slowly deliquesced into a reedy rustling hum of light. And later, after some stifling journey, I rediscovered myself unexpectedly drooped at people's feet. Trying to sit up on the floorboards, and reeling; trying to lift my arms that had gone numb and heavy: my small, sombre face turned more

179

than white, they told me – turned grey.

This feeling keeps returning, that there is someone nearby. I wish that you would touch me, if you are really there.

What was I trying to think, though.

There are reddish smears on the pillows. It doesn't matter. Seem to hear my own thoughts lifting and falling. Or perhaps it is the wind racing down from the mountain: veering into rain; carrying the scents of earth and ash.

You. You are the real author of my meaning, aren't you.

Can already feel the wicker handle of my basket, digging into my fingers. Because tomorrow is another school day and I have to be ready: at half past six I must have rinsed my face, and dressed, and swallowed down my coffee; I must be ready to head off into the north-wester. Why. Why all that. Having to fuss with plastic bags tucked around the papers in my basket, to protect them from the wet. That feeling of the skin across your sternum turned transparent almost, and tightly stretched: with the rain dashing against you, infiltrating the turned-up collar of your raincoat. I keep trying to remember: there is someone I have to keep constantly in mind.

This is not right, though – that I can't seem to keep my hands pressed over the images that rustle in my mind. There's something that pushes me away, welling up; the silence inside words breaking out under my hands. And there is something forcefully streaming, carrying her further and further away from me. There is nothing but a hollow left now, gouged-out niches where the images of words should be standing. Light-filled, faintly dusty spaces accuse me. She's staring back, with those deep-set, flecked hazel eyes: staring out from shadows that shift and then disappear behind the fronds of ferns, the pale, budding croziers that are lifting – isn't there a trembling of green light. The plants are set out in front of her, ranked along the top of the veranda wall. Punnets filled with dark earth and the young seedlings – petunias and marigolds that she's seeded herself, in the ramshackle backyard greenhouse. And in old coffee tins, displayed in a row against the wall there are the ferns: maidenhair and sword ferns, and the bristling, vividly green asparagus ferns. Thanks, Anna, sweet of you to think of me. She is saying something? Oh hang on a sec, I've got something for you. Turning away: there is a woman, faceless, beginning to turn on her heels. She's trudging slowly, wearily back into a house. No, but she's going away, I can't be expected to reach her anymore: there are only words in the end left spurting up against the hard, translucent parts of my hands. I'm holding up my hands to the light bulb, higher than my heart they have to be. Is this true, I wonder. Can see the bones faintly visible under the skin: phalanges and metacarpals, white against the glow of light falling through the flesh. They're uniquely mine, these particular bones. And yet they've nothing to do with 'me'.

No, but I'm too tired now. And this isn't where I want to be at all.

I'd like to go away for a few days – ja, into the country. It won't be difficult, I'll put a few things into my rucksack, that's all, and hitch from the start of the national route in Mowbray. I want to go up the west coast, maybe to Elandsbaai.

It must be drizzling. The wind seems to have choked itself off into silence, and there's a feeling of calmness, of sweetness in the air.

I've never been to Elands in the winter. Wonder if it's the season for the rains there. Although that must be immaterial – there's been drought upcountry for years now. I remember the dust road we took from Het Kruis; and the tumbleweeds that came drifting down off the sandy verges into the path of the Land-rover – dried into shapes of bleached spikiness. And that hard-baked, reddish-yellow sand; the dead river-courses in the bottom of the valleys. It's a mesem scrub there, adapted to an arid climate. Lithops and conophytum cluster crowded amongst stones or in rock crevices; and aloe plants sprawl along the ground, healthily green- and ochre-flecked, even flowering at the tip – but with the long leaves at the base withered away into a papery greyness.

This is what I want. I want to be walking across that dry country; tramping over sand; low succulent plants; pebbles; scattered, glistening fragments of quartz. Have to carry water with me – remembering how François scowled when I wanted to drink from the farmer's rain-water tank. Anna, that's all they've got, hey.

I remember seeing pumpkins piled up in a corner of a broken-down thorn-kraal: giant white vegetables that were cracked open; been left there with the red inner pulp rotting away to a stringy mess of dried seed and fibre. For the goats to eat, Frans said. He explained about the reeds then, how one summer when there was

181

nothing left for the sheep and goats in the entire valley the farmers set fire to the river, to all those miles and miles of densely clustered bulrush, so that the animals would have the green shoots of the re-growth to nuzzle at.

I'm thinking about those tall, shivering reeds. The herons that beat their way out from somewhere near the remote, rustling centre of the vlei. Nesting there, probably. And the red bishops: I remember how there were dabs of singing bright colour scattered across the vast lake of reeds. And weaver-birds; crane; wild duck; cor-morants; pelicans; coot. François pointed out the names for me, finding them in the colour plates of his field-guide. We saw king-fishers – black and white ones, far more dazzling than all the other tiny, jewel-coloured kingfishers and bee-eaters in the book. They were poised above the stream when we glimpsed them, in a glis-tening, daredevil trio, weightlessly quivering right at the apex of some swiftly skimmed, upward lunge, and the three beaks already dipping downward, readied for the moment of the sheer drop down.

I'd camp at that abandoned station on the bywoner's land, where the giant, forked bluegum reared up above our sleeping place on the stone stoep. I remember being startled into wake-fulness at five in the morning: dismayed by a colossal, shimmering din of weaver-birds who seemed intent to destroy, over and over, the clumsy disc of the sun that had come in amongst their grass nests. That tree draped with their woven, straw-coloured nests wavering at the end of thin, stripped twigs – hundreds of them there must have been, and each nest with four or five or six birds. I remember the papery slips of the eucalyptus leaves – moving and rustling with all that imperious racket; and the sun's breaking repeatedly in amongst the dim grey, the burning white of those crystalline light forms.

François was grinning at me from the camp-fire, where he crouched next to the embers, prodding at them to let through the breeze and fan up the heat; paring the twigs he would use to set up the billycan over the flames. He reached over without looking, scrabbling for something: and then he was clutching the bowl of his pipe in one hand. I smelt the tobacco, before drifting con-fusedly back into a haze of second sleep, with the sunlight burning down on my face.

182

I'd have to ask the bywoner for permission. François always knew how to cope with that sort of thing. 'Dag, Oom. Gaan dit met Oom?' Having to sit politely in the dark voorkamer while François and the old man courteously tried each other's tobacco. Having to listen to an account in detail of sheep ailments; having to grin admiringly in response to some interminable, obscure anecdote about trapping a rooikat in the veld. Frans never seemed to care when it came round to the inevitable racist jokes. But a flush always sets in across my cheeks then, and I start to feel achingly thirsty, sick: imperilled, almost. No. I don't think I should call in at the cottage. He'd look askance, in any case – a woman on her own, in the mountains? So I'd be a trespasser. But I'm always careful to close the farm-gates, and I wouldn't light any fires.

He might even be dead by now.

The way the werf was littered with those tiny bottles of patent medicine. Drained and tossed out on the grey sand, in amongst the cowpats and the chicken feathers, the rusted tin-cans, the drab slivers of eucalyptus leaves. About ninety-eight per cent alcohol that stuff is, Frans said; with tiny fractions of orange oil and quinine sulphate added. He must have been addicted. But then he had a constant, groaning pain in his side – a cancer, maybe.

Dead. Who, Anna? Who might be dead.

I remember the view from his stoep, looking out across the wide stretches of reed-bed to the low hills in the distance. Stony, they looked, boulder-strewn, and dotted with some scrub of low, desolate bushes. The sand on those collapsing, wind-scoured slopes was blinding almost, in the sunlight, and even from several miles away. The top-soil has been lost from over-grazing, shoddy farming, miserliness, drought. Suppose if the heavy rains ever return in some miraculous torrent – the whole valley will be swept away in catastrophe, washed out instantly in the havoc of a flood; because there is no vegetation now to filter away the water.

That was a fucken pipe-dream, man. Maybe once, once there was the means to hold down agrarian production. But now? Come right, man.

You got to think again, man.

I suppose the fishing boats still go out from Saldanha Bay, Lamberts, Paternoster, Stompneus? Even if the factories are closing down up north at Walvis, and the workers are being turned away.

What do they catch now, I wonder. If the pilchard stocks are almost exhausted. Suppose anchovies; and maasbankers, and jellyfish, squid, lantern-fish and rooi-oog herring are landing up now in the nets of the pelagic trawlers. Wonder what the labourers of Elands-baai can have to eat these days. Maybe fish and kreef that they've caught for themselves. The landowners' kids don't see a future in farming with yellow sand and quartz bits and locusts. And if they're moving away to the bigger towns or the city, there can't be much work on the farms anymore. In the dorps perhaps there's domes-tic work, and in the summer there's work at the hotel in Elands, when students and tourists and young artisans on leave drive up for the surfing and to stun themselves with alcohol in the evenings. Suppose there's money to be got from working in the kitchens, or serving at table; washing people's cars; polishing the stoep of the hotel; ironing clothes for the sunburnt Madams with gold chains clinking and jimmering at their wrists and thick necks; maybe looking after children on the beach; cleaning fish for people; sel-ling bundles of rooikrans for braaivleis fires.

Think again.

That bywoner was never lost in any nostalgia for his own en-vironment: the veld for him consisting of the scrub that tore at his arms when he strode through it, of plants that should be hacked out and burnt, and of plants that the farmer's sheep could eat safely. Anton would approve. Smiling faintly, and with his hands clasped behind his head in a moment of unusual expansive-ness. 'But of course . . .' His eyebrow quirking dangerously. 'Any-one who needs to *enthuse* about nature is precisely the person who is alienated from it. Anna, wouldn't you agree.' He wanting me to detect then the latent, ironic theme of his own *Stedelike Kuns*.

Papa is one to attribute an intellectual glamour to sullen ignorance and then reject it all the same, as beyond his personal capacity. Niceties of paradox and benignly regretful self-reference.

François seems to have felt the same thing, almost: except that he couldn't bear to leave it at that, insisting that he would win back his lost, innocent world of oneness. At least Papa knew the futility of that yearning quest. But then, why did he let his useless dreams collapse inward, into self-gratification. . . . I suppose despair is the brave excuse for decadence. But he could have waited. He might have trusted that his children would grow up in authenticity,

even if he himself could never escape the incorrigible state of consciousness.

But Anton was only speaking for his own time, after all. And
maybe he's entitled to his disillusionment. If that's what it is. Perhaps he was simply too perceptive to set much store by socialist
utopias that are dreamt up by the sad, alienated intellectuals out
of an inner discontent.

The silence seems to be flickering somehow, lightlessly through
my own mind.

Anton isn't really my father, I think. Well; maybe twenty-six
years ago the seed from his body flowed silkily into Constance's.
But fatherhood is a social function: and abiding.

No.

I don't care about that anymore; I don't.

I want to be heading out across the hard-baked, yellow sand.
Want to watch the shiny black beetles scurry across the ground and
plummet absurdly into the flimsy shelter of a bush or white grass
stalks. To see the mudworks of the harvester termites' foraging tun-
nels; and the spiderwebs across the entrances to abandoned porcupine lairs. This is what I want. It'll be cold, this time of year,
Anna. Will it? Will it be cold. Maybe it snows along the Piketberg
range. I don't know. But I'll go in my corduroys; take a sweater,
I can carry it over my shoulders. Desert country. Only a hundred
kilometres from Cape Town; yet you can tell from the plants. The
pelargoniums are adapted there, with spiky, thin-bladed, tough
leaves; and the leaves of other plants are finely silvered with hairs
or wax. Where I want to be. Brushing through the thorny scrub;
trailing my hand through the prickly, aromatic kapok on the roos-
maryn bushes.

Does it rain there. Perhaps in the shadow of the Piketberg itself.
I seem to think of the whole sky darkening over, with faintly
livid patches: and then a heavy, iron-coloured rain spurting down
into the dust.

Why would François not accept. He hated to kill any creature,
even for the sake of learning something. Why couldn't he accept
that you have to kill a part of your most vivid, richest experience –
before you can enter into systematic knowledge. Isn't that it. The
small murder that inaugurates each symbol. François would protest
against partial knowledge. But then that is written into the philo-

sophy of modern science. Wasn't it that man Heisenberg. If you pin down sub-atomic particles to know their position, then their velocity must elude you. François always with his wistful, sombrely angry holism. Anna, I – the way I see it, we're already a part of the whole set-up, you know: like, what we trying to look at in the first place.

Sometimes I think he was wanting to deny the fact of time that passes: bitterly hunting for some static world of perpetual simultaneity. Strange universe that would be: without beginning or end, and all meaning founded in symmetries – insubstantial as music.

It's cold. And my hand's burning for some reason.

François will be walking ahead, sweeping methodically at the bushes with that heavy, wire-rimmed net of his, till the flowing bag is dust-coloured and stuck full of thorns and twigs. And he'll stop every once in a while – reaching in to sort through his haul, head and shoulders right inside the frame of the thing: lifting out tenderly the lace-wings and dragonflies, the katydids, spiders, and the tiny, bud-green leafhoppers. His favourite trick is to stalk the sound of a persistent cicada, and then lunge brilliantly into a woody shrub: striding back with the shrieking thing held gently between thumb and finger. Once I held it too, when he let me take the thorax in a firm grip; and I felt the urgent, powerful vibrations of the wing muscles readying themselves before I let it fly free. Pretty creatures, with strong, lacy wings held in a glistening roof over the abdomen; and that intricate, miniature stippling of enamels and gilt on the head and thorax.

I want to walk close behind Frans's shoulder, so that he can show me the things in the veld.

Skilpadbessie – that low, untidy bush with the small, translucent globes that hang and dip in amongst its spiky leaves. I tasted the flesh of those berries once – watery and faintly tart; and spat out the remaining seeds hurriedly. François was crouching idly alongside, with a hand draped carelessly over one knee; staring absently into the heart of the bush. He reached inward a moment later with an unhurried, brief flick of the wrist, to draw out the wirily struggling tortoise. Small, scaly legs of the animal writhing, fully protruded from under the carapace: Frans showed me the vermilion plates across his belly; the dark, bright eyes; and the horny beak. The scrambling haste of it too, once it was released.

186

Anna? You see, I can go along with you, that you get knowledge out of being detached from a thing. Maybe what you say, even about science being a dialectic. Don't know about that. But, so then, how can a scientist ever talk about the *non*-alienated things, hey? I mean, like – like man when he's a species of animal, and . . . about the animals *in* their ecological relations.

But we aren't merely animals. Because of having a human history, because of changing our environment. Ja, the whole of the Elands-baai country is littered with the traces of artifice: dozens of skil-fully struck flakes you find, lying on the surface of the stony ground, and sometimes the bulbous core where the flakes came from. Grubby, ochreous beads ground out of ostrich eggshell. And if you scramble up to the rocky overhangs, sometimes there are paintings still visible, in the colours of ash, sand, mud and clay and blood. The weather-dimmed portraits of men wearing brimmed hats – priapically invested, and crudely drawn, really: lacking prototypes, maybe. But also the softly polychrome paintings of eland and giraffe, friezes of them lining some of the bigger caves.

This whole region was teeming once with eland, they say – the bushmen's cattle. Two hundred, maybe two hundred and fifty years ago. Is that recent? Or a long time ago. Can't tell anymore.

No. And it is something else I was supposed to remember.

I was explaining something. Why I want to be with François. He has a way of driving me on with his own rugged fitness, forcing a walk of almost twenty kilometres – so that we'll get back to camp and sink into a luxurious, blazing warmth of sleep almost straight away, after chewing drowsily at charred, fire-roasted slices of bread. It's not a country you can escape. There's nowhere else to go, Anna: historical advancement has taken the place of romance, comedy, religion, exploring . . . But I know that, Papa, I know: who do you think I am?

I can hear the drip beginning from that rusted section of the gut-tering in the alley. It's raining more heavily now.

François will be taciturn mostly on the long walks; and even when he spots something, he may do nothing more than indicate quietly with his hand or the tilt of his head. A kestrel overhead; or a slim, silver-striped skink already disappearing; or the blue-headed koggelmander, pushing himself up warily on small, leathery legs to peer out across a rock. Or there may be the lost scale from a tor-

187

toise shell lying in the sand, near the tip of Frans's boot; or a scatter of bleached limpet shells and ancient alikreukels, carried inland once – maybe centuries ago.

What I want: to feel the grazes and scratches on my forearms, and the dustiness. I want to feel the veld, not my body. There may be skulls, sometimes, lying half-buried in the sand, of dead cows and sheep. But I don't want to see those. No. Only dassie skulls up in the caves along the ridges. And porcupine quills I might find, the long, quivering, almost pure white ones; or shorter ones that are tougher, and yellowish. I want to dip my hands into the warm, butter-warm pools of sunlight that lie in the hollows of the stones, just above the lichen. And I want to dig down with my hands into that charred, grey sand at the roots of certain bushes, to dig out the rough gold, amber-coloured grains of the scale insects: ground pearls, they call them. Anna, it is winter. I want to see the smooth clay cells, big as acorns, that lie wedged in along the vertical crevices of huge rocks, and sometimes are cracked open, where the wasps have flown out. Winter.

I don't care: I am dreaming of summer. Well, Anna, my dear: you must know that *pastoral* – that the country is dead? . . . Ja, Anton. Ja: do you imagine that I am not mourning.

Papa. You with your conceits, your poësy – ja, jou digkuns. En wat is glas, dan, as dit nie 'n ware solied is nie. Something fluid, 'n helder, stromende vloeistof – dis wat jy wou sê: iets wat deur die mens vervaardig word, something that is wrought; but which remains in its essence organic. You with your penetrating mind, Papa, your sharpened, careful conjectures. Your thoughts have found their way into me, I know: miskien is dit jou skerp, ruwe besinnings wat my in my stille wese gesteek het.

I'm going to go back to that sandy field, where we found a few withered peas still lying in the blackened pods, and there were other plants in rows that we could not name, because they had no crop on them. And there were locusts – a plague, we thought, but the bywoner only shook his head, bewildered, as though they were commoner than dust-storms. Glossy crimson and black things, creeping over the cauliflowers, to gnaw at what was left of the scorched white flowerets, and the thick-veined parts of the drooping leaves. Vat maar gerus, vat van die kool. What is it called in agriculture where monoculture leads to infestation by vast swarms of insects. We saw them everywhere we went, on the dust roads even, crushed under car tyres, or clinging sleepily to the shrubs at the roadside. And the different instars: Frans showed me the patternings. Nee, vat maar: anders gaan die rooibaadjies sommer alles opvreet.

Anna, you tell me why there is a difference, hey. Why people want to treat the wild plants any different from the cultivated ones. Hey? They all sustain us, all vegetation supports us, you know: it's not just the peas and the mielies and the wheat. Like the difference between killing people outright or enslaving them. You want the vegetation to keep working for you, then you got to, well – like, perpetuate the conditions that are going to ensure it keeps coming back. Hey. Like the bushmen did: never wipe out the basic stock of anything. Okay, well, like in farming too. All I'm saying is, Anna: you got to have that attitude towards *all* of nature.

I'm too tired.

I want to head up towards the kloof, I want to find a path for myself, kicking aside the fragments of quartz; hauling myself up over jutting rocks with the help of roots and trailed succulent plants. Up to that immense overhang where the swallows nest under the ledges, and the soft laughter of rock pigeons is amplified by the backdrop of stone till it sounds like a clattering fusillade of gunfire. Where I want to go. Climbing upward, and grabbing at thorn bushes, stones, earth, vygies. To see nothing but a blurred, constant image of stoniness at my feet – some general system of earth-smeared crystals and wind-eroded pebbles. Sometimes the startling particular – patches where the ground is littered with the broken emeralds of wing cases from buprestid beetles, smashed and discarded by predatory birds. Dassie skulls. And the relics of human industry, in flakes, blades, scrapers. . . . Holding on to something, a hardy bush, I want to turn and look back down the valley. To see the meandering stretches of the reed-choked river. And to the west, to guess at a coastline from the dense white mists of dune-sand and sea-spray. The beaches there are still strewn with the debris of blue-black mussel shells, that people must once have feasted on. Below me the bywoner's cottage lies half hidden amidst the stand of bluegums. An ancient, rusted ploughshare has been drawn up under one of the trees, and the sand is building up against it.

I imagine that he must be dead.
    Fallen, perhaps, on a concrete floor; in shadow.